Be Careful What You Pray For

Kimberla Lawson Roby

WILLIAM MORROW
An Imprint of HarperCollinsPublishers

HarperCollins books may be purchased for educational, business, or sales promotional use. For information please write: Special Markets Department, HarperCollins Publishers, 10 East 53rd Street, New York, NY 10022.

FIRST EDITION

Library of Congress Cataloging-in-Publication Data

Roby, Kimberla Lawson.
  Be careful what you pray for / Kimberla Lawson Roby. — 1st ed.
    p.   cm.
  ISBN 978-0-06-144311-4
  1. African American women—Fiction. 2. Children of clergy—Fiction. I. Title.
  PS3568.O3189B4   2010
  813'.54—dc22

                                                              2009029268

10 11 12 13 14   OV/RRD   10 9 8 7 6 5 4 3 2 1

*In loving memory
of my wonderful friend and fellow writer,
the talented Mr. E. Lynn Harris*

Acknowledgments

First and foremost, I thank God for guiding my direction and for protecting and blessing my family, friends, and me. Without You, absolutely nothing would be possible.

To my loving husband, Will. I love you from the bottom of my soul, and thank you for loving me to the fullest and for being my greatest support in all that I do.

To my loving brothers, Willie Jr. and Michael; my wonderful stepson and daughter-in-law, Trenod and LaTasha, and the boys, Lamont, Tre, and Troy; my beautiful nieces and nephews, from the oldest to the youngest—Jamaal, Malik, Ja'Mia, Ja'Mel, Shelia, William, and Nakya—and their wonderful mothers, Karen, Danetta, and April; my loving cousin, Patricia Haley (also a fellow writer); my aunts, Mary Lou, Fannie, Ada, and Vernell; my uncles, James, Cliff, Luther, Ben, Charlie, and Earl; and all of the rest of my cousins, in-laws, and other family members who I love so very much. And to my girls who have my back no matter what—Kelli, Lori, Janell, and Victoria (also a fellow writer).

To Eric Jerome Dickey, Trisha R. Thomas, Lolita Files, Mary B. Morrison, Trice Hickman, Eric Pete, Victor McGlothin, ReShonda Tate-Billingsley, and all my other writer friends. I also still have to acknowledge my friend who I miss dearly: the very kind and compassionate E. Lynn Harris. You will remain in my heart always.

To the best assistant in the world (and I sincerely mean that), Connie Dettman; to my very talented editor, Wendy Lee—thank you for just being you; to Richard Aquan, Tavia Kowalchuk, Ben Bruton, and Aurora Hughes, for putting forth so much effort when it comes to my books; to the entire sales and marketing teams and everyone else at HarperCollins/William Morrow/Avon for all that you do for me daily; to my wonderful agent, Elaine Koster, for absolutely everything; to my amazing freelance publicist, Shandra Hill Smith, for doing such a splendid job with getting my work noticed by the media and beyond and for being so kind; to Luke LeFevre, my fabulous and exceptionally talented website and e-blast designer for everything; to every bookstore and retail outlet that sells my books; to Patrik Henry Bass, senior editor, and everyone else at *Essence* magazine for the best support in the world (I am beyond grateful for all that you've done); to the wonderful and hugely syndicated Michael Baisden (thank you so much for having me on your fabulous show—I am so very proud of you); to my local media family in Rockford, Illinois, for promoting my work and events: *Rockford Register Star* (Georgette Braun and Jennie Pollock), WIFR-TV (Andy Gannon and Aaron Wilson), WXRX (Stone and Double T), WREX-TV (Laura Gibbs), WTVO-TV, Comcast Cable, WZOK/WROK, 106.3 FM, and all the other wonderful people in radio, TV, and print nationwide who publicize my work to the masses. Thank you for all that you've done for me over the last thirteen years.

Finally, to the people who make my writing career fun, enjoyable, and possible: my very caring and loyal readers—thank you for all the love and support you always give and know that I love each of you with everything in me.

Much love and God bless you always,
Kimberla Lawson Roby

Be Careful What You Pray For

Prologue

He was almost too good to be true, what with his at least six-foot-two body frame, flawlessly smooth skin, coal-black wavy hair, and pearly white teeth. He somehow didn't seem real, but Alicia knew he *was* real because at this very moment, she was sitting directly across the table from him at one of the most upscale restaurants in downtown Chicago. He was by far one of the finest-looking men she'd ever laid eyes on, and there wasn't a woman she could think of who would disagree with her findings. The man looked that good, and as if that wasn't enough, he also conveyed exceptional charisma and an alluring smile, and was the founder of New Life Christian Center, a five-year-old church that already had more than five thousand members.

Yes, Pastor JT Valentine was the kind of man Alicia had been hoping and praying for, particularly ever since her marriage to her first husband, Phillip, had ended just a few months ago, and she could barely contain herself. But since her father, stepmother, and a couple of Pastor Valentine's deacons and their wives were also dining right along with them, she took a deep breath, drank a sip of water, and coolly leaned back in her chair.

"Pastor Black," Pastor Valentine said, and Alicia couldn't

help noticing the very elegant and obviously tailor-made suit he was wearing. "I just want to thank you again for agreeing to come speak at our church this morning. Your words were even more powerful than the last time I heard you deliver a sermon, and I hope you'll consider blessing us with your presence again sometime in the future."

"I would be happy to, and I'm glad you were satisfied with what I had to share today."

Pastor Valentine chuckled. " 'Satisfied' isn't even the word. You have been the one man I've truly looked up to for a while now, even before I accepted my call into the ministry, so having you accept my invitation has been the highlight of my year."

"Well, I'm glad and it was an honor."

"And I also want to thank you, Mrs. Black," he said to Charlotte, "for taking time to make the trip here as well. I know you live only about an hour and a half away, but I do still remember what it was like for my wife, God rest her soul, and how demanding a first lady's schedule can really be."

"This is true, but unless our son, Matthew, needs me to be home to attend one of his football games or something else school related, I pretty much travel with my husband to most of his out-of-town speaking engagements. Which actually works out fine because Matthew loves staying with my aunt when we're gone, and Curtis doesn't travel nearly as much as he used to anyway."

Curtis lifted a forkful of Caesar salad from his plate. "No, these days, I tend to turn down far more opportunities than I take on, but after traveling around the country for so many years, I eventually decided that I wanted to spend as much time as possible with my family."

"Totally understandable," Pastor Valentine said, and then looked at Alicia. "So, Miss Alicia, and I guess I'm sort of changing the subject a bit, but your father tells me that you've written the next worldwide bestseller."

Alicia smiled. "Well, I don't know about all that, but I did just finish writing my first novel."

"That's really impressive. It takes a lot of patience and diligence to write a book, fiction or nonfiction, so I'm very proud of you."

"Thanks," Alicia said, smiling at him again, her stomach fluttering.

"She worked on it just about every single day over the last six months, and it's great," her father added. "She definitely poured her heart into it and that makes all the difference, regardless of what anyone is writing."

"It really is wonderful," Charlotte said. "I read it in one sitting, the same as I do with all the other books I read by well-known authors."

Pastor Valentine raised his eyebrows. "Wow, then maybe I should read it, too. That is, if you don't mind sharing it with me."

"No, I don't mind at all, and actually, I would love to have someone else's opinion. Someone who doesn't love me so unconditionally that they would tell me anything as long as it doesn't hurt my feelings."

Everyone laughed and then her father said, "You're right. I do love you, but at the same time, I would never tell you something was good if it really wasn't."

Pastor Valentine turned his attention to Alicia again. "So, you'll send me a copy next week?"

"Yes, I'll mail it tomorrow," she said, and it was all she could do not to blush like some teenage schoolgirl. She was pleased to know how interested he seemed to be in her work but what she was most thrilled about was how interested he was in her—

something she could tell more and more as they continued making eye contact. The chemistry between them was discreetly intense, and it was the reason Alicia suddenly realized something. JT wasn't just some man she was attracted to. It was true that she'd known him for only a few hours, but at this very moment she knew he was the man of her dreams. She knew it with all her heart.

She knew she was going to be the next Mrs. JT Valentine. No doubt about it.

Chapter 1

Seven Months Later

It was a fine and very warm first Sunday in May, and Alicia sat in the front row of the church, admiring her wonderful husband. He was actually sitting right next to her but was only minutes from heading into the pulpit to deliver his sermon. Alicia and JT had been happily married for one full month now but she was still in awe of his entire being, the same as she'd been the first day she'd met him. It was still so hard to conceive of how truly blessed she was to have found him—the perfect spouse, who, ironically, was ten years her senior, just like her first husband had been—not to mention how soon it all had happened. She'd sent him her manuscript as planned, he'd called her two days after receiving it, saying he'd read it and loved it, and the next thing Alicia had known, they'd found themselves on the phone for two hours. They'd talked about everything imaginable, and one thing had led to another. He'd driven over to Mitchell the next day to take her to dinner, and just one month later, JT had presented her with a three-carat, princess-cut, solitaire diamond ring. He had slipped the huge rock onto her finger and had asked her to marry him. For a few seconds, however, and only a few seconds, Alicia had been speechless and in tears, but then she had quickly told him yes three different times. She could still remember how happy she'd been, happier than she'd ever been in her life, and how even though they'd been together only for six short months, she felt as if she'd known this man for years.

There was one unfortunate aspect, however, that she couldn't push out of her mind: Her father didn't approve of JT and still hadn't accepted the idea that she'd gotten married to him. She'd tried her best to forget her father's words and all the reasons he'd given in terms of why she needed to end things with JT— reasons he'd given her for the umpteenth time the night before the wedding. But she couldn't.

"Baby girl, I really wish you'd think long and hard about what you're getting ready to do tomorrow," her father said. "Because all JT Valentine cares about is money, power, and women, and he'll never do right by you."

"Daddy, why can't you just be happy for me? I mean, why can't you just support my decision the same way you did when I married Phillip?"

"Because JT is nothing like your first husband. Yes, he's a minister like Phillip and he's thirty-three like Phillip, but that's where their similarities pretty much end. JT is all about JT, and when it's all said and done, all he's going to do is cause you a mountain of pain."

Alicia pleaded with her father to understand. "He loves me, Daddy. He really does, so I'm begging you. Please, just give us your blessing."

"I can't do that. I can't be happy about any man who I know is going to hurt you in the end."

"Daddy, the only person who's going out of their way to hurt me right now is you."

"I'm sorry for any harm this may be causing you, but I can't help the way I feel. I can't help the fact that I'm able to see straight through this man you're so desperately in love with. Or should I say who you *think* you're in love with, because I'm not sure if you actually love him for him, or if what you're really in love with is the amount of money he earns."

"I really resent that, Daddy. I resent it, and I'm shocked that you would have the audacity to say something like that to me. I love, trust, and believe in JT with all my heart, and regardless of what you or anyone else thinks about him, JT is the one."

Alicia sighed at her last thought and remembered how her father hadn't said another word and how he'd eventually walked out of her bedroom. Then, that afternoon, he'd pleaded with her one last time to reconsider, but when he'd finally realized she'd made up her mind to go through with the ceremony, with or without him, he had reluctantly escorted her down the church aisle and given her away.

JT peered at the crowd in front of him, and Alicia gave him her undivided attention, the same as everyone else in the sanctuary. "It is so good to finally be back in the house of the Lord," he said. "Although I must say, while I really did miss seeing all of you, I definitely enjoyed having an entire month off to spend with my beautiful new bride," he said, and a vast number of "Amen's" could be heard throughout the congregation. "Most of you know how hard it was on me when Satan robbed me of my first wife two years ago and how I never thought I'd find true happiness again. But I'm here to tell you today that through God's grace, not only did I find true happiness, I also found the kind of genuine love every man ought to experience at least once in his lifetime."

"Glory to God," one woman said.

"Praise His holy name," another added.

JT glanced down at his wife. "Sweetheart, stand up and say hello to everyone."

Alicia smiled, stood, faced their parishioners, and waved. Many of them smiled back at her, chuckled, and chattered approvingly among themselves, and Alicia felt like a celebrity. In the beginning, she hadn't known how receptive the members of New Life Christian Center would actually be toward her. Especially since they'd clearly been very fond of their former first lady and also because JT hadn't known Alicia very long before popping the big question. So, she was very relieved to see how pleased they were to have her there.

She continued waving in a number of directions and then took her seat.

JT grinned and said, "And just for the record, don't think that the only thing my wife has are her noticeably good looks, because she's also a very talented writer. She's written a novel and once she finishes up a few revisions, it'll only be a matter of time before multiple publishers begin making offers for it."

The congregation applauded, and Alicia appreciated their kindness and obvious support of her endeavors.

"Most of you know, too," JT continued, "that I have lots of new goals for NLCC and a vision of how quickly I want to see our ministry grow, so I thank God for giving me a woman who loves me the way Alicia does and for all of you, the people who make all that I'm trying to do here so possible."

Alicia listened as JT spoke more about his future plans for the ministry, but she couldn't stop thinking about her new husband and how attentive and generous he'd been over the last seven months. He'd given her dozens and dozens of roses, spent every minute of his free time with her, and had surprised her with the kinds of gifts most women could only dream about. Alicia had wondered if she would ever find a man who loved her the way Phillip had but at the same time earned a salary that was well into six figures, and she was happy to say she'd found every bit of that and so much more.

Over the years, she'd heard a number of people insisting that it simply wasn't possible for any one person to have everything all at the same time, specifically lots of wealth and a perfect marriage. But Alicia was pleased to know that she and JT had proved every single one of them wrong. JT was such a loyal and honest man of God—the kind of man who had made it clear from the start that even though he was dying to make love to her, he wanted them to do the right thing and not have sex until after they'd taken their vows. He'd talked a lot about how he didn't want them doing anything that would defy God's Word or something that might diminish their very strong moral values and how he was more than willing to wait. Needless to say, Alicia couldn't thank God enough for bringing such a decent and wholesome man into her life. She was thankful that the fairy tale she'd prayed for actually wasn't a fairy tale at all. She was elated to know that the fabulous life she and JT were so happily living was clear-cut reality.

Chapter 2

"Oh, that's it!" Diana Redding screamed at the top of her lungs, and JT felt like he was going to pass out. His heart beat violently, he panted uncontrollably, and it was all he could do to try to catch a few breaths of air. In all honesty, he felt like he was going to die . . . but it was a chance he was always willing to take when it came to this wildcat who was old enough to be his mother.

JT rolled to the side of her. "You have got to be the most amazing woman I've ever met."

"Oh yeah?" she said. "Well, let me tell you . . . that's nothing compared to all the other tricks I plan on showing you before you leave here tonight. That is, if your little young behind can handle all of them."

Diana was incredible, to say the least, and strangely enough, JT had known from the first day he'd laid eyes on her, one year ago, that he had to have her. He'd known she had to be at least in her early to middle fifties, especially since she had a daughter who appeared to be the same age as him, but she looked not a day past forty. She was lively and vivacious and her perfectly shaped body, youthful skin, and erotic smile had lit a raging fire right under him—the kind of fire that simply had to be put out. And he'd let her *put* it out five nights later at this very same condo out in Oak Brook, which was one of the many properties Diana and her real estate tycoon husband owned in the Midwest. They were multimillionaires in their own right and by far the wealthiest members of his congregation.

JT had originally seen Diana, her daughter, and her husband one Sunday at church and had spent days trying to figure out how he might be able to connect with her. He'd known he couldn't just simply walk up to her during one of their services, but as luck would have it, he had run into her at an Italian restaurant not far from where he lived. He'd been dining with his two assistant pastors and a couple of other church officers, but then he'd seen Diana, dressed to the hilt in some vogue-style, cream-colored suit and looking over at him. Shortly after, he'd spotted her heading toward the restroom, so he had quickly excused himself from his table and followed her. It had only taken him seconds to catch up with her and when he had, she'd smiled seductively and handed him a small piece of folded paper with an address and what time to meet her but never said one word. She'd then walked away, and less than twenty-four hours later, JT had found himself in bed with a fifty-five-year-old cougar who could run wide circles around just about any woman he'd been with.

Diana propped herself onto her elbow and caressed JT's chest. "You really gave a wonderful message this morning. I mean, you always give great sermons, but this one was another winner for sure."

"I'm glad you liked it."

"I did, and I'm always so proud to sit and listen to you. I'm so proud of who you are and who I know you're eventually going to be."

"Your support means everything because I never got that when I was a child."

"Meaning?"

"I know I've never told you much about my childhood, the same as I haven't told most people, but my years as a child were flat-out pitiful. My father spent most of it telling me how I was never going to amount to anything and how I was going to end up just like him: working myself to death for just a few dollars more than minimum wage and living my entire life in shame. He pounded those words into me every chance he got and for a long time I believed him."

"Oh, sweetheart, I am so sorry, and why haven't you ever shared that with me?"

"Because I try my best not to think about my father and the horrible person he was. He practically ruined any self-esteem I might have had back then and by the time I turned ten, my mother passed away from uterine cancer and he turned to alcohol. He drank himself into a complete stupor seven days a week, and after a couple of years of dealing with it, I ran away."

Diana frowned. "At twelve years old?"

"Yeah, but thankfully my aunt was willing to take me in. She was my mom's older sister, and she treated me like her own child. Which was fine until I started my senior year in high school and she passed away from the same kind of cancer my mom did."

Diana slowly shook her head in disbelief. "You poor, poor thing."

"Okay, that's enough of that," JT said, refusing to release tears that had suddenly filled his eyes. "Let's talk about something else."

"No, we have to talk about this, because I can't believe what you went through. And looking at you now, no one would ever guess it in a million years."

"I know. I've definitely come a mighty long way, and it's all because of how wonderfully God has blessed me. He took care of me when I wasn't quite able to take care of myself, and then one night about six years ago when I was at my lowest, He set things up so that this ended up being the same night my now father-in-law was on television, preaching this awesome sermon. At the time, I had never even heard of anyone named Reverend Curtis Black, but he still had my attention from the moment I flipped through the channels and saw him. Then, when he finished, I got on my knees and asked God to forgive me for all of my sins and to use me in whatever way He saw fit."

"That's really profound, and you know, I think it would really help if you started telling your life story to a lot more people. Especially to our congregation, because they'll certainly feel a lot closer to you once you do. People like knowing that their leaders, or that any man in power who they look up to, is just as human as they are. They like knowing that you haven't always had the success you have now and that you had to work very hard to get to where you are today."

"Well, they already know I wasn't always this successful in ministry because I'm always mentioning how I started out with only a few members but now have more than five thousand."

"Still, they'll sympathize with you a whole lot more if you tell them about your childhood. They'll listen to you a lot more closely, and they'll tell others what you've been through, which in turn might bring in new members. At the least, it might get new people to come and visit New Life to see how they like it."

JT sighed deeply. "Maybe."

"Just think about it. I know it's not an easy story to tell but having any real success in this day and age means putting your heart and soul into every aspect of what you're trying to do."

JT smiled at Diana. "That's what I love about you the most. Well, it's *one* of the things I love about you, anyway."

13

"Yeah, right," she said, chuckling, "because we both know what you love more than anything else."

JT reached toward her and caressed the tip of her chin. "You're right about that. But seriously, what I love about you is the way you constantly encourage me to be the best person I can be and how you always have such strong faith in all that I want to do. I mean, I have so many plans and goals till I can barely think straight. I want to double the size of the congregation within the next five years, and my biggest dream of all is to begin televising nationally."

"And, sweetheart, you will. You have everything it takes, and as long as you continue satisfying me the way you have over the last twelve months and you keep spending a respectable amount of time with me, I'll do whatever I can to help you financially, emotionally, and otherwise."

"Hey. You'll always be my girl and nothing will ever change what you and I have together."

Diana's face turned serious. "Not even the fact that you have a new little wifey? That sweet young thing who's only twenty-three years old?"

JT sighed; he hated having this particular discussion with Diana because he knew she still wasn't happy about him getting married. "Now, baby, you know I didn't have a choice. You know when a pastor doesn't have a wife, it opens the door for loads of ridiculous rumors. As it was, people were starting to gossip and whisper about a couple of other women in the church they thought I was sleeping with, and that's when I knew it was time to get married again."

Diana looked at him but didn't comment one way or the other. JT wasn't sure what he should say next because he could never tell her his other reasons for taking a wife: that he'd had the opportunity to marry *the* Reverend Curtis Black's firstborn child, that he could already see how becoming Curtis's son-in-law would eventually do great things for his career, that he wanted to have a couple of children who would be able to carry on his legacy, and that deep down there was a part of him that really did love Alicia.

"So, do you love her?" Diana asked, almost as if she could hear what he was thinking.

"I care about her," he said, not wanting Diana to think he loved anyone more than he loved her. He didn't want her even considering the idea that what the two of them had together really wasn't love at all and that their relationship was purely based on the rough and very passionate sex they regularly engaged in and, of course, based on the money she didn't mind providing for him. He cared about Diana, but love had nothing to do with it.

"Well, if you don't love her, then I don't see why you had to up and get married," she said, shifting rather forcibly away from him and onto her back. JT knew he needed to explain things a lot better.

"Baby, come on now," he said, pulling her back toward him so they were facing each other. "I care about Alicia, but I *love* you. Plus, it's like I keep telling you, I only got married because I knew the congregation would be happy about it. And of course with Alicia being Curtis Black's daughter, they love her."

"Yeah, I could tell that today, but if you ask me, that's just plain silly. I mean, who decides to like someone just because their father is famous?"

"Well, for whatever reason, lots of people are obsessed with having even a remote connection to any celebrity, and to prove it, our membership increased by two percent within a month after he served as guest speaker."

"But according to you, he's not all that thrilled about you marrying his daughter in the first place."

"Yeah, but he'll come around. He's just a little hesitant right now because of all the rumors and lies floating around about me, but I'll eventually gain his total trust. Before long, he'll love me like his very own son."

"I hope you're right, because there's nothing like a father-in-law, especially someone as powerful as Curtis Black, who despises the man his daughter is married to."

"Everything'll be fine. You'll see. He'll change his whole tune before you know it. Plus, even if for some reason he doesn't, I have you, right?"

Diana smiled in a captivating sort of way. "As long as you keep up your end of the deal, I'll give you all the money you need to promote both New Life and yourself throughout the entire city of Chicago. And I'll also do whatever necessary to help you go national. But there is one other condition."

JT wasn't sure he liked the tone in her voice but said, "And what's that?"

"With the exception of me, you're to have no other mistresses. Your wife is one thing, but I don't ever want to hear about you being with anyone else. Not ever."

"You have my word," he said. Then he rested his body on top of hers and kissed her more ravenously than he had earlier. He did what he had to do. For the sake of his ministry and its future.

Chapter 3

Alicia sat up, stacked a couple of pillows behind her back, glanced over at her husband, who was still slumbering peacefully, and smiled. Right after leaving church yesterday afternoon, the two of them had gone to this quaint little Chinese restaurant, and then around five P.M., JT had left for a couple of hours, well actually four hours, to go visit a family who was losing a child to cancer, and also so he could drop by the home of another family who had a sick relative. Alicia had wanted to go with him but since she was still working on a few revisions her father's literary agent had asked her to make and she wanted to get the manuscript shipped back to her in a few days, JT had told her she should stay and work on that instead. He was so supportive of her dream of being published, and she was very thankful for that. He encouraged her to write and do whatever was needed to get her work acquired by a major publishing house, and she was happy to say she was well on her way toward doing just that.

JT quietly breathed in and out, and Alicia scanned every section of their master suite. First, she looked at the thick, royal blue velvet drapes covering the huge picture window, and then she eyed the lavish-looking, king-sized mahogany bed, dresser, and matching nightstands. Next, she glanced at the forty-inch flat-screen HD television, two winter white chaises, and all the royal blue, black, and gold accessories. The entire setting reminded her of something she'd seen in a recent issue of *Architectural Digest,* and Alicia was impressed at how good a job JT had done as a bachelor. Although, he had told her that because his wife had died before the house was completely built, he'd hired an interior decorator to help him make quite a few decisions.

Alicia continued admiring all the expensive beauty that surrounded her and whispered, "Thank you."

"You're quite welcome, beautiful, and good morning," JT said, stretching both his arms toward the headboard and smiling at her.

Alicia leaned over and kissed him. "Good morning, baby. And while I hate saying this, I wasn't really thanking you . . . I mean no offense . . . but what I was doing was thanking God for giving me everything I've ever wanted. I was thanking him for bringing you into my life and for allowing us to have so many wonderful things."

"There's not a single thing wrong with that, and I'm glad you're happy."

"I am. Actually, I couldn't be happier, and not many people in this world can say that."

"That's very true, but in all honesty, I want to give you even more than what we have now. You grew up in a very wealthy household, and I don't ever want you feeling like you have to live with any less than what you've always been used to. That's why I took you on that little shopping spree when we got back from our honeymoon."

Alicia stared at JT, and tears rolled down her face.

"Baby, what's wrong?" he asked, drying her face with the

back of his hand and then stroking her hair. "Why are you crying?"

"Because I spent the majority of my first marriage trying to explain to Phillip how wrong it was for him to expect me to settle for less than what I'd become accustomed to. I do admit that there were a few things I could have handled a whole lot better, but regardless, Phillip never understood any of what I was saying and he always made me feel bad about who I was."

JT positioned his back against the pillows the same as Alicia had. "Well, now that you're married to me, you don't ever have to apologize or feel bad about anything. I'm not nearly as well-off as your father but if you decide you want a pair of five-hundred-dollar shoes on a Monday at ten A.M. just because you like them, then I want you to get your five-hundred-dollar shoes and not think twice about it. Okay?"

"I love you so much, JT," she said, kissing him again.

"I love you too, baby, and I promise you, this is only the beginning. Your happiness is very important to me, and I'm very blessed to have such a loyal and loving wife by my side. When I lost Michelle in that horrible car accident, I thought my life was over, and I wasn't sure I'd ever find the right person to marry again."

"I'm still so sorry about that," she said. "I'm so sorry you had to experience such a tragic loss. The entire thing is unfathomable, and I can't even imagine how you must have felt."

"It literally was the worst thing I've ever encountered, and I wouldn't wish it on anyone I can think of. I mean, it was terrible enough losing my wife, but then finding out after the fact that she was three months pregnant—well, that made the entire ordeal even more devastating."

"I remember you mentioning that before, but I wonder why she hadn't told you about it."

"Well, when I spoke to her doctor, she told me that Michelle had taken an at-home pregnancy test the week before and had just come into her office the morning of the accident to confirm the results. So, I guess she never had a chance to tell anybody."

"Gosh."

"Yeah, but unfortunately, that's life. And thankfully, you and I will have our own babies, just like we talked about. I know right now you want to focus on getting your writing career off the ground, but in another year or two I want us to start trying."

Alicia nodded, pretending to agree, because while she did want to have a baby, she'd been hoping they wouldn't even make their first attempt at it until maybe five years from now. It was true she wanted to focus on her writing career, the same as JT had just mentioned, but she also wanted to spend as much time as possible with just him before starting a family.

"So, what do you have planned for today?" he asked.

"Not much except more writing. I have a few more scenes to add and a few more to revise, but I should be finished by the end of this week and ready to do my final read."

"I'm so proud of you, and how wonderful that your dad's agent wants to represent you."

"I know. At first, I wanted to find my own agent because I didn't want publishers and reviewers showing interest in my work just because of how successful Daddy's books are. But after I received back all those rejection letters, I sort of changed my mind about that."

They both laughed and JT said, "Hey, there's nothing wrong with taking advantage of all the contacts your dad is willing to connect you with. You should consider it a blessing to even have a father like Curtis."

"Yeah, I guess. But I just want my work to sell because people really like my writing and not because Curtis Black's daughter wrote it."

"I hear what you're saying, but I'm sure the publishing business is the same as any other. It's more about who you know than what you do."

"Yeah, I'm sure it is."

"Still, though, you have a really strong story line, and this will be your main driving force when it comes to sales. Your dad's name will help you get more publicity than most new writers would ever get, but trust me when I say your story is what will make all the difference. When people read your first novel and see how great it is, they'll automatically pick up your second one as soon as it's published."

"I hope you're right."

"I know I am."

"So, what about you?" she asked. "What are you doing today?"

"Well, if you don't mind, I'll probably meet a couple of minister friends for lunch."

"That's fine, because like I said, I need to get some writing done."

"I'll be back by late afternoon, though, so if you want, we can go out to dinner."

"That'll be fine, too," Alicia said, turning toward the ringing phone. When she saw that it was her best friend, Melanie, she reached over to answer it. That is, until JT stopped her.

"Hey," he said, pulling her on top of him. "Let it go to voice mail."

"Why?"

"Because."

"Because what?"

"Because I wanna make love to my gorgeous wife."

"Is that right?"

"Yes, that's exactly right. So, is that okay with you?"

"It's more than okay. And just for the record, I wanted you last night."

"I know but, baby, after delivering the message yesterday morning and then visiting two separate families in the evening, I was exhausted."

"Yeah, yeah, yeah," she said playfully. "Whatever."

"I was. I was beat."

"Well, I sure hope you're completely rested up now."

"I am," he said, kissing her. "I'm rested and totally ready to prove it."

Chapter 4

Lying on his back, JT crossed his feet and locked his hands behind his head. Then, when the woman returned from the bathroom, he eyed her up and down, from head to toe. "No, wait," he said as she moved closer to the bed. "Just stand there for a few seconds. Let me look at you. Because there's absolutely nothing more beautiful than a naked woman who has curves in all the right places."

"So, you like what you see, huh?" she said.

"Love it."

JT had been having an affair with Carmen Wilson for a little more than four years and no matter how many times he'd tried breaking things off with her, he'd never been able to do it. He'd tried and tried and tried, but the sex between them was so explosive, he just couldn't seem to go more than a few days without having his way with her. It was true he loved having sex with Diana and he even loved having sex with Alicia . . . but he also loved having sex with Carmen.

He didn't want to love sex as much as he did, and he certainly wasn't proud of the fact that he'd just had it with his wife this morning and only minutes ago with someone else. But for years now, particularly ever since he'd gained more power and respect in the ministry, he hadn't been able to control his extreme desire toward stunningly attractive women. Deep down, he knew adultery and fornication were wrong, but it was as if he simply couldn't help himself. So much so, he found himself craving all the attention those women in the church went out of their way to give him. Single ones. Married ones. Women, period. And he found joy in knowing that he really could have just about any of them if he wanted to. They sometimes threw themselves at him, even those who didn't look so hot, but whether they were ugly or as good-looking as any woman could be, JT got a huge and very satisfying rush from all of it.

Carmen finally slipped back into bed and cuddled up next to him. "So, Pastor Valentine, was it as good as always?"

"The best," JT said, closing his eyes and smiling.

"Well, if that's true, then why in the world did you marry that tramp Alicia?"

His eyes reopened. "What? Oh, please, please don't tell me that you're going to start that nonsense up again."

"I wanna know why, JT. I wanna know why you chose that tramp-trick over me."

"First of all, she's not a tramp, so please don't call her that."

"Oh, really? Well, then, you must have forgotten what we saw in the national headlines just one year ago. You know . . . the news about her having an affair with some big-time drug dealer named Levi, how she was arrested and also how her husband left her."

"Carmen, why do you always have to ruin the great time you and I have together? Why do you insist on bringing up these unnecessary subjects?"

"Why? Because I'm tired of hiding out at my apartment with you and tired of being treated like some second-class citizen. I've been doing this ever since my college years and also while you were married to your first wife. Then, to add insult to injury, when she died, you still went and married someone else."

"Look—" he began, but Carmen interrupted him.

"Look, nothing! When Michelle died, you kept telling me that the reason you couldn't marry me was because it wouldn't look good to the congregation if you married someone so much younger than you, but then you ended up marrying someone my exact same age. Not to mention, before that, I even stopped attending NLCC because *you* didn't want to take any chance that someone might see you and me making eye contact or that they might pick up on any chemistry between us."

JT heard what she was saying but didn't dare tell her that the real reason he'd wanted her to leave New Life Christian Center when his first wife was still alive was because he hadn't thought it was a good idea having two mistresses attending service together every Sunday—Diana and Carmen—even if there were five thousand members and little chance that they'd ever bump into each other.

"Carmen, baby, come on now. We've gone over this a thousand times, and you know why I married Alicia. I married her because of who her father is, and just being able to tell people that I'm Curtis's son-in-law has and will continue to be a major benefit to me and to the church as a whole."

"Do you think I care about any of that? So, what I want you to do is divorce Alicia. I want you to end things with her and marry me."

"I'm sorry, but I can't do that."

Carmen sat up, spun her legs over the side of the bed, and stormed across the room. "I've been out of college for a whole year, JT," she yelled. "So, whether you realize it or not, I'm ready to settle down, and I won't continue being some part-time woman."

JT got up and walked over to where she was standing, but

when he wrapped his arms around her from behind, she jerked away from him. "No! You need to make a decision. It's either that tramp Alicia or it's me."

"Carmen, you know I'm the founder and senior pastor of a very large church and that I don't have the privilege of getting rid of my wife just so I can marry someone else."

Carmen's face went blank. "Like I said, it's either that tramp or it's me. Period."

"Then I guess I have no choice but to end things with you."

Carmen cracked up like he'd just said something funny. "Fine. If that's the way you want it, fine."

"Carmen—"

"No, I want you out of here," she said, putting on a hot-pink terry-cloth robe. "I want you out of here right now."

"Baby, it really doesn't have to be this way. I know you're upset, but let's talk about this. Tell me what I can do to make this right."

"Tell you what you can do?! I already did. It's either her or me."

"Why are you being so unreasonable?"

"JT, please get your clothes and get out of here."

JT gazed at her but finally did what he was told. He slipped on his pants, polo shirt, socks, and shoes and then grabbed his keys.

"You are so, so low-down, JT. You're low-down and you've never cared about anyone but yourself. I've made so many sacrifices for you. I mean, even when my employer started offering us flex hours and said we could take off any afternoon we wanted, I chose Monday. I wanted to take Friday afternoons off instead, but I chose Monday because it was your day off from the church. And don't get me started on all that illegal crap I did for you. I was so stupid, but I did everything you asked because you had me believing that you loved me."

"I do love you."

"Just shut up! You don't love me. You don't love anyone except JT," she said, and then snatched open the top of her jewelry case and tossed one necklace and bracelet after another, hitting him with each of them. "Bringing all these expensive gifts over here like you really cared about me. You make me sick."

JT shook his head and walked out of the bedroom and down the hallway to the front door. He looked back and then realized that Carmen's decision to break things off with him was probably a blessing in disguise. Over the last few months, she had started to become much too demanding, anyway, so maybe it really was time she moved on and found someone who could give her what she needed. JT would miss the remarkable way she had always pleased him, there was definitely no denying that, but in the end, he had a feeling her decision was best for everyone involved. He was sure Carmen would be much better off without him.

Chapter 5

Alicia grabbed a bottle of Perrier from the stainless-steel, dual-door refrigerator and looked over at the double ovens, one stacked on top of the other, and then at the granite and cherrywood island that included built-in burners and a sink. A few feet away were a large sitting area, with two oversized chairs and a fireplace, and a breakfast area that contained a rectangular glass table that seated six people. The kitchen was so large, she and JT could easily host a moderate-sized party in it and never have to use any other area of the house.

No matter how many days passed, no matter how many times she strolled from room to room, Alicia never got tired of exploring the home she and JT lived in. Even as she walked into the living room and observed the exquisitely arranged light-tan furniture, she felt as if she were seeing every single piece for the first time. Then, as she continued on her self-directed tour, she glanced into the dining room at the lacquered wooden table, surrounded by ten comfortable chairs, and also at the china cabinet that seemed almost too perfect and delicate to touch. She loved this room and couldn't wait to have both sets of her parents and both of her siblings over for dinner.

Alicia finally unscrewed the metallic gold cap from the bottle she was holding, drank some of her water, peeped inside of JT's study—the kind of study one might find at any of the top law firms in the country—and headed down the winding staircase and into the lower level. Once there, she observed the bluish-gray leather furniture and sixty-inch black television located in the family room, and then walked into another room that housed an even larger viewing screen and four rows of theater chairs.

After she'd gone into the workout room and turned off the light she must have left on earlier this morning, she went back up to the first floor and then up to the second. On the way to the master suite, she passed three guest bedrooms, one of four bathrooms on that level, as well as her office. When she arrived, she went into her walk-in closet and scanned all of her clothing, some of which she'd had for a while and some she still hadn't even removed price tags from and had a chance to wear yet. Then there were the multiple rows of dress shoes, casual shoes, and athletic shoes.

Alicia loved her life and wouldn't have traded it for anything. She loved her husband and the lifestyle he was able to give her. She loved everything about him and was planning to be the best wife she knew how to be. She honestly couldn't have been more satisfied than she was right now, but suddenly, Phillip crossed her mind. Her ex-husband and her first real love. She couldn't believe it had been a whole year since she'd last seen or heard from him, but no matter how much time passed by, she still felt a little sad about the way things had turned out between them.

She still remembered the first day they'd met and how in love they'd been with each other from the very beginning. But she also remembered how horribly they'd gotten along with each other. Their marriage had been a total disaster and she couldn't deny all the pain and trouble she'd caused Phillip, and she hoped he was doing okay. She prayed that life was good for him now and that he'd found the perfect mate, the same as she had.

Alicia went into her office and sat in front of her computer. But when she signed on to AOL, she saw a headline about prisons, and for whatever reason, she quickly thought about Levi and the feelings she'd once had for him. She'd known it was wrong for any married woman to have feelings for another man, but she hadn't been able to help herself. He was so smooth, and he looked so good. She'd been drawn to him as a teenager but even more so when she'd become an adult, and, drug dealer or not, there had been something very special and compassionate about him. Levi knew, wholeheartedly, how to satisfy a woman, how to treat her with respect, and whenever Alicia had been with him, she'd always felt this noticeable sense of security. When they were together, she'd felt loved and protected in a way she couldn't explain to anyone. But that still hadn't changed reality: Their relationship just wasn't meant to be.

Alicia still remembered the day Levi was preparing to drive her back to the public parking lot where she always left her car whenever she wanted to spend time with him at his home, and how multiple policemen had stopped them from exiting the driveway. Levi had turned off the ignition and then demanded that she toss out of her purse the five thousand dollars he'd given her to pay off some of her bills, so she wouldn't be charged with possession of drug money. She remembered how she hadn't wanted to give any of the money up because she'd needed it so badly, but once they'd been arrested and she was quickly released on bond, she'd been glad she'd done what Levi had told her.

After reading a few articles online, Alicia flipped through some of her manuscript pages and got excited about the idea of being a published author. She only had maybe another two days' worth of revisions to work on, and then she'd be resubmitting it to her dad's agent. Joan loved the idea that Alicia's novel was centered on two young people who meet, fall hopelessly in love, and then get married barely six months later. She'd said she liked the fact that the characters were an example of so many young married couples in America who never truly got to know each other as well as they should before agreeing to make a lifelong commitment and then ended up miserable, hating each other, and ultimately in divorce court. Alicia, of course, had loosely based part of the story on her marriage to Phillip, but at the same time she'd used much of her very vivid imagination to tell the majority of it.

Writing felt so natural to Alicia, and she was glad she was in a position to work on her novel full-time. Creating characters and story lines were the two things she enjoyed doing and would have done them even if there was no chance of getting paid for it.

She read through a few more pages that she'd edited this morning and then her cell phone rang.

"Hi, Daddy," she answered.

"So, how's my baby girl doing today?"

"I'm good. How's Charlotte? And Matthew and Curtina?"

"They're fine. Curtina is giving a whole new meaning to the saying 'terrible twos,' but she's doing well."

"I haven't seen her in forever, so I'll have to drive over sometime next week. I haven't seen Matthew since the wedding either, and I really miss him."

"He misses you, too, and he was just saying yesterday how he was going to call you to see if he could come spend the weekend with you."

"I would love that, and I'll make sure to call him tonight when he's home from school."

There was a short pause and then Curtis said, "So, you're really doing okay? Because you know I worry about you."

"Yes, everything is wonderful, and I'm very happy."

"I'm glad. So, what else is going on?"

"Okay, Daddy, wait. Can I just ask you something first?"

"Sure, honey, go ahead."

"Why is it that you hardly ever ask how JT is doing?"

At first her father didn't say anything but then he said, "So, how's your husband, Alicia?" His tone was sarcastic, and Alicia didn't like it.

"He's fine, Daddy, and he's taking very good care of me."

There was another pause, and Alicia was losing her patience.

"Why can't you just accept how much I love JT and how much he loves me back? Why can't you just be happy for me?"

"What I accept is that you're a grown woman who has the right to make her own decisions. But there's no way I'm going to pretend I'm happy about you being married to JT Valentine. Alicia, the man has a long history of women, and word is that he messed around on his first wife the entire time they were married."

"But, Daddy . . . so did you. You did the same thing to Mom."

Curtis didn't say anything, and Alicia immediately regretted what she'd said.

"Daddy, I'm sorry. I don't mean to be disrespectful and you know I love you, but at the same time, I want you to see that JT is no different than you. He may have done things he's not proud of, but he's a totally changed man just like you are."

"Have you ever asked him about the affairs he supposedly had?"

"Yes. And he admitted that he wasn't perfect when he was married to his wife, but also that he only went out on her one time with one woman."

"Hmmph."

"So, what are you saying? That you don't believe him?"

"To be honest with you, I don't. And I'll tell you why. It's because of what you just said: He's no different than me. At least he's no different than the old me, anyway, and I can see straight through him. I'm telling you, he's no good, baby girl, and I regret the day I ever invited you to come with us to visit his church. I'll regret it from now on."

Alicia was livid. "Daddy, I have to go. And just for the record, I'm not your baby girl anymore, so please stop calling me that. It's one thing for you to call me that because the words are endearing, but it's another when you do it because you think I'm still some child living in your house and one you need to watch over."

"Alicia, you're taking all of this the wrong way, and I just wish you'd listen to me."

"I *have* listened and now I think it's best that we just agree to disagree and leave it at that."

"Fine. But I'm still your father, I love you, and I'll be here when you need me."

"I'll talk to you later, Daddy," Alicia said, and then pressed the off button and tossed the phone onto her desk. She couldn't remember when she'd ever been angrier.

Chapter 6

"Hi, Mom, can you talk?" Alicia said when her mother answered her phone. Tanya was the director at an abused women's facility not far from New Life Christian Center and sometimes had little time for personal phone calls.

"Actually, I'm eating lunch so this is fine. How are you?"

"Terrible."

"Why, what's wrong?"

"It's Daddy. He just made me so mad, Mom."

"About what?"

"JT and the fact that he doesn't like him."

"Look, sweetheart, I totally understand your frustration, but you also have to realize that your father loves his children more than anything and he's only trying to look out for your best interest. He's only acting this way because he doesn't want to see you get hurt."

"Well, I don't care what his reasons are because what I want is for him to stop being so ridiculously overprotective of me, and I want him to accept JT the same as he accepted Phillip."

"He'll eventually come around. It may take him a while, but he will."

"Maybe, but Daddy has a lot of nerve judging JT when he

did all sorts of crazy stuff when I was a child. He messed around on you all the time."

Her mother didn't say anything, and Alicia knew she'd hurt her feelings. She'd spoken too much too soon and without thinking, and the only thing she could do now was change the conversation.

"So, how's Dad James?"

"He's good. Just getting ready for golf season. Actually, he and some of his buddies have already been out to the course a few times."

"I know how much he loves that."

"So, how's the revising process coming along?"

"Very well. I'm almost finished, and I really hope Dad's agent is happy with the rewrites I've incorporated."

"I'm sure she'll be fine with them. Do you want me to read it one last time?"

"Will you, Mom? You've read it twice already, so I didn't want to ask you again."

"Please. What are mothers for?"

"I really appreciate it, and I'll print out a copy and overnight it to you tomorrow."

"Sounds good. And you should probably let your father read it again as well."

"I don't think so."

"Alicia," her mother said, obviously disappointed in her answer.

"I'm sorry, Mom, but I don't want to talk to Daddy for a while."

"Do you think distancing yourself from him is a good idea?"

"Actually, I do, and if you want to know the truth, if Daddy can't accept JT, then I don't see how he can accept me as his daughter."

"Alicia, I know you don't really believe that, do you?"

"Well, if he doesn't start treating JT like a son-in-law, then I won't be going around him as much. JT is my husband, I love him, and if Daddy can't deal with that, then so be it."

"I really wish you and your father would work out your differences."

"I'm sure we will at some point but not today."

"Well, hey, I need to get going. But make sure you mail the manuscript to me, okay?"

"I will, and thanks again, Mom."

Alicia dialed her best friend, Melanie. Her phone rang four times and then went to voice mail, so Alicia left her a message, asking her to call her back when she got a chance. After that, she signed in to NLCC's computer system. Since she wouldn't be able to spend much time at the office the church had given her, at least not until she got her book shipped off, she checked her assigned e-mail account daily from home. She'd only been a member for one month but already she was getting lots of notes from members, welcoming her to the church family. Some talked about how they would eventually make it a point to stand in line to meet her one Sunday after service, and others said they were e-mailing her because they wanted her to know how happy they were to have the Reverend Black's daughter as their new first lady. Alicia rolled her eyes with irritation. Yes, there had been a time when she loved being recognized or given special treatment because of her father's notoriety, but not at the moment. Not when she was so perturbed with him. Actually, she didn't like it much at all anymore because what she wanted was for people to love her for her and not because of how famous one of her parents was.

Alicia skimmed through more e-mails and smiled at all the

nice things people had to say, and then she saw one that had "From a Good Friend" as the subject line. So, she opened it:

> Hi Alicia,
>
> I have a message for you from a very good friend of yours so please call me at the number below.

She wondered who the note could be from but picked up her home phone and dialed *67, so she could block her number, and then dialed the number on the computer screen. It rang a couple of times, and then a guy picked up.

"Hello?" he said.

"Hi, you sent me an e-mail and asked me to call you?"

"Are you Alicia?"

"It depends."

"I'm assuming you are because I didn't send my number to anyone else."

"Okay, yes, I'm Alicia."

"How are you? I'm Darrell, a longtime friend of Levi's, and he wanted me to give you a message."

Alicia's stomach quivered, and strangely, her heart did the same. Finally she asked, "Where did you get my e-mail address?"

"Levi heard about you getting married to the pastor of New Life Christian Center and asked me if I could maybe find you online. So, when I went to the church's website, I saw your photo and an address listed for you."

"I guess I'm not sure why he wanted you to contact me."

"Levi is in a federal prison in Indiana, but he really wants to see you. His attorney is in the process of appealing his conviction, and because those detectives went into his home without a proper warrant and basically found nothing, he has a pretty good chance of getting out."

"Even after all the millions of dollars that were found in off-shore accounts? And the testimonies that were given by narcotics officers and a ton of other people Levi had been paying off for years?"

"Yeah, but the good news is that Levi has also cooperated with the authorities in a number of ways, including his providing proof of the person who really owned the drug manufacturing location. And the list basically goes on and on."

Alicia was stunned by what she was hearing. "I guess I don't know what to say."

"I know it sounds far-fetched but none of those testimonies or anything else matters if the police entered Levi's home improperly and his attorney can get him a new trial and prove he wasn't the ringleader. If so, Levi could be cleared on a technicality."

"Still, why does he want to see me?"

"He just does. He talks about you all the time, and I would be happy to take you to visit him."

"I can't. I just got married again, and there's no way I can ever have any contact with him. But please give him my best, and tell him that I wish him well."

"Will you at least take some time to think about it?"

"I'm sorry."

"Well, all I could do was try. Levi will definitely be disappointed, but I'll relay your message to him."

"I really appreciate it, and again, I'm really sorry."

"You take care."

Alicia set the phone down and tried to calm her nerves. She wasn't sure why she was reliving and remembering all the feelings she'd once had for Levi, but she was and she didn't like it. Why did he have to try to contact her now? It was bad enough that she hadn't been able to resist his advances when she was married to Phillip and now here he was causing the same problem again through some friend of his. She hadn't even heard his actual voice, but just knowing he wanted to see her made her uneasy. Not because she thought he would do harm to her but because she knew, without even hearing him say it, that he still cared about her. She knew he was still in love with her.

But she wasn't in love with him. Not anymore. She loved her husband, JT. She loved *him* and no one else, and she was going to pretend she'd never gotten some anonymous e-mail or made a phone call to anyone named Darrell.

She would go on with the rest of her day, business as usual.

Chapter 7

*J*T drove his black BMW M6 convertible into the driveway and heard his BlackBerry ringing. He smirked when he saw it was Carmen.

"So, I guess you've finally come to your senses," he said, waiting for the garage door to open.

"Actually, I was giving you one last chance to come to yours," Carmen shot back.

"And what is that supposed to mean?"

"Exactly what I said. I'm giving you one last chance to acknowledge all that I've sacrificed and how long I've waited to be Mrs. JT Valentine. How long I've waited to be the one and only woman in your life and the first lady of your congregation. I've earned all of those privileges and then some, fair and square, and I want what I have coming to me."

JT laughed out loud and wasn't sure how she expected him to respond to such nonsense.

"Oh, so now you think I'm funny?" she said. "You think this is some sort of game I'm playing with you?"

"Look, Carmen, what we had was good, but since you've decided that you no longer want our relationship to continue, let's just move on. Let's end this thing peacefully so we can both get on with our lives."

"I hate the day I ever laid eyes on you," she said, sniffling, "and this isn't the end, JT. This isn't the end and that's a promise you can count on."

JT opened his mouth to speak, but before he could, she hung up on him.

He took a deep breath and maneuvered his car inside the garage. *Women* was all he could think, and he wished Carmen had stayed on the phone long enough for him to tell her to never dial his phone number again. She knew she wasn't supposed to call his cell phone anyway, unless there was some sort of dire emergency. But he'd been willing to let it pass, just this once, if she was calling to apologize and tell him she'd made a terrible mistake when it came to cutting things off with him. For as long as he'd been seeing both Carmen and Diana, the rule had always been that they would arrange their next meeting days and times while they were with him, so that actual phone conversations were never necessary. Then, if for some reason he did need to talk to them, he would do the calling—which wasn't a problem because Carmen was single and could take calls from anyone, and Diana always kept her phone on silent when her husband was around. Their system had always worked fine, but apparently Carmen had forgotten the guidelines and needed to be reminded of them.

JT shook his head out of sheer annoyance, parked his car, and went inside the house. Alicia was removing a pan of dinner rolls from the oven, and JT went over and pulled her into his arms.

"So, how'd your afternoon go?" he said, kissing her.

"Good. How about yours? Did you enjoy your lunch?"

"I did. And after that I ran by the church to do a little work."

"Well, everything should be done in maybe twenty minutes or so."

"You know, I'm actually glad you decided you'd rather cook than go out this evening because I really do enjoy being right here at home with you."

"Me too. You know I love going out, but sometimes there's nothing better than having a nice quiet dinner with no interruptions."

He kissed her again and then said, "I think I'm going to head upstairs to change and get washed up."

"Okay. See ya when you come back down," she said, and he left the kitchen.

Alicia really was the perfect wife for him, and it was for that very reason that he sometimes regretted the way he was sleeping around on her and the way he lied to cover it up. He frequently told himself that he'd mainly married her because of what he'd thought being in the Black family could mean for his long-term career in ministry, but he couldn't deny his feelings for her and how they seemed to grow stronger with each passing day. As a matter of fact, he was glad his affair with Carmen was over because now he'd be able to spend more time with Alicia, and he wouldn't have to lie about where he was every Monday afternoon, his day off, or on some of the other days in the week. He'd still have to sneak out to be with Diana, but at least he no longer had to juggle two steady mistresses and a wife all at the same time. When his first wife had passed, he'd been able to see Diana and Carmen without much pressure at all, especially since neither of them knew about the other. But ever since marrying Alicia, he'd begun feeling the stress and strain of sleeping with three women on a regular basis—not physically, because he always had the kind of bodily strength he needed to keep up with all of them, but mentally the whole scenario was starting to wear on him. Actually, Carmen was the reason he'd started feeling this way, what with all her demands and possessive behavior, and he wasn't sure why she couldn't leave well enough alone. Why she couldn't just appreciate their situation for what it was. He wasn't sure why she couldn't accept reality: She wasn't his wife; she was his fling on the side. She was a woman no one could ever know about, not under any circumstances, and it was as simple as that. Yes, the more JT thought about it, he was glad to be rid of Carmen for good.

When he stepped inside the bedroom, he slipped out of his clothing and then went into the bathroom and took a quick shower. Normally, he never had sex with another woman and then came home without showering, but since Carmen had basically kicked him out of her apartment, he hadn't had time to do so. Thankfully, he'd convinced her years before that he preferred a woman's natural, God-given scent and that he didn't like smelling a lot of perfume when he was making love. Of course, that couldn't have been further from the truth, but it guaranteed his never having to come home with any fragrances that might have caused his first wife, Michelle, and now Alicia, to become suspicious.

After drying off, saturating his body with lotion, and then putting on a T-shirt and a pair of jogging shorts, JT started downstairs. But then his phone rang, so he went back into the bedroom, removed it from his pants pocket, and frowned when he saw that it was Carmen again. His first notion was to hit ignore, but then he decided he'd better take care of this problem once and for all.

"Why are you calling me again?" he asked, walking toward the bathroom and lowering his voice.

"Because."

"Because what?"

"Because I love you, JT. I love you more than anything or anyone, and I can't imagine not being with you."

"Well, you need to make up your mind, one way or the other, because you can't keep calling me like this. Alicia is right downstairs, and—"

"Alicia?! Why are you always talking about her? I'm the one who's been there for you for all these years, and I'm the one who would give my life for you if I had to."

"She's my wife, Carmen. Like it or not, she's the one I married and nothing is going to change that."

Carmen burst into tears. "JT, please. I'm begging you. Please just leave her."

"Look, I'm sorry things didn't work out the way you wanted them to, but let's just try to end this on a friendly note. We had some very good times, but what you need to do now is find someone who can give you the kind of love and commitment you're looking for."

"I don't want someone else. I want you and only you."

"Like I said, I'm sorry. And I have to go."

"JT, I'll do anything."

"Good-bye, Carmen," he said, ending the call, and then switched his phone to silent mode. First thing tomorrow morning, he'd have to call his cell phone provider to see what he needed to do to block incoming calls from both Carmen's home and mobile numbers. Maybe then she would take a hint and leave him alone.

Chapter 8

With most of the church staff being off on Mondays, Tuesday mornings tended to be filled with all sorts of meetings and personal counseling sessions, and right now, JT was sitting in his office with his two assistant pastors—both of whom contributed to the ministry in extremely positive ways but clearly couldn't have been more different. Steven Payne was in his late twenties, full of energy, and thought the world of JT; and Glenn Weaver was a fortysomething straitlaced and strictly by-the-book kind of person. Truth be told, there were times when JT could either take or leave Minister Weaver, but because he was consistently dependable and had an exceptional knowledge of God's Word, JT couldn't imagine him not being a part of NLCC.

JT leaned away from his cherrywood desk, making himself more comfortable in his high-backed chair. "With summer being barely a month away, I just want to make sure we have each of the Sunday services and Wednesday-night Bible studies covered through September."

Both of the ministers looked over the spreadsheets in front of them and Minister Payne said, "The only date I might have to change is the last Sunday in August because I have a family reunion."

"I'll be out of town as well," JT said, and looked at Minister Weaver. "So, Glenn, do you think you can cover that Sunday instead?"

"I'm sure I can. I have a family reunion as well but it's a couple of weekends before that."

"Great."

"Then I'll take one of your other Sundays or Wednesday nights," Minister Payne offered.

JT pushed the summer schedule to the side and rested his elbows on top of his desk. "The other thing I want to discuss is our membership objectives. Both of you know that my goal is to double the number of members we have within the next five years, so I want to begin having weekly meetings to discuss it."

"Bringing in another five thousand people in such a short period of time won't be an easy task," Minister Weaver said, and JT wasn't all that surprised because Glenn could be a bit on the pessimistic side when he wanted to be.

"It won't be easy, but it's not impossible."

Minister Payne had a lot more faith in JT's vision. "Well, if you turned fifty members into five thousand during these first five years you've had the church, then I don't see why you won't be able to pretty much do the same thing once again."

"Exactly," JT agreed. "It'll take a lot of planning and promoting, but I definitely think it can be done. What we have to do is figure out a way to attract more of the Chicago and surrounding-area communities, and we can start by creating multiple committees to work on various projects. There are also a number of seminars being offered that I'd like the three of us to attend, and actually, I'd like some of the ministers who report to both of you to attend as well. Then, once we appoint the heads of each committee, we'll have them go, too."

"So, when were you wanting to move forward with creating the committees?" Minister Payne asked.

"Either next week or the following, because the sooner we get those in place, the sooner we can get started."

JT looked at Minister Weaver, who seemed uninterested, and said, "Is that okay with you, Minister Weaver?" They were all on a first-name basis but every now and then, JT liked referring to Glenn's official church name because he took things so seriously.

"Whatever you wanna do, I'm fine with it."

"The other thing I'd like to do is bring in a Christian marketing coach to spend some time with us," he said, and then dialed his executive assistant. When she answered, he said, "Janet, can you bring me a couple of those seminar and coaching catalogs we received last month and give us an update on what you were able to find out about them?"

"Sure. I'll be right in."

They chatted for a few more minutes until Janet came in and took a seat. As usual, her clothes fit her tall and slender body frame perfectly, and JT wanted to laugh at the way Minister Payne was practically drooling over her. He wasn't even being discreet, but Janet did what she always did: ignored him.

She passed two booklets over to JT and said, "There are so many resources available to churches, more than I imagined, but just to give you an idea, one of the coaches teaches how Christian organizations can gear their marketing efforts toward lots of different kinds of people, whether they be saved, unsaved, believers, nonbelievers, and so on. He even talks about the fact that our message needs to inform potential members why it would be a benefit for them to attend our church, because many times churches talk at length about what programs they have to offer, but they don't necessarily keep their focus on how people's attendance will benefit them directly."

JT nodded. "That's a very good point."

"So, after reading through most of the material and doing a little research online, I think we need to do more advertising on the top radio stations, local TV stations, and in local magazines. We need to target the market we're specifically trying to reach. We need to tie in secular activities with Christian activities so that people will be more interested in participating."

"You know, I heard about a church out east that did something like that," Minister Payne said. "If I remember correctly, they had this huge Super Bowl party that was open to any man who wanted to attend. You didn't have to be a member, and there was no charge."

"Those are the kinds of things I'm talking about," Janet commented.

"The other thing we need to do," JT added, "is create something family oriented that hasn't been done before. Something that would get an entire household of people excited."

Janet stood up. "That would be great, too, because in these economic times, families are looking for activities that they can do together and won't cost them an arm and a leg."

"Thanks for the update," JT told her.

"I'm expecting a call in about five minutes, but let me know if you need anything else," she said.

"I think that's it for now," JT replied, and Janet left and closed the door behind her.

Minister Payne had watched her every move and now looked at JT. "Mm, mm, mm. It's a pitiful shame for any woman to look that good."

"Okay, Reverend Payne," he said playfully. "Please try to control yourself."

"Man, I can't help it. Because you *know* I would get with Janet Wingate in a heartbeat, and all she'd have to do is say the word."

Minister Weaver finally spoke up with a touch of attitude in his voice. "I don't think I have to remind you that Janet is a very married woman."

Minister Payne frowned. "And?"

"And you need to respect that."

"Man, please," Minister Payne said, waving Minister Weaver off.

JT couldn't help laughing but said, "Okay, you two, back to the business at hand."

"Well, as far as the seminars and coaching go, I'm all for it and can't wait to get started," Minister Payne said. "I'm ready and willing to do whatever you need."

"And you, Glenn?" JT asked.

"Whatever you need."

"Good. I really appreciate both of you, and of course, the more the church grows, the more your salaries will increase as well."

"That's nice to know, but I'm just thankful for what I'm already earning now," Minister Payne commented.

"Well, I look forward to any raise that might come out of all of this," Minister Weaver said matter-of-factly, and JT wasn't sure he liked the tone Minister Weaver was using and wondered where it was coming from.

But he decided to ignore it and said, "Well, I think that's it for now, so unless the two of you have something else—"

"Actually, there is something I'd like to speak to you about . . . in private," Minister Weaver said, and looked at Minister Payne.

"Oh, so what you mean is you want me out of here," Minister Payne said, chuckling and standing up. "I'll see you later, Pastor."

"Take care," JT said, and Minister Payne left the office. Then JT returned his attention to Minister Weaver. "So, what's up?"

"I need more money."

JT leaned his body forward, pretending to be interested. "Okay. Can I ask why?"

"Minister Payne and I and all of the other ministers and deacons are working our behinds off trying to keep up with our responsibilities, and I don't feel we're being compensated for it. Then, on top of that, you've got all these other plans you were just talking about today, which are only going to add even more to our plates."

JT was a bit taken aback, specifically because of how serious Minister Weaver was looking. "First of all, I think you get paid very well, and I know for a fact you're being paid more than many other assistant pastors who are employed by churches similar to the size of this one."

"I disagree. And we certainly don't earn anything near the half million dollars you take home, not to mention the other couple of hundred thousand a year you collect from member love offerings, speaking invitations, and from other sources— we certainly can't afford to buy twelve-hundred-dollar suits the way you do on a regular basis."

JT folded his arms and realized he was going to have to put this man in his place and remind him of whom he was talking to. He'd just had to put Carmen in her place yesterday because of the outlandish demands she'd been trying to make, so he wondered if maybe they'd both been stricken with the same kind of insanity.

"I earn what I earn because I founded this church and have done everything I can to make a name for myself here in Chicago and in a few other cities and even states. I also built up this congregation from a small storefront location, not far from here, with only fifty members."

"Yeah, I know all about the fifty members and how you

turned those fifty into five thousand," Minister Weaver said, sounding unimpressed and like he was tired of being reminded of it. "But I'm still barely earning eight thousand dollars a month, and sometimes I work more hours than you do."

"We all work a lot of hours. We have different responsibilities, but we all work more than we would like."

"Maybe, but what you need to do is either hire a few more ministers or pay the ones you have a whole lot more than what we're getting now."

JT took a deep breath and tried calming his emotions, because if he didn't, this discussion was quickly going to turn worse, and Minister Weaver would find himself in the unemployment line.

"I guess I didn't realize you were so unhappy with your job."

"I've been pretty displeased for some time now, but I kept hoping things would get better. Either that or I thought you would at least recognize and acknowledge all the work the rest of us are doing around here. What I thought was that you would eventually see that every one of us helped turn this church into what it is today."

"I do recognize it," JT said, still realizing it was best for him to end this dialogue before he said something he might regret. "And over the next month or so, I'll reevaluate everyone's salary and responsibilities."

"That's all I'm asking, Pastor, because I think once you do that you'll see exactly what I'm talking about."

"Is there anything else?"

Minister Weaver got up. "No, that's pretty much it, and thank you for taking the time to hear me out."

"No problem," JT said, but as soon as Minister Weaver left and shut the door behind him, he added, "I'll reevaluate your salary when hell freezes over and not a second before that."

Chapter 9

The day had finally arrived. Alicia had just sent off her revised manuscript a couple of hours ago and couldn't have been happier. She'd been thinking she would have it finished by last week, but when she'd realized there were a few new scenes she wanted to add, she'd spent a few extra days working on them. Now, though, it was well on its way to New York City, thanks to FedEx's overnight shipping service, and Alicia felt like celebrating. She was excited and relieved, and it was the reason she was now walking through the dress section of Neiman Marcus at Oakbrook Center. She hadn't been shopping in over three weeks, since right after she and JT had returned from their trip to St. Thomas, but she had to admit she'd gotten just about everything she wanted. Or at least she'd bought enough suits to wear to church for the next six Sundays and had also gotten a really great deal on them. They hadn't been St. John, which she loved, but they were made by some of the other top designers she admired, and they'd only cost around six hundred dollars each. Neiman's had had a rare sale that day and JT had insisted she take advantage of it, so that was the reason she'd purchased so many outfits at one time. Well, actually, *he'd* purchased them, but he'd made it pretty clear that his money was her money and that she should never think otherwise.

"What's mine is yours, and I don't ever want you to forget that, okay?" he'd told her.

"I won't," she said.

"Because what I want is for you to look good at all times and eventually be able to get anything you want."

"Well, if you want to know the truth, I sort of already feel like that right now—like I have everything."

"Maybe, but it's not like we have a Bentley to drive around in, and we definitely don't have the kind of house a first lady like you deserves to be living in. Sixty-five hundred square feet is respectable, but what we need is a house that's at least as big as your father's. Or larger."

Alicia loved how ambitious JT was and how he was never satisfied with the existing conditions. She loved his unwavering hunger, his desire to succeed, and his drive toward being the best, and she knew one day he really was going to give her all that he promised and so much more. If only Phillip had had the same personality, things might have worked out so much better between them. JT never complained about her love for shopping or the amount of money she spent, so why couldn't Phillip have felt the same way? Instead, all he'd done was swear she had some sort of addiction and there hadn't been a thing she could say to change his mind about it. She couldn't deny that she'd run up a few credit card balances behind his back, a number of cards that were in his name only, but still, Phillip could have been a lot more understanding than he had been. Especially since Alicia had really loved him and he had claimed he loved her just the same. But if she'd said it once, she'd said it a trillion times: Sometimes love just wasn't enough.

After Alicia had strolled around in Neiman's and hadn't

found anything that caught her attention, she went outside and walked down to Nordstrom. First, she looked at a pair of four-inch-heeled sandals, which she purchased, and now she was in the handbag section, picking up a small, pure-white Kate Spade tote. She turned the purse around to the other side, realizing she sort of liked it, but then put it down when a woman walked up to her.

"Alicia Valentine, right?"

"Yes," Alicia said, feeling as though she'd seen the woman before.

"Hi, I'm Donna," she said, shaking Alicia's hand. "I used to be a member of New Life Christian Center until a few years ago. But I did come visit the Sunday your father was the guest speaker, and I said hello to you and your stepmother on my way out."

"Yes, I thought you looked familiar. There were a lot of people there, but I rarely forget a face. It's nice to see you again."

"Likewise. So, how does it feel being first lady of such a large church?"

"Wonderful. Everyone has been so kind and that makes a huge difference in itself."

"I can imagine."

"I've been working on a project at home, but now that I'm finished with that, I'm really looking forward to getting more involved with the women's ministry. I'd also like to begin bringing in a featured female speaker every month and then hold open discussions afterward."

"That sounds like a great idea. When I was there they had a pretty organized women's ministry, but when the former first lady passed away, they stopped sponsoring so many events," she said, looking at Alicia with sad eyes.

"I'm sorry. Was Michelle a friend of yours?"

Donna sighed and then said, "Hey, I know we really don't know each other but just the idea that you and I would bump into each other out of the blue, not to mention in the middle of a department store on a quiet Tuesday afternoon, well, I just don't believe in coincidences. I believe in fate and that every single thing that happens is somehow in God's plan."

Alicia wasn't sure where Donna was going with this conversation but kept listening.

"I hope I don't regret this, and my prayer is that no matter how negatively this might affect your marriage to Pastor Valentine, I'm doing the right thing by telling you the truth."

"Telling me the truth about what?"

"Pastor Valentine's first wife and how she may not have been killed accidentally."

"What?"

"Some people think she was murdered . . . and that Pastor Valentine was behind the whole thing."

Alicia frowned, immediately taking offense to what this Donna woman was saying. "If that's true, then why haven't I heard anything about it?"

"Probably because when the police did their investigation, they found no evidence of foul play and had no choice but to rule it an accident."

Alicia's heart beat faster. "Well, if that's the case, then why would anyone think otherwise? And who are these *people* you're referring to?"

"Some of her friends and also her parents and siblings."

"This is crazy."

"I'm sorry, but I really thought you should know about this."

"JT loved his first wife and would never have hurt her like that."

Donna looked at Alicia calmly and then said, "Well, he had

I don't know how many affairs on her, and I know she wasn't happy about it. As a matter of fact, she was so fed up that for the last four or five weeks of her life, she didn't even attend church services and she told a few of the women she was close to that she was planning to divorce him."

Alicia was overwhelmed. Her father had basically told her the same thing, that JT had regularly messed around on his first wife, but Alicia refused to believe any of this. She didn't believe her father, and she didn't believe the woman standing in front of her. Especially since JT had denied sleeping around any more than the one time he had admitted to and because he talked a lot about how much he'd loved his first wife. Plus, what could he possibly have had to gain from her death? Insurance money maybe, but as far as Alicia could see, JT didn't have millions of dollars stashed away in some bank account. He earned quite a bit of money through his ministry, but he certainly didn't have the kind of millions that people committed murder over.

"Look, I have to get going," Donna said. "But again, I thought it was only right that you know. And please, please take care of yourself."

Alicia smiled, acting as though she hadn't been shaken one bit, and the woman went on her way.

But Alicia *was* shaken. And she couldn't wait to talk to JT.

Chapter 10

H i, baby," JT said after walking into the bedroom and pecking Alicia on the lips.

"Hey."

It had been four hours since that Donna woman had made those disturbing accusations about JT, and still, Alicia couldn't stop thinking about them. She'd tried focusing on something else but no matter how much time had passed, she just hadn't been able to. She had even tried to do a little more shopping; however, for the first time since she could remember, she'd found no interest or excitement in it. She hadn't been able to enjoy herself because, whether she wanted to admit her true feelings or not, she was very troubled by all of this.

"So, what did you buy at the mall?" JT asked, removing his navy blue suit jacket and dropping it onto the bed. Then he loosened his classic red tie and unbuttoned his French-cuffed sleeves.

"Nothing."

"Nothing?" he said, laughing. "Alicia Black Valentine went shopping and came back with nothing?"

Alicia never acknowledged his comment and instead leaned against the dresser and crossed her arms. "There's something I need to ask you."

JT went into his closet. "Okay, go ahead."

"I've tried to figure out the best way to ask you this, but I've decided that there's no other way except to just do it. When your wife died in that accident, was there an investigation?"

"Yes. All accidents are investigated, but why do you ask?"

"Were you a potential suspect?"

"Suspect for what?"

"Murder."

JT quickly stepped back out of his closet with only his underwear on. "Excuse me? Who told you that?"

"A woman came up to me while I was in Nordstrom."

"What woman?"

"She said her name was Donna and that she used to be a member of NLCC a few years ago. Then she said that Michelle's parents and siblings and some of her friends thought you had something to do with her death."

"I can't believe this," he said, exhaling loudly and taking a seat on the edge of the bed. "What did she look like?"

"She had a medium-brown complexion, was a little taller than I am, and had very long hair."

JT sighed again. "Baby, come here and sit down next to me."

Alicia did what he asked.

"Sweetheart, yes. There was an investigation, but in the end I was cleared."

"But why would anyone think you were involved in something so horrible in the first place?"

"Envy, of course. Some people just don't want to see others do well, mainly because they're miserable themselves. And so they thrive on starting vicious rumors such as this one."

"This Donna woman also claims that you messed around on Michelle repeatedly and that Michelle was planning to divorce you."

"Lies, lies, lies. Baby, Michelle and I were the happiest couple I knew. We loved each other, we were committed to each other, and we'd planned on spending the rest of our lives together."

"Well, why didn't she come to church for the last few weeks she was alive? Because this Donna person mentioned that to me as well."

"She stopped coming because she was tired of hearing all those lies and rumors about me and other women. She was so humiliated, and she just couldn't face people at the church anymore."

Alicia stared at him with uncertainty.

"I mean, baby, look. This sort of thing happens all the time with men who hold the kind of leadership positions that I do, and it especially happens with pastors like me who have thousands of members in their congregation. People love trying to destroy any man who's been called by God to teach His Word and one who is being completely faithful to his wife and his ministry."

"I just don't understand why anyone would say these kinds of things."

"Because, baby, people are very cruel, and unfortunately as first lady of our church, you're going to have to deal with these kinds of rumors all the time. I'm sorry that this woman approached you out of the blue the way she did, but sadly I doubt it will be the last time. Sweetheart, there are so many women out there who would do or say anything if they thought they had even the slightest chance at breaking up our marriage, just so they can have a chance at becoming my wife."

Alicia wanted to believe him, but she couldn't stop thinking about her father and all the women he'd slept with over the years. All the lies he'd told her mother whenever she had confronted him about them. All the plotting and scheming he'd done with not just one wife or two, but with three. Alicia thought about how long her father had gotten away with so much wrongdoing. Mostly, though, she thought about herself and how she'd plotted and schemed, too, and told effortless lies to Phillip the whole time she'd been having an affair with Levi. She thought about the fact that she'd always been able to keep a straight face, the same as JT was doing right now.

But maybe she was reading too much into this and JT really was being honest with her. Maybe he wasn't like her father at all. Maybe he wasn't anything like the way she'd once been either. She just didn't know what to think, and she was very confused.

"Alicia. Baby," he said, grabbing both her hands. "You have to believe me. I'm your husband, and you have to trust me. You have to trust that I love you with all my heart and that I would never hurt you."

"I love you, too, JT, but I could never tolerate you messing around with other women. I could never do that, not under any circumstances."

"And you won't have to because I'll always be faithful to you. Always," he said, leaning her body backward and onto the bed. "You're the only woman I want and the only woman I need, and I promise you that won't ever change."

Alicia gazed into his eyes, praying he was telling the truth, and JT kissed her. He kissed her the way he had the night of their first date, gently yet insatiably, and she couldn't help loving him with everything in her. She loved him hard, and her feelings were so intense, she had no control over them. She was powerless, and that was the one thing that frightened her the most.

Chapter 11

*J*T scrolled through the list of contacts in his BlackBerry, searching for his father-in-law's phone number, and hated having to call him. His plan had been to at least wait until he'd been married to Alicia for three or four months before asking Curtis for any help, but now with this whole mysterious Donna woman entering the picture, something told him he needed to act without delay. He'd done everything he could, trying to convince Alicia that this woman was lying through her teeth and was only trying to cause problems in their marriage, but he could tell Alicia was still feeling uneasy. This woman, whoever she was, had caused Alicia to question his past as well as who he was currently, and he had to do whatever necessary to keep her happy. This, of course, included making a lot more money than he was, because Alicia loved living the high life. She wanted to be rich, and while she'd insisted she would never tolerate any extramarital affairs, he had a feeling that if he gave her more than she could ever dream of—more than what her father had given her—she would think long and hard before ever leaving him. JT wasn't planning for Alicia to find out about Diana, Carmen, or any of the other women he'd been with since meeting her, but he knew it was better to be safe than sorry. It was better to start preparing for what could eventually happen, because he didn't want to lose his wife.

He also didn't want to lose his five thousand followers, which could easily come to pass since his congregation loved having Alicia as their first lady. They loved the idea that she was the daughter of a world-renowned minister, a man they all cherished, and without her, it might be twenty years before JT saw the kind of success he longed for—he might never become the leading televangelist in the United States and build the largest church in history. If Alicia left him, there was a chance his loyal congregants would leave, too, because he wasn't sure they could deal with yet one more scandal. Two years ago, he and the other ministers and officers at NLCC had been able to stifle all that murder investigation gossip and keep it out of the media, but there had still been a few nosy members who'd found out about it, had spread the word, and had decided they wanted nothing else to do with JT. Thankfully, the majority hadn't believed any of what they'd heard, not about his being a potential suspect or about all the women he'd consorted with, but still, he wasn't sure they'd be as understanding this time around. Especially since he knew he was guilty of more allegations than he cared to think about.

When JT located his father-in-law's number, he picked up his office phone and dialed it. Curtis answered after the second ring.

"Hello?"

"Curtis. Hey. This is JT. How are you?"

"I'm well. You?"

"Fine, fine. And how're Charlotte and the children?"

"They're good."

"I'm glad. Look, the reason I'm calling you . . . well, actually I'm calling you for two reasons, and the first is that I wanted to ask when you might have time to come speak here at the church again. You could do any Sunday morning you want during the main service because we can certainly work around your schedule."

"Actually, my schedule is pretty booked for the rest of the year, but maybe sometime next January or February."

Curtis spoke with no enthusiasm, and JT just couldn't understand why he always sounded so distant whenever he spoke to him or saw him. He'd seemed fine that day he served as NLCC's guest speaker and even while they'd been at dinner that afternoon, but as soon as he'd learned that JT was dating Alicia, he'd begun acting as if he wanted nothing to do with him. Oh, he was cordial enough in front of other people, but JT had a feeling Curtis hadn't wanted Alicia to marry him. JT had even asked Alicia exactly that, and while she'd denied it and insisted her father was fine with him, his gut told him otherwise.

"Well, whenever you can will be good," JT finally said. He really needed Curtis to make an appearance much sooner than eight or nine months from now, but he didn't want to push the issue. Especially when he had a much more important request.

"The other thing I wanted to talk to you about is my ministry and a huge favor I'd like to ask of you."

"What kind of favor?"

Curtis's tone was snappish, but JT continued. "I'm really trying to build up my ministry and wondered if you would write me a letter of recommendation so that I can approach some of the megasized ministries regarding speaking engagement opportunities."

"Well, the thing is, I've only heard you speak one time. I've also only known you for seven months, so I really wouldn't feel comfortable doing that."

JT frowned and swiveled his chair around so that he was facing the window of his study. "But you know how successful I've been as founder and pastor of my church."

"I know what you've *told* me. And yes, I saw how many members you had when I was there. But let's be honest, JT, I really don't know you well enough to vouch for your character, let alone your overall abilities as a minister."

JT hated the way Curtis was dismissing him but realized he had no choice except pulling out the big guns. "Well, if you can't do it for the reasons you mentioned, then can you do it because I'm your son-in-law and because, with the exception of God, I love your daughter more than life itself?"

"No. I can't." Curtis spoke callously, and it was all JT could do not to slam the phone onto its base.

But instead, he said, "Okay, fine. I understand your position, and while I'm a little disappointed, I completely respect your decision."

JT waited for Curtis to respond but when he didn't, he said, "Well, I should go, but thank you for taking my call."

"No problem."

JT hung up the phone, but only long enough to end Curtis's call and then dial his assistant. "Janet, can you come in here for a few minutes?"

"Sure. I'll be there in a few seconds."

When she walked in, JT asked her to shut the door, and then she took a seat directly in front of him.

"First, I'd like you to call the florist and have them deliver two dozen long-stemmed roses to my wife every day for the rest of this week. And I'd like them to start this afternoon."

"How romantic."

"Then I need you to work on another project for me."

"Okay."

"I want you to go online and research the top one hundred

churches in the country according to the size of their congregations, as well as all of the ministries that broadcast on television. Then, once you've compiled a list and you and I have had a chance to go over it, I want you to draft a cover letter to each of the senior pastors. I've been thinking about this a lot because, even though I get a respectable amount of invites from various churches throughout the year, it's now time I seek out as many upper-echelon churches as I can. It's time I become a lot more well-known in those kinds of circles."

"That's understandable and I think very doable," Janet said.

"In the letter, I want to introduce myself to them, let them know I'm the Reverend Curtis Black's son-in-law and that if they're interested in having me serve as a guest speaker at their respective churches, I would love to come. I also want you to include some of my personal history as well, such as how my mother was a drug addict, how I have no idea who my father is, and how I was tossed around from one foster home to another until I finally ran away from the last one when I was sixteen. Then mention how after that, I basically raised myself on the street and for about a year, I even got mixed up with a gang. But thankfully, when I turned twenty-seven, God called me into the ministry, and after hearing my father-in-law for the first time on television, I was inspired to found New Life Christian Center. Of course, you already know to include how many people I started out with and what we have now."

"Definitely," she said, writing down a few more notes. Then she looked at him with a confused gaze.

"I know all of this is a shock to you, but if I want to get people's attention, it's time I market myself through my own personal testimony," JT said, knowing he had exaggerated his story quite a bit in comparison to the true scenario he'd shared with Diana a little over a week ago.

"I had no idea you'd had such a hard childhood, and I'm so sorry."

"Hey, it was what it was, but now I want to share it with everyone. Most ministers share their entire histories, but I don't think I ever did because I've always been ashamed of what I went through. I've always felt like no one would respect me if they knew I had parents who cared nothing about me and that I'd even been homeless for a period of time."

"But it wasn't your fault," Janet said with tears in her eyes, and JT felt somewhat guilty for telling her such a fraudulent story. However, he didn't have a choice if he wanted to move forward with his plans.

"I realize that now, but it's taken me years to come to terms with that. Still, I haven't even shared this with my wife or any-one else, so for now, I want this information to remain between you and me and the pastors you'll be sending the letters to. Then, once they begin calling to schedule engagements with me, I'll tell my wife and our church family so that they'll hear my testimony first."

"I won't say a thing. You have my word."

"I really appreciate your help with this."

"No problem at all," she said. "There is one other thing, though. Since you're going to mention Reverend Black's name in the cover letter, do you think he would write you a letter of recommendation? Because I think it would do wonders for you if we were able to include something like that in the package."

If JT hadn't known any better, he'd swear Janet was reading his mind. Which was the reason he smiled and said, "He'll be writing it this week. I just got off the phone with him, and he was more than happy to do it."

Chapter 12

"Hey, girl," Alicia's best friend, Melanie, said.

"Hey, Mel. How are you?"

"I'm fine. I hadn't spoken to you in a few days and thought I'd give you a call."

"I'm glad you did, and I'm so sorry we haven't been able to talk very much over the last few weeks. First it was the wedding and then the honeymoon, and then I had to work daily on the revisions for my book."

"You know I completely understand. So, did you get it finished and sent off?"

"Yes, just yesterday, and actually I was going to ask you to read it one last time but didn't want to bother you."

"Bother me? Now, Alicia, you know I'm happy to read it as many times as you need me to and all you had to do was say the word."

"I know. But my mom reread it, and so did I, and I think it'll be fine."

"Well, I still want you to send me a copy."

"I'll make sure to put one in the mail tomorrow."

"So, what else is going on? And how's JT?"

"He's fine," Alicia said, thinking about the horrible rumors relating to JT's first wife. She wanted so badly to tell Melanie, but she couldn't. Melanie was her best friend and if there was anyone in the entire world she could trust with her life it was her, but she just didn't want her thinking negatively about her new husband. She didn't want her feeling any ill will toward him.

"Good. You seem really happy and content, and that makes me happy."

"I truly appreciate that, Mel. You have always supported me, even when I messed up my marriage with Phillip, and I never could have gotten beyond all of that without you."

"Girl, please. That's what friends are for."

"I know, but you're the kind of friend most people never get a chance in life to have, and I just want you to know how thankful I am."

"I'm thankful to have you as well. I sort of hate that you had to move ninety miles away, but that will never change how close we are."

"No. It won't. Distance is one thing, but you'll always be like my sister, no matter what. As a matter of fact, what we should do is schedule a lunch or dinner date right now."

"Well, actually, I have next Thursday off, so if that works for you, we can get together then."

"Thursday is perfect."

"Do you want me to drive over there?"

"No, I'll just come to Mitchell because that way I can drop by to see Matthew and Charlotte before I head back home."

"Okay, that's fine. So, will your dad be out of town?"

"I don't think so, but why do you ask?"

"Because you said you wanted to see your brother and Charlotte."

"Well, if you really wanna know the truth, I'm not all that happy with my dad right now."

"Oh. And why is that?"

"It's a long story, and I'll fill you in when I see you."

"Are you sure you don't want to talk about it now? I mean, my break is almost up, but I can extend it and get one of the other nurses to cover for me if you need me to."

"No, it's not that serious at all."

"Okay, well, then I'd better get back to work."

"I'm sure I'll speak to you again before next week but I'm really looking forward to seeing you, Mel," Alicia said, signing on to her computer.

"We'll have a great time."

"All right then, well, take care."

"I will, and you do the same. Love you."

"I love you, too."

Alicia hung up the phone and smiled. It really was wonderful hearing Melanie's voice, and Alicia missed her a lot more than she'd realized. She loved her new life with JT, but there was a part of her that missed her old surroundings and the people she'd known and cared about since she was a child. She was sort of shocked to be feeling this way, what with her finally having all that she'd ever prayed for. But deep down, she did miss attending her father's church on Sunday mornings, seeing her family on a daily basis, and visiting Melanie a lot more than she was able to now. She did have her mother and stepfather right there in the area, but she still felt a tiny void in her heart. In a perfect world, everyone she loved would reside in the same city, but sadly she knew that wasn't possible.

After browsing Neiman Marcus's website and that of Marc Jacobs, she checked some of her NLCC e-mail. She read one after another and was elated to see she was still receiving so many responses from church members. Their words continued to show such amazing support and approval of her marriage to their pastor, and she couldn't wait to become more involved with the overall ministry.

She read a few more messages but got nervous when she saw the last one, which said, "Guess who?" She didn't recognize the address and hoped Levi hadn't found some way to e-mail her. She wasn't sure if inmates even had Internet or e-mailing privileges, but just the fact that Levi had asked his friend Darrell to contact her one week ago was enough to put her on edge.

But she clicked on the message and felt relieved when she saw that it was from a girl she'd gone to elementary and junior high school with. She hadn't seen Renee in years, not since they were children, and she was so excited to be hearing from her. They'd been such good friends, but when Renee's parents had divorced, Renee's mother had no longer been able to afford private school tuition and Renee had been transferred to one of Chicago's public schools instead. She and Alicia had talked on the phone for almost a year and sometimes visited each other, but eventually they'd lost touch.

Alicia read the rest of the e-mail and thought about how wonderful it would be to have a girlfriend close by. No one could ever take Melanie's place, of course, but it would certainly be nice having someone she could get together with, every now and then, on a moment's notice. It would be neat having someone to shop with, do spa days with, and maybe even confide in from time to time. It would feel good having someone she could laugh and talk with face-to-face whenever she wanted to, so she printed out Renee's e-mail message and called her.

JT's heart plummeted, his chest muscles tightened, and he knew he must have been dreaming. Had to be if Carmen was sitting in *his* living room with *his* wife and acting as though they were best friends for life.

Alicia smiled when she saw her husband and went to go greet him. "Hi, sweetheart. I'm so glad you got here in time to meet Renee. Well, actually, I should say Carmen, but when we were kids, I always called her by her middle name. Anyway, this is Carmen Wilson."

Carmen stood and reached out her hand. "It's very nice to meet you, Pastor."

JT wanted to rush back out to his car but tried acting as calmly and as unsuspectingly as he could. "It's nice meeting you as well."

"I was going to call you," Alicia said, "but since Carmen got here, we've pretty much talked nonstop. She's been here for three hours, and we've been catching up on everything. Oh, and thanks, baby, for the beautiful flowers."

JT looked at both of them in a stupor.

"Are you okay, sweetheart?" Alicia asked.

"What? I mean, yeah, I'm fine. So, how did you guys meet?"

"In kindergarten. We went to school together all the way through eighth grade but we haven't seen each other since right after we started different high schools. But thanks to you, Carmen was able to find me."

"What do you mean by that? What did I have to do with it?"

"Well, since you decided to make me your wife and someone told her I had just gotten married to the senior pastor at NLCC, she went to the website and saw my e-mail address. And that's how she was able to send me her phone number."

"Oh, really?"

"Yes, and I'm so glad she did. We've had the best time this afternoon, and it's almost as if we were able to pick right back up from where we left off nine years ago."

JT was dumbfounded and wondered what Carmen was up to. He wondered why she'd had the audacity to come into his home like she was welcome and why she'd never once told him she knew his wife personally. He wanted to kill her, but he stood there pretending he couldn't have been happier about their reunion.

Alicia started out of the family room. "When you came in, I was just on my way upstairs to get some photos of my parents and of Matthew and Curtina, so I'll be back in a few minutes."

Carmen picked up what looked to be a glass of iced tea. "We'll be right here," she said, taking a sip of her drink. Then she set it back onto the coaster on the coffee table and made herself more comfortable on the sofa.

When Alicia was gone, JT looked at his former mistress and spoke in an angry whisper. "Carmen, what in the hell are you doing here?"

"Wow! The good reverend is now resorting to four-letter words? Shame, shame, shame," she said, snickering at him. "I mean, not the man who's always claiming he loves God so much. The man who despises curse words of any kind."

"Look. I'm not playing with you, Carmen. What are you doing here?"

Carmen's face turned cold. "And I'm not playing with you either. I told you this wasn't the end for you and me, and that's exactly what I meant."

"You're crazy. You're sick, and you need a psychiatrist."

"Maybe. But if you don't end your marriage to Little Miss Thing, you'll regret it for the rest of your life. Oh, and I suggest you unblock my numbers on your phone, too. Unless you want me calling the church or calling you here at home."

"Why are you doing this?"

"You know why."

"Carmen, if you know what's good for you, you'll leave right now and you'll never come back here ever again."

Carmen laughed at him and crossed her legs. "And if I don't?"

"If you don't, you'll wish you had."

"Oooooh," she said, feigning fear. "I'm so scared I don't know what to do."

JT opened his mouth to respond but closed it when he heard Alicia coming back down the stairs.

"Here they are, girl," she said, walking back into the room and sitting down next to her friend.

"Oh my. Your little brother is such a handsome little thing, and your sister is a cutie, too."

"I know," Alicia said, and then showed Carmen a photo of her father and Charlotte and then one of her mother and James.

JT looked on for a few seconds but then politely excused himself and went up to their bedroom. When he arrived, he removed his blazer, slammed it onto the bed, and gritted his teeth. He was fuming and couldn't believe Carmen had been willing to do something so psychotic. He'd dumped a number of women over the years, but not once had any of them been this obsessed with him.

JT paced back and forth across the room, trying to figure out the best way to handle this situation. What he wanted more than anything was to get rid of her. Not just for the moment, but permanently, so he'd never have to lay eyes on her again.

Chapter 13

*I*T pulled open the door, slipped onto the patio, and then closed the door behind him. Alicia was getting dressed for a publishing seminar she'd registered for a couple of weeks ago, and this gave him ample opportunity to call Carmen. His first instinct was to wait a day or two before contacting her, but when he'd thought about all the trouble she might end up causing, he'd decided it was better to deal with her as soon as possible.

He dialed her number, and she answered right away. "Hi, baby," she said. "Miss me already? I mean, I just left your house not even a whole hour ago."

"This has to stop, Carmen."

"Does it?"

"Yes. It does. But one thing I wanna know is why you never told me you knew Alicia. I wanna know why you kept that hidden all this time."

"Why? Because you're a liar and a cheat. And when I found out you were dating that high-priced ho, I knew my relationship with her just might be the insurance policy I needed."

"Insurance policy?"

"Yes. You heard me. You'd been dating me for all those years and had me believing I would eventually be your wife, and then you betrayed me with that tramp. Then, when I saw that you were really going to marry her, I realized my past friendship with Alicia was well worth keeping a secret."

"You're acting like a complete fool, you know that?"

"Well, your wife certainly doesn't think so. Because as it turns out, she's thrilled to have me back in her life. She's excited to have someone right here in Chicago that she can spend time with, and I'm going to be there for her as much as she wants me to. Before you know it, I'll be her best friend in the world."

"No, what you're going to do is stay away from my wife *and* me. Or else."

"Or else what?"

"If you don't leave us alone, you'll be sorrier than you've ever been about anything."

"I don't think so. Not with everything I know about you. Not with all the dirt you've done, all the horrible things you had me do, and all the people you've hurt in the process. If you push me, JT, I'll tell everything I know. To your congregation and the whole city of Chicago."

JT clenched his phone tightly. He hated this. Hated ever having gotten mixed up with the likes of Carmen and then being careless enough to confide so many incriminating pieces of information to her. Although, he knew those moments of sharing had only come right after they made love, a time when he was most vulnerable about everything.

Carmen continued, "Look, it doesn't have to end this way. We don't have to be enemies, JT."

"Hmmph. Well, from where I'm sitting, I don't see where we have any other choice."

"Oh, there're always other options. Because don't get me wrong. I do despise the fact that you married Alicia, but I also understand your reason for doing it. You wanted to use her father as a way to grow your ministry, and I don't blame you for that. Actually, I don't blame you in the least, and that's why I'm willing to give you six months to do what you need to do . . . and then I want you to file for a divorce. And in the meantime, I expect things between you and me to go back to the way they were. We'll spend time together the same as in the past, and everyone'll be happy."

JT wanted to yell "No!" as loud as he could, but he knew it wouldn't change anything. He knew Carmen really did know way too much and could ruin him on a moment's notice. So he said, "Fine. Whatever you want, but you have to stay away from Alicia."

"I'll keep my distance, but now that we've reconnected, it's not like I can just cut her off for no reason."

"Then make up something. Tell her that you have to go away for a while to take care of a sick relative. Tell her whatever you have to."

"I'll see what I can do."

"Good," JT said, and looked inside the house, making sure Alicia hadn't come downstairs yet. "Hey, I need to get going."

"Okay, JT, but just let me say one more thing."

"What?"

"You know I'm only doing this because I love you, right?"

"I guess."

"I do, JT. Sometimes I think I love you more than I love myself. Sometimes I wonder if life would even be worth living if I can't be with you, and that scares me."

JT raised his eyebrows. He didn't dare respond to what she'd just said, but little did she know, he was scared, too. He was afraid of any woman who thought that lowly of herself.

But he said what he could to pacify her. "Everything is going to be fine."

"You promise?" she said, sniffling, and now he was even more worried. Here just a few minutes ago, she'd been threatening him to no end, and now she was sobbing into the phone.

"I promise," he hurried to say.

"Then I feel better about this whole thing. I feel better than I have in over a week."

"I'm glad, but I really have to go, okay?"

"I love you, JT."

"I'll talk to you later," he said, and ended the call.

Right after he did, he went back inside the house. It was barely in the nick of time, though, because Alicia was already walking down the staircase.

JT waited for her to come into the kitchen.

"I sort of regret not being able to go to Bible study with you this evening," she said. "But I'm also really looking forward to this seminar. The main focus is actually going to be on self-publishing, and while it doesn't look like I'll have to go that route, I still want to learn everything I can about the business side of the industry."

"Of course. With anything you do, it's always good to learn as much as you can."

"Over the last year, I've read a ton of books on writing, publishing, and marketing, but it'll be good to hear someone talk about it in a class setting."

"All the time you're putting in, baby, is definitely going to pay off, and it's only a matter of time before you see all the rewards."

Alicia strode closer to the door leading to the garage. "The seminar is from seven to ten, so I guess I'll see you around ten thirty or so, okay?"

"So, you're not even going to kiss me good-bye?"

"Oh, I'm sorry, baby," she said, walking back toward him. Then she gave him a peck on the lips.

JT grabbed hold of her. "I really do love you, Alicia. I love you more and more as the days go on," he said, and meant every word.

"I love you, too, and I'll see you when I get back. Oh, and enjoy Bible study."

JT watched her leave and sighed deeply. He sighed because if he didn't leave now, he'd be late getting to Diana's.

"I've been looking forward to seeing you all day," Diana said with her arms wrapped solidly around JT's neck. "It's been over a week since you last came here, and that's much too long for me."

"I know," he said, looking at her diamond stud earrings, which were at least two carats each. "And that's why I asked Minister Payne to lead the Bible study session tonight. So I could see you."

"But what about the last four or five days? Why couldn't you be with me then?"

"Well, for one thing, I've had a lot of church business going on."

"Really? Because I thought maybe it might be because you're spending a lot more time with that young wife of yours."

"No, that's not it at all," he said, but knew he had in fact spent every evening with Alicia over the last few days.

"I need to see you more often, JT," she said with conviction. "I need to see you at least once or twice every week."

"I'll do better," JT acknowledged, but wasn't sure how he was going to make that happen. Especially since Carmen was now demanding that he spend time with her again and also because he didn't want Alicia becoming suspicious about the amount of time he spent away from her. Not to mention he really did want to be at home with his wife the way he was supposed to. When he'd married her, he hadn't counted on falling in love with her, but just at this very moment, while embracing Diana, he realized he had. For weeks, he'd begun admitting to himself the fact that he did love Alicia, but it wasn't until now that he knew just how deep his love for her actually ran.

"All I ask is that you try," she said. "Because it's like I told you: If you keep up your end of the deal, I'll be more than willing to keep up mine."

"Of course," JT said, kissing her, and Diana stepped away and started unbuttoning her snow-white, sleeveless silk blouse.

"So, how are your marketing plans going?" she asked.

"Fine. We're planning to appoint a committee and then attend a few seminars, but what I'd like to work on right away is a major media blitz. We do have money in the church's PR account, but if your offer is still on the table, I'd really like your help. I really need it because the more funding we have to work with, the more TV and radio stations we'll be able to advertise on for three to four weeks straight. We'd also be able to do ads for the same period of time in both the *Chicago Tribune* and the *Chicago Sun-Times*."

"How much do you think you'll need?"

"I'm not completely sure, but we'll be hiring an ad agency soon."

"Well, if I had to guess, I'd say you're probably going to need at least a hundred thousand dollars just to start. That is, if you want to do this campaign the right way and make it as memorable as possible."

"Yes, probably at least that much."

Diana unzipped her St. John jeans and stepped out of them. "Whatever you need, sweetheart, it's yours," she said, still undressing herself.

JT finally pulled his shirt over his head and then slipped off his pants.

Diana slid into bed and gazed at him with enticing eyes. "You know, it really ought to be a crime for a man to look as good as you do."

JT smiled. "Thank you for the compliment."

"You're welcome. Now, take off those sexy little briefs I bought you and come to Mommy."

JT wasn't sure why those words always turned him on— "come to Mommy"—but they did. Maybe it was because of how old Diana was and because of how fascinated he was with their age difference. Maybe it was because he'd lost his own mother when he was just a young boy and he liked the way Diana sometimes nurtured him. Diana was his lover, but in a quiet sort of way, she was also his protector. She cared about his success, she was willing to do whatever she could to help him, and JT was grateful for her. Grateful she had no problem giving him the two things he craved most: mind-blowing sex and lots and lots of money.

He didn't want to keep sleeping with Diana, not with him just realizing how in love he was with his new wife. But God forgive him, he didn't want to *stop* sleeping with her either. Diana was sort of like an addiction, except there were huge benefits involved, and he just didn't see how he'd ever be able to give her up. Although, once he figured out how to fix this Carmen fiasco, he'd only have to split his time between two women, and that wouldn't be hard to do at all. He'd see Diana once or twice a week the way she wanted him to, and he'd spend each of his other days with Alicia. He'd keep both of his women happy, and there wouldn't be a single thing to worry about. If anything, life was only about to get better for him.

Chapter 14

It had been a full week since Diana had agreed to give JT six figures, but even now, all sorts of advertising and promotional wheels were still spinning in his head. But more so, he fantasized about the kind of results each of these efforts was going to bring. He could see himself now, heading up a church with ten, twenty, and at some point, maybe even thirty thousand members, and eventually being seen on television by millions of people worldwide. He would first move forward with televising locally and then regionally. But in five years or less he'd go national on TBN, TLN, BET, or TV One, or even better, his sermons would air on every one of those networks on different days of the week. What he wanted was to be bigger and more recognized than any of the leading well-known televangelists out there today.

JT thought even further into the future and burst out laughing. Not because anything was funny but because he was literally overjoyed about all the wonderful things God was getting ready to do for him. He was thrilled about all the blessings he would soon be receiving, and he was ready to contribute his part to the process. He'd learned a long time ago that God helped those who helped themselves, and it was the reason he'd asked

Janet to pull a very important file for him. The administrative staff kept a separate folder for every minister they invited to come speak, but little had JT known this orderly procedure of theirs would now be extremely beneficial to him.

JT opened his father-in-law's file and saw Curtis's lengthy and very impressive bio, a few articles outlining some of his major accomplishments, and then the speaker's agreement he'd signed and returned to them months before his date of appearance. Next, JT flipped past the first two pages, but when he came to the last of them, he leaned all the way back in his chair and grinned. At first, he'd had second thoughts about doing this, but now that Curtis's signature was staring him straight in the face, he realized that this was going to be much easier than he'd planned on. He'd wondered if maybe a big-time pastor like Curtis might scribble his signature the same as some physician, but based on what JT saw before him now, this definitely wasn't the case. His handwriting looked pretty straightforward, and JT couldn't wait to start practicing it. He would learn every curve of every letter. He would pay close attention to the way Curtis dotted the *i* in his first name and the way he looped the *l* in his last. JT would practice multiple times a day until he was able to replicate it perfectly. He would master it so well, not one person would ever consider the idea of forgery. Not Janet and not any of the pastors each letter of recommendation would be going out to.

On the other hand, however, there was a chance a few of them might call Curtis, not necessarily to confirm the authenticity of the letter, but possibly just to make small talk and to mention that they'd received it. This, of course, did worry JT slightly, but in the end, he was sure the majority of these ministers wouldn't bother wasting their time. They would either decide to invite him to their churches or not, and that would be the end of it. Still, if word did get back to Curtis and Curtis confronted him about it, he would simply play the role of a very desperate and very apologetic son-in-law, the kind who'd *only* been trying to create a better life for Alicia—Curtis's beloved daughter. He would beg Curtis's forgiveness and promise to never do anything so deceitful again—he would do and say whatever he had to, squashing any thoughts Curtis might have about pressing charges against him. JT would overcome any obstacles Satan placed in front of him. He would rise above any stumbling blocks, the same as always.

As soon as Alicia looked at the Caller ID screen and saw that her father's agent was calling, she hurried her mother off the phone and answered the other line.

"Hello?"

"Alicia?" she said.

"Yes, this is she."

"How are you? This is Joan Epstein."

"I'm great, how are you?"

"Well, actually, I'm feeling fabulous now that I've had a chance to read your novel again. Alicia, it's absolutely wonderful."

"Really? You think so?"

"Yes. I just love it, and I have no doubt that your future readers are going to feel the same way. As a matter of fact, I haven't felt this motivated and sure about the future of a brand-new author since quite a few years ago when I first agreed to represent your father."

Alicia closed her eyes, wanting to scream with joy, and said, "Oh my God. I can't believe you're so happy with it."

"I really am, and I think it's because you've incorporated so much honesty and so much feeling into it without being preachy.

You've written a story that so many young couples will be able to relate to, and you've also shown just why so many of their marriages end in divorce."

"Well, unfortunately, it's like I told you during our first conversation: I was basically writing what I know. There are so many plot points that have nothing to do with my own life, but there are plenty of scenes in the book that resemble or, in some cases, are almost identical to what happened between my first husband and me. We went through premarital counseling, but for the most part, I think the only reason we did it was because my father insisted on it. At least that was my reason anyway."

"It's probably why even though many young couples do participate in counseling, they never really get to know each other as well as they should before taking their vows. Most people fall in love with the idea of being in love, and they truly believe this is all they'll ever need to be okay. Thirty years ago, even I was naïve enough to believe that love was all my first husband and I would ever need. But as your character so clearly states in the book, love just isn't enough. A successful marriage requires so much more than that, and my hope is that when couples, married or engaged, read *When the Honeymoon Is Over*, they'll be encouraged to communicate all of their likes, dislikes, and expectations. There is no doubt that we want your novel to entertain readers, which it certainly will, but if people can relate or learn something in the process, this will be all the better."

"So, does this mean you're taking me on? I mean, I assume you are, but . . ."

"Yes, absolutely, and I guess I should have said that as soon as I called, right?"

They both laughed and Alicia said, "I'm just glad you feel so good about it."

"You've got a winner here, and I'm going to get started on the submission process right away."

"Do you have an editor or two in mind?"

"More like six."

"And you think they'll all be interested?"

"I do, and I also think we'll end up having to do what we did with your dad. I'll set up meetings with each editor and her publishing group and have you fly in to meet with each house individually."

Alicia couldn't believe this was really happening. She was actually going to be a published writer with a real book in real bookstores being read by real readers. This was so implausibly outrageous.

"What we want," Joan continued, "is to connect you with a very talented editor who honestly loves your work and who will be committed to helping you make your novel the best that it can be. What we want is to find someone who will allow you to create your characters and story line completely and then offer editing suggestions based on what a general audience will want to see and will be satisfied with. The goal is less about personal preference on the part of the author or the editor and more about selling as many books as possible to as many people as we can. Meaning, we have to give your readers what they want and what they'll be able to relate to. We have to give them something that they'll enjoy so much, they'll rush to tell all their friends and family members about it."

"I agree."

"The other thing is that while I'm not sure how you'll feel about this, I'd really like to include something about your father in my cover letters. I can imagine that you probably want to stand on your own merit and not enter the industry as Reverend Curtis Black's daughter, but because your father is so successful and is loved by so many millions of people, using his name will definitely make a difference for you."

Alicia was disappointed. "I was hoping I wouldn't have to do that."

"I totally understand. However, on the other hand, since you write fiction and your dad writes nonfiction, your work will still sell based on the story line, but if your publisher is allowed to include your father's name with the initial publicity and promotion, it will almost guarantee you a ton of sales right out of the gate."

"My husband was saying the same thing a couple of weeks ago, so if you think this is what we should do, then I'm fine with it. You've always done right by my dad, so I trust your judgment."

"I'm glad. Also, on a side note, I want you to know how discreet I am and how confidential I keep all of my clients' information. I represent your father and will now be representing you, but I won't ever discuss your business with your father unless you authorize me to. I would have even asked your permission first before calling to ask him if I could use his name when I contact potential editors, but as it turns out, he began suggesting I do that before you'd even finished writing your novel. He really loves you, Alicia, and one of the last things he said to me was that his hope is that you'll sell ten times more books than he has."

Tears filled Alicia's eyes. She'd been so angry with her father for being so hard on JT and for not accepting him, but deep down she knew her father loved her more than anything. She knew he wanted to see her happy and would do anything to help her.

Finally, she said, "My dad is the best, and I appreciate you sharing that with me."

"Well, I'd better let you go, but please look for the author-agent agreement that I'll be overnighting you this afternoon. My signature will be on both copies, and then all you'll have to do is sign both of them as well and then return one to me. That way, we'll both have originals."

"Sounds good."

"Oh, and you may already know this, but I take a fifteen percent commission on anything I sell relating to your books, including foreign rights and film rights."

"Yes, my dad showed me his contract last year when I first started researching the industry."

"Wonderful. Well, it was great speaking to you, and of course, if you have any questions at all, please call me anytime."

"I will, and Joan, thanks so much for everything."

"It's my pleasure. Take care."

Alicia hung up the phone and said, "Thank you, thank you, thank you. Thank you, Lord. And thank you for my dad."

Before Joan had called, she'd still been furious with her father and hadn't intended to say much, if anything at all, to him when she stopped by his house this afternoon. But now she looked forward to seeing him. She would have lunch with Melanie and then head straight over there right afterward. She would apologize to her father for not speaking to him for just over two weeks now, and they would go back to being as close as ever. It would seem as if they'd had no spat or disagreement in years.

Chapter 15

irl, can you believe all of this is happening?" Alicia said, dipping one of five jumbo shrimp into a dish of red sauce the waitress had brought with her appetizer. She and Melanie were having lunch at one of their favorite Mitchell restaurants, The Tuxson, and were sitting at a linen-covered table overlooking the river. They would have much preferred to have sat out on the patio rather than near a window, but even though the weather was sunny and in the low seventies, there was still a slight chill in the air.

"Yes, I believe it, and you know I always said you would be a published novelist someday. And I'm so, so happy for you."

"Thanks. My dad's agent—"

"You mean *your* agent," Melanie said, interrupting her.

"Excuse me," Alicia said, beaming. "*My* agent still has to find a buyer for it, but it doesn't sound like she's worried at all."

"She'll sell your work in no time."

"I hope so, but I'm just so happy she liked it as much as she did. She had a lot of good things to say about it and was able to tell me why she thought it would do well once it's in print."

"Well, you know I loved the first draft you ever gave me. It's a page-turner no different than any of the other novels I read, and you know I read a lot. I read just about everything."

"Thank you for reading it so many times for me and for giving me some really great suggestions."

"You are quite welcome, and as soon as you write another one, I'll be ready to read that one, too."

"Actually, I've already started outlining it but still need to think it through a little more."

"Well, whenever you finish, I'll be looking forward to it."

"I called my mom when I was driving here, and she sounded prouder than I've ever heard her. And JT was ecstatic."

"I can only imagine. And what about your dad? Because I know he's been wanting this for you for a very long time."

"I was going to call him, but I decided I would wait and tell him in person later today."

"Gosh. I should go over there with you, just so I can see the look on his face. I'm sure it will be priceless because I don't think I've ever met any man who cherishes his daughter the way Dad Curtis cherishes you."

"I know."

"Which reminds me," Melanie said, after eating some of her cream of mushroom soup. "Why were you so upset with him?"

Alicia sighed and relaxed farther into her chair. She wanted to tell Melanie everything, but she just didn't think she could do it. She would tell her parts of it, though. "I never told you this, but my dad was never happy about my marrying JT."

Melanie looked at her but didn't seem shocked.

"What?" Alicia said.

"Nothing really, but when we were at the rehearsal dinner and at the wedding, it was pretty obvious that your father wasn't very happy. I mean, he didn't seem angry or sad, but he also didn't seem excited or like he approved of JT."

"Well, if you picked up on that, I'm sure other people did as well."

"Why doesn't he like him?"

"I think it's mainly because he loved Phillip and can't see having any other man as his son-in-law," she said, knowing this wasn't even close to being true.

"That's too bad."

"It really is. Because I love both my father and my husband. But if my father keeps refusing to accept him, then I won't be seeing my father very much anymore."

"Maybe you should talk to him."

"I have, but the last time we spoke, all we did was argue."

"Maybe all your dad needs is some time. Maybe once he sees how in love you and JT are with each other and how well JT treats you, he'll eventually be okay with everything."

"Maybe."

"It'll be fine. You'll see."

Alicia wished she could be sure of that, but she wasn't. Not when her father kept insisting that JT was no earthly good and was only going to hurt her in the long run. Not if he ever found out about the supposed murder investigation JT had been involved in regarding the death of his first wife.

But Alicia wouldn't breathe a word of that to Melanie. Instead, she would pretend that life with JT couldn't have been better.

"Well, regardless of what my father thinks, I really couldn't have asked for a better husband, Mel. He showers me with gifts, and he never complains about anything I do. And best of all, JT is faithful to me. He loves and honors me, and that's all I expect."

"You're really blessed to have him."

"I know, and I'm very thankful. I mean, I was blessed to have Phillip as well and I loved him, but with JT, I get to love him and live in peace. I never have to yell and scream with him or hear him criticizing my spending habits the way Phillip did."

"But do you ever think about him?" Melanie asked right when the waitress walked over to them.

"Can I take this?" the twentysomething, exceptionally tall young woman asked Alicia.

"Yes, please."

"And yours?" she said to Melanie.

"Yes."

"Is there anything else I can get either of you?"

"No, I think we're fine," Melanie said.

"Yes, we're good," Alicia added.

"Your entrées should be ready shortly," the woman said, and strutted away.

"So, back to my question," Melanie continued. "Do you?"

"Sometimes. But why do you ask?"

"I just wondered because I know you were so in love with him, and he certainly still . . ."

"He still what?"

"Nothing."

"Mel?"

"Really, it's nothing."

"Come on, Mel. Phillip still what?"

"He still loves you, Alicia, but I'm so sorry for letting that slip. You know I love Phillip like a brother and always will, but I would never try to undermine the love you and JT have together. I respect your marriage, and you know I'm very happy for you."

"Did he actually tell you that?"

"Sort of."

"Meaning?"

"He did."

"When?"

"He was here in town the day after you got married. He delivered the morning message at your dad's church."

"Really? My dad never told me that."

"Well, he was here, and then afterward, he and Brad and I went to dinner."

"So, how is he?"

"He's fine."

"And his mom?"

"She's fine, too."

"I think about her from time to time because she was always so wonderful to me."

"She's definitely a great lady."

"So, how did you guys get on the subject of Phillip and how he feels about me?"

"Well, it wasn't like it was planned. We were talking and out of nowhere, Phillip asked me how the wedding was and I told him it was nice."

"Then what?"

"He said he was happy for you and that he hoped JT loved you as much as he still did."

Alicia's heart sank. After all this time, she still felt bad about the way things had turned out between her and Phillip. It was one thing for them to end their marriage because of how terribly they'd gotten along, but it was another for her to have had an outside affair and run up his credit cards without his knowing it. Now, on top of that, Melanie was telling her the man still loved her.

The waitress set down their entrées, both of which consisted of stuffed flounder, potatoes, and sautéed vegetables, and then she walked away.

Alicia sliced some of her fish with her fork. "Sometimes I feel just awful when I think about the way I hurt Phillip. He had his faults but what I did to him was the worst."

"We all make mistakes," Melanie said, chewing some of her spinach. "And the good news is, he doesn't hate you for it."

"Still, I just wish he could find someone like I have, fall in love, and be happy."

"I'm sure he will, but it's only been a year since you guys separated, and I don't think he's interested in finding anyone else just yet."

"Well, I wish he would, because he really is a good man, and he would make some woman a great husband."

"I never should have brought this up, and I'm really sorry."

"It's not a problem at all. Plus, best friends are supposed to tell each other everything, right?"

Melanie smiled. "I guess. But your life is with JT now, and that's all that should matter."

"I'm sure Brad couldn't care less one way or the other," Alicia said, referring to Melanie's boyfriend, but Melanie didn't say anything. "He still hates me, doesn't he?"

"He doesn't hate you. He just doesn't like what happened between you and Levi. I mean, he and Phillip have been extremely close since childhood, and it killed him to see Phillip in so much pain."

"I guess. But maybe one day, he'll be able to forgive me."

"I'm sure he will."

"So, are you guys thinking more about marriage?"

"We talk about it a lot more than we used to."

"Well, you've been dating for two years, so what's the holdup?"

"We just want to be sure."

"Sure of what?"

"Sure that we want to settle down and be with one person

for the rest of our lives. We love each other but forever is a very long time."

"So, are you saying you're okay with waiting just as much as Brad is?"

"Yeah, I'm fine with it. We enjoy our time together. We're loyal to each other. We're completely happy with our relationship."

"Well, as long as you're both okay with it."

"We are."

Alicia and Melanie chatted awhile longer about Melanie's parents, the master's degree in nursing she was very close to completing, and how she was considering going back to school full-time to be an anesthesiologist. Alicia had no desire to go back to school, especially for multiple years, but she could definitely see Melanie doing it. She would do fine and she had no debt, so she would be okay financially, too. Alicia also realized that maybe Melanie's desire to become a doctor was the reason she wasn't pushing the idea of getting married.

When they finished their meals, Alicia took care of the check, and they headed to the mall. This was certainly not the norm for Melanie, but Alicia was glad she'd been able to talk her into going. What Alicia wanted was to enjoy as many hours with Melanie as she could, because she knew it would be a while before they saw each other again.

Chapter 16

It was amazing how extraordinary her father's impeccably designed mini mansion always looked, Alicia thought as she drove JT's BMW up the long driveway. She still owned her silver-blue ragtop BMW, the one her father had given her as a college graduation gift, but JT's car was much sportier and barely two months old. He'd purchased it not long before they'd gotten married, and she loved the way it raced down the highway. It was the reason she always drove it whenever she made a trip over to Mitchell.

Once she parked and turned off the ignition, she walked up the brick sidewalk and rang the doorbell twice. Shortly after, Agnes, the housekeeper, answered.

"Hi, sweetheart," she said, smiling at Alicia. "It's so good to see you. Give me a hug."

Alicia loved Agnes. She hadn't so much in the beginning because she couldn't help comparing her to their former housekeeper, Tracy, but now Agnes was just like family to her. "It's great seeing you, too, and how are you?"

"Wonderful. And how's that gorgeous husband of yours?" she asked, closing the door.

"He's fine. I wanted to spend the day with Melanie, so he stayed in Chicago."

"And how is she?"

"She's good."

"You should have brought her with you."

"She wanted to come, but she has plans this evening with Brad."

"Well, you make sure you tell her I said hello when you talk to her again."

"I will. Where is everybody?"

"Matthew had track practice and should be home any time now, but your dad and stepmom are out back with one of the landscapers."

"I have some news for them, but I may as well tell you now. My dad's agent loved the revisions, and she's getting ready to try to sell my manuscript."

"Oh, honey, that's wonderful! Good for you. We all knew it was going to happen, but it's good to know that it's now a reality."

"I know. I'm so relieved and can't wait to see what offers we're able to get."

"I'm so, so proud of you," she said, hugging Alicia again.

"Thank you. Also, thank you for always being so kind to me, Agnes. I know I've told you this many times before, but thank you for not judging me or treating me any differently when I had to move back in here. When Phillip and I split up, it was a very tough time for me, but you made me feel very special."

"I would do it again in a heartbeat."

Alicia looked up when she saw her dad and Charlotte coming down the hallway.

"Hey, Alicia," Charlotte said, embracing her.

"Hey," she said, and then looked at her father and smiled. "Hi, Daddy."

"Hi, baby girl—I mean, Alicia."

" 'Baby girl' is fine," she said, hugging him, and she could tell he was just as happy to see her as she was to see him.

"Let's go in the family room," Charlotte said, but when they did Alicia heard a child saying "Lee Lee" and saw her baby sister, Curtina, walking toward her and rubbing her eyes. She was clearly just waking up.

"Hi, little one," Alicia said, picking her up. She kissed her repeatedly, and Curtina squealed with laughter. "You're getting so big."

"Isn't she?" Curtis added. "She's only two, but she looks more like three or four."

"She's such a doll, though," Alicia said. "And I'm so glad I got to see her while I'm here."

Curtis sat down on the sofa. "Actually, she's been here all week because Tabitha hasn't been doing so well."

Alicia looked at Charlotte and wondered why she hadn't said a word since Curtina had come into the room, but then looked back at her father. "What's wrong with her?"

"She's been having a lot of complications, and we're not sure when she'll be coming home from the hospital."

Charlotte sighed loudly, and Alicia knew she still wasn't happy about this little girl her husband had conceived out of wedlock with his mistress. Alicia could tell she wasn't happy at all and that the last thing she wanted was to have Curtina living with them indefinitely.

"I'm sorry to hear that," was all Alicia could think to say.

"You know she's had HIV for a while," Curtis said. "So, all we can do now is pray it hasn't turned into full-blown AIDS."

Her stepmother still didn't comment, so Alicia changed the subject. "So, how are your mom and dad, Charlotte?"

"They're fine. They were down for a visit this past weekend, and we had a great time. Mom and I went shopping, of course, and then they went to church with us on Sunday."

Alicia switched Curtina from one side of her lap to the other. "I really miss Deliverance Outreach. I mean, I love all the people at New Life, but I've known the people at Deliverance for so many years."

"You should come visit one Sunday," Curtis suggested.

"I'll try, but when you're first lady, you're sort of expected to be at your own church every Sunday."

"That's true, but maybe they'll excuse you every now and then so you can come hear your dad," he said.

"I'll see what I can do about that," she said, and they all laughed, including Charlotte, and Alicia was glad Charlotte's spirits were back up.

"So, what else is going on?" Curtis asked her. "Have you heard from Joan yet?"

"Welllll . . . ," she said, smiling.

"Well what?"

"She's sending me the author-agent agreement, and she's getting ready to submit my manuscript to six editors."

Charlotte's face lit up. "Oh my God. Why didn't you call us right when you heard?"

"I knew I was coming by this afternoon, so I figured I'd wait and surprise you with the news."

"Congratulations, baby girl. This is the beginning of a truly great career."

"This really is wonderful, Alicia," Charlotte said. "And words can't even express how proud I am of you."

"We're beyond proud," Curtis said. "And in only a very short time, you'll be hitting the *New York Times* list and receiving all kinds of awards."

"We'll see."

"Well, I already told Joan to use my name, connections, and anything else to get you the most publicity available."

"I know. She told me, and thank you for doing that, Daddy."

"Of course."

"Hey, big sis," Matthew said, strolling into the room. Alicia set Curtina to the side of her on the love seat, got up, and hugged her brother.

"Hey, how's it going?"

"Good. Just got out of practice," he said, and then picked up Curtina and kissed her on the forehead.

"When's your next meet?" Alicia asked.

"Saturday afternoon. You wanna come?"

"They're having a meet on Memorial Day weekend?"

"Yep."

"Let me check with JT to make sure we don't have anything else going on, and if not, we'll be here," she said, thinking how this might be the perfect opportunity for Curtis to get to know JT a whole lot better.

"Oh, and did Mom and Dad tell you I only have one session left at driving school?"

"No, but good for you."

"I got the car I want all picked out, too."

Curtis and Charlotte both shook their heads, but Alicia obliged him. "Really? What kind is it?"

"The same as yours, of course. What else do you expect me to get?"

They all laughed, because for as long as anyone could probably remember, Matthew had always looked up to his sister and looked forward to getting many of the same things she already had.

"I'm serious. I don't want the same color you have, but I do want a plain silver one or maybe even red."

"We'll see next month," Curtis said. "Because the deal was that you had to get straight A's the entire school year."

"Well, if that's the case, then we might as well head down to the dealership right now, because I'm definitely getting all A's again."

"You can't beat that," Alicia said.

"No," Charlotte agreed. "I guess you really can't. Also, Matthew, your sister found out today that your dad's agent is going to represent her and that she's getting ready to submit her novel to some editors."

"Wow. Congrats, Alicia. Now, that's what's up!"

"Thanks," Alicia said, and her cell phone rang. She pulled it out of her tote and smiled. "Hi, baby."

"Hey, you havin' a good time with your family?"

"I really am. What are you up to?"

"I just left the church, and now I'm headed home."

"I wish you were here with us."

"I wish I was, too, but maybe next time."

"Well, actually, if we don't have anything else to do this Saturday, Matthew wants us to come over for his track meet."

"That would have been great, but remember we have that Pastors' and Wives' Luncheon downtown."

"Oh yeah, that's right. But do we really have to go?"

"Well, we don't have to, but since Janet RSVP'd for us a good while ago, I definitely think we should."

"Oh," she said.

"Baby, I can tell you're disappointed. I can hear it in your voice, and I'm really sorry."

"No, it's fine."

"It wouldn't be so bad if there weren't going to be a lot of top

Chicago pastors attending. Pastors who I really need to connect with more closely."

"You're right. And really, I'm okay with it."

"So, when will you be home?" he asked.

Alicia looked at her watch, seeing that it was just after six. "Maybe around nine or ten."

"Okay, well, tell everyone I said hello and drive safely."

"I will. I'll call you when I'm on my way."

"I love you."

"I love you, too," she said.

JT ended his call with Alicia, looked down the hallway, and wondered what was wrong with him. He did love Alicia. Or at least he thought he did anyway. But if that was the case, then why was he getting ready to walk inside a room at The Ritz-Carlton downtown on East Pearson? Why was he getting ready to sleep with a woman he'd just met for the first time and was willing to take a chance on getting caught with her? Because it wasn't like The Ritz was some low-rate motel where you didn't have to walk through a public lobby. It wasn't like this particular location was situated out in some suburb the way the one in Dearborn, Michigan, was—the one he'd spent two days at when he'd spoken at a church in Detroit and had invited over the wife of one of the deacons.

No, this Ritz was popular and very busy around this time of day, but he hadn't cared. The ironic part in all of this, though, was that the only reason he'd driven downtown in the first place was so he could pick out a gift from Tiffany's for Alicia. He'd wanted to find something very special as a way to celebrate the news from her literary agent, but once he'd made his purchase and had started on his way back to the parking ramp, he'd stopped inside a nearby Starbucks. He'd gone in, gotten in line to order his mocha Frappuccino, and that's when he'd seen her walking in right behind him. A stunning thirtysomething woman whom he hadn't been able to take his eyes off of. A woman who looked so much like his first wife, they easily could have been sisters.

Still, he'd tried ignoring her. But before long, they'd struck up a casual conversation and had sat down together at a table. They'd talked for over an hour, and then JT had made his move. He'd told the woman that he wanted her, and she had willingly given him one of her room card keys.

He hated doing this to Alicia but the good news was, the woman lived at least six hours away in Minneapolis and was only in Chicago for a few days on business. So, after today, JT would never have to see her again. He would be with her just this one time, she'd be flying back home tomorrow, and that would be the end of it.

It would seem as if nothing had happened between them at all.

Still, though, he hesitated for a few seconds. He stood in place, not making a single move. He stood, debating his decision, but finally said, "God, forgive me," and then slid the plastic card into the key slot.

Alicia untied the white satin ribbon, opened the small aqua-blue box, and pulled out a white gold and diamond bracelet. "Oh my God, JT, this is absolutely beautiful."

"You really like it?" he asked, leaning against the doorway of their bedroom and feeling thankful he'd made it home a half hour before she had.

Alicia reached her arms around his neck, kissed him, and

then hugged him. "Yes, I love it, and it was very thoughtful of you to drive all the way downtown. Is that where you were when you called my cell phone?"

"I was actually in the car and on my way, and that's why I wanted to know how long you were going to be at your dad's."

"You're too much."

"I just wanted to surprise you with a little something because I truly am proud of you, baby."

"You're always doing so many nice things for me."

"I do them because you're my wife and because I love you."

"Will you put it on me?" she asked.

"Of course," JT said, taking the bracelet and placing it around her wrist.

When he'd fastened the clasp, Alicia turned her arm back and forth, admiring it. "You couldn't have chosen anything better."

"Well, actually, I could have, because there's always something bigger and pricier to choose from when you're shopping at Tiffany's. But I thought this was pretty appropriate since I saw an asterisk marked by it in their catalog that came last week."

JT saw the embarrassment on Alicia's face, but then she said, "I hope you don't think I was trying to throw you some sort of a hint, because I really wasn't. I never even expected you to see that."

"But even if you had, that would be fine, because how else will I know what it is you really want? I mean, yeah, you could simply just tell me. But this way you had no idea I was going to get it for you, and that made receiving it a lot more enjoyable. Right?"

"Yes," she said. "It did. More than you know."

"Then that's all that matters," he said, taking her into his arms again. His feelings were mixed, though, because while he was glad to be holding his wife, he couldn't stop thinking about the woman he'd just slept with less than three hours ago. Veda Scott. The woman who not only resembled Michelle but who also felt like her in bed. He'd told himself this was just another impromptu tryst, the kind he enjoyed having on occasion, but he couldn't push the woman's beautiful brown eyes, her perfectly structured cheekbones, or her soft lips from his mind. Then there was the gentle way she'd stroked his face and the way she'd held him. The sex had been as wonderful as he'd expected, but what he couldn't seem to let go of was the emotional connection. He knew it didn't make sense, not with them just meeting each other, but he'd felt a certain level of closeness when he'd been with her. He'd felt as though he'd known her for years, and it was the reason he had to see her again.

Chapter 17

JT lifted his shiny black Montblanc pen away from the yellow legal pad and marveled at how good he'd gotten at writing Curtis's signature. His diligence about practicing it over and over had paid off tremendously and only in one day's time, too. He'd worked on it yesterday and then again all this morning, and he was now ready to move forward with the next phase of the process.

He picked up his desk phone and dialed his assistant. "Hey, can you come in for a few minutes to go over the ministry listings you've been looking up?"

"Sure. I'll be right in."

JT set the phone back on its base and slipped the pad of paper he'd been working on inside his desk drawer.

When Janet walked in and took a seat, he said, "So, how has all your research been going?"

"Wonderfully. And as it turns out, I was able to find a really neat website that lists congregations with five thousand or more members. It even included NLCC, so that was nice to see as well."

"That's very good to know because this means we truly are considered a megachurch. A mini megachurch, but still a megachurch nonetheless."

"Absolutely."

"Were you able to find anything else that might be helpful?"

"As a matter of fact, I found another listing that highlights only pastors who televise their services. Some locally, some regionally, and some nationally."

"It's amazing what you can find on the Internet these days."

"I know, and all I did was Google a few different keywords and that was basically it."

"Well, then once you have the addresses typed into a data file, we should be ready to mail out everything. Then I want to review the cover letter I wrote a couple of more times, and I should have my father-in-law's recommendation letter on Tuesday or Wednesday. At first I was going to ask him to sign an original for each package, but since there will be so many of them, I figured I'd just have him sign maybe ten or twenty for the top ministries and then we can send Xerox copies to the others."

"I agree, and since you'll have Pastor Black's letter by Wednesday, then I should be able to ship everything by next Friday. I'll print all the documents and then have Martha assemble them," she said, referring to one of the other secretaries who reported to Janet. There was a total of three of them, but Martha was the most efficient, and JT was glad Janet was assigning her to his mailing project.

"Then, after that, it'll just be a waiting game," he said.

"Oh, I think they'll begin calling right away. You're an excellent speaker and you're the son-in-law of a very famous pastor, so what more could they ask for?"

JT sighed heavily. "I hope you're right."

"Of course I am, and if anything, you'll have to figure out which engagements to turn down."

"That would be an absolute dream. I mean, I know traveling

is going to take me away from NLCC a lot more than some of our members will want, but if everything goes as planned, I'll only have to do this for a year or two. Then, after that, my prayer is that our ministry will have grown in great numbers and we'll be broadcasting nationally."

Janet smiled and nodded her head in agreement. "It's all so exciting, and I can't wait to see it come to pass."

"Well, I couldn't do any of what I do without you, and I want you to always remember that. Hiring you a couple of years ago was the best decision I could have made, and I'm very grateful for all your loyalty and dedication."

"You are quite welcome, and I just appreciate having the opportunity to be a part of New Life's mission and the lives of the people who will eventually be helped by this ministry."

"If I have things my way, we'll be able to reach millions of souls on a regular basis," JT commented, and then his cell phone rang. But when he looked at it and saw the word "private" displayed on the screen, he hit the ignore button. He'd unblocked Carmen's phone number, thanks to all her petty threats, but he'd also made it very clear that if she couldn't help calling him, he would much prefer she disguise her number before dialing his.

"So, what are you, Richard, and Kayla doing for the holiday?" he asked Janet, trying to forget about Carmen and the fact that she wouldn't stop bothering him.

"We're eating at my parents'. They do a huge cookout every Memorial Day, and all of my aunts, uncles, and cousins usually attend. What about you and Alicia?"

"We're going to my in-laws'. Alicia's mom and stepdad."

"Oh, okay. Will there be a lot of people there?"

"No, I think just the four of us, and to be honest, I'm really looking forward to not having to mingle with a whole lot of people. It'll be nice just to hang out and enjoy a day of peace."

"I don't blame you," she said, looking at the wooden clock on JT's wall. "Gosh, I didn't realize it was so late. So, if that's all you have, then I'm going to head out to meet Richard for lunch."

"Yep, I think that's it for now."

"Sounds good, and just let me know if you want to add something else to the package."

"I will," he said. "Also, if you don't mind, can you shut the door behind you?"

"Sure."

When Janet was gone, JT picked up his cell and dialed into his voice mail system. There was only one message, obviously from Carmen, and he dreaded listening to it. Still, he pressed 1 to play it.

"Hi, baby. I didn't want anything but was hoping to speak to you for a few minutes. Anyway, I'll see you in a few hours, okay? I love you."

JT rolled his eyes toward the ceiling in disgust and pressed 7 to delete. This woman literally made him sick. She irritated the heck out of him, but sadly he had to go along with the program for now and there was no sense in complaining.

Next, JT scrolled through his BlackBerry until he saw an entry for Victor Scott—the name he'd typed in when he'd entered Veda's phone numbers, just in case Alicia ever saw reason to snoop through his contact listing. He'd given each of his women male first names, David Redding for Diana Redding and Carl Wilson for Carmen Wilson. This method had always worked in the past, even when he'd been married to Michelle, so he hadn't seen a reason to discontinue using it now. He'd also asked Verizon years ago to stop sending itemized pages listing all of his incoming and outgoing calls, so he never had to worry about Alicia questioning any particular phone numbers. He never had to worry about her suspecting anything out of the ordinary when it came to the women he communicated with.

He selected Veda's cell number and dialed it.

"Hello?" she answered.

"Hey, pretty lady. How are you?"

"I'm fine. How are you?"

"Couldn't be better."

"Wonderful."

"So, are you at the airport?"

"Yes. It sounds like we'll be boarding in just a few minutes, though."

"That's what I figured, because I remember you said your flight was leaving around noon."

JT waited for her to say something but when she didn't, he said, "I know this is going to sound strange, especially since we barely know each other, but I'm already missing you."

"Yeah, right," she said, slightly chuckling.

"I'm serious. I mean, I really like you a lot, and no matter how hard I try, I can't get over the fact that you remind me so much of my former wife."

"So, is that the only reason you wanted to be with me?"

"Well, I do have to be honest. Your resemblance to her is what initially attracted me to you, but now after being with you last night, I'm attracted to you as a person. There's just something very special about you."

"You think so, huh?"

"I do."

"And I'm what, maybe the hundredth person you've told that line to in the last week?"

They both laughed and JT said, "Come on now. You're not being fair."

"I'm just saying."

"I won't lie to you, I meet lots of attractive women, but you can't deny that there's some pretty noticeable chemistry between you and me. Am I right?"

"I guess."

"Well, I don't guess. I know this for sure because it's very unusual for me to feel like this so quickly."

She didn't respond again, so JT said, "I do have one question for you, though."

"What's that?"

"Are you seeing anyone?"

"Actually, I'm married. Unhappily. But still very married."

"So am I, but I'm sure you already figured that out."

"Yeah, I did. I saw the wedding ring on your finger, remember?"

"True. But on the other hand, I didn't see one on yours."

"Stopped wearing it a long time ago."

"Then you're on your way out, I take it."

"Eventually. I have an eighteen-year-old who's graduating next Friday, so once he's off to college this fall, I'm planning to file for a divorce."

"So, it's that bad?" he asked, wondering how old she was, because she definitely didn't look old enough to have a child who was about to finish high school. Not that it mattered to him one way or the other, though.

"I'm miserable."

"I'm really sorry to hear that, but if it's any consolation to you, I'd certainly like to see you again."

"Oh yeah?"

"I would. So, when are you going to be back in the area?"

"I'm not sure, but I'll let you know when I have another visit planned. My company sends me here at least a couple of times per month, so chances are I'll be back in a couple of weeks."

JT heard what sounded like the gate representative preparing to begin the boarding process.

"Hey, they're calling first-class, so I have to get going."

"That's fine, but, Veda, I really want to see you again, and soon."

"Just call or e-mail me, and we'll talk about it."

"I will, and you have a safe flight, okay?"

"I will, and you take care."

JT ended the call, laid his phone on his desk, and looked at the picture-perfect five-by-seven wedding photo of him and Alicia. He wasn't sure why she simply wasn't enough. He wasn't sure why he couldn't resist being with other women. He honestly didn't want to hurt Alicia, but he also couldn't control his sexual desires or impulsive feelings. He couldn't help doing a lot of the terrible things he did, and he wished there was something he could do to modify his way of thinking. He wished he could be a better man and stop lusting over this woman he'd just hung up with. But he knew that was never going to happen. He knew JT was going to be JT and that there wasn't a thing he could do to change that.

Chapter 18

hank you so much for treating me to lunch," Carmen said
to Alicia, and then leaned against her little red Nissan.
The two of them were standing in the parking lot of a popular
Asian restaurant located a few blocks down from the office where
Carmen worked, and Alicia was glad they'd had a chance to get
together.

"You're welcome, and I'm really glad we could do this."

"And thank you, too, for bringing me the manuscript," she
said, holding the brown envelope close to her body. "I'm so
excited, and I can't wait to read it."

"Well, I just hope you like it."

"I know I will, and I'll be calling you as soon as I finish it. I
also can't wait for the actual book to be released, because then
I'll be able to tell everyone that I'm close friends with a published author."

"You're funny," Alicia said, smiling.

"I'm serious. I'm so proud of you and everything you've
accomplished."

Alicia leaned against the side of Carmen's vehicle but closer
to the front of it. "Well, I'm just happy you made the decision to

look me up online and then e-mail me, because if you hadn't, we might not have ever connected with each other again."

"I know, and now I'm sorry I didn't try to contact you before now. Although, you know what they say, better late than never."

"This is true."

Carmen looked at Alicia for a few seconds and then said, "Can I ask you something?"

"Of course. What is it?"

"Did you ever in your wildest dreams think that your father would eventually be known all over the world and that you would ultimately marry a man like JT? A man who's clearly on his way to being just as famous himself?"

"No, not really. I mean, I knew my father was very successful, but I don't think I ever guessed he would do all the amazing things he's been able to do."

"Girl, you are so blessed. You have everything you could ever want, and most of us will never get to know how that feels."

"I am blessed and very thankful for the life that I have."

"You're beyond blessed. And didn't you say you only met JT because your dad spoke at NLCC one Sunday?"

"Yeah, and normally, I don't even go with my dad and Charlotte when they visit other churches. But this time I'm glad I did."

"I'll say. And then there's that huge rock you have on your finger," Carmen said, reaching over and lifting Alicia's hand. "I mean, my goodness, it must have cost a fortune."

"JT is definitely very good to me."

"Girl, he's better than good, and I just pray that I'll eventually find a man just like him."

"You will."

"I don't know. I keep thinking that all I have to do is be patient, but what I want more than anything is to find someone and get married. Sooner rather than later. What I want is to love someone, have them love me back, and then live happily ever after just like in the fairy tales."

Alicia set her take-home container on the car hood. "Have you been praying about it?"

"Every day."

"Then all you have to do is trust and believe and keep praying for the kind of husband and life you want just like I did. God always gives us the desires of our heart, and you have to keep your faith in that. My first marriage turned out terribly, but now I couldn't be happier."

"Maybe I just need to pray a little harder and a little more often."

"It certainly won't hurt, because you can never talk to God too much. My dad is always saying that the more time you spend with Him the better off you'll be, and I think he's right."

"I'm sure he is," Carmen said, turning the top of her wrist upward and looking at her watch. "Well, girl, I'd better get going. I hadn't told you, but the other reason I took this afternoon off was because I have a hot date."

"Oh, really?"

"Yep."

"And when do I get to meet this hot date of yours?"

"Maybe at some point."

"Okay, well, do your thing, girl," Alicia said, hugging her. "Have a great time."

"I definitely will. That you can count on."

JT had just finished showering and now stood in front of the gold-trimmed, full-length, oval mirror in Carmen's room, putting his clothes back on. She was sitting on the side of her bed watching him.

"I'm so glad you came by, baby," she said, but all JT could think was how, for the first time since he'd met her, sex with Carmen had been average at best. He hadn't even wanted to do it at all, and the only reason he had was because he hadn't wanted to hear any of her whining.

So he pretended as though he couldn't have felt better. "I'm glad I came over, too."

"I've missed you so much."

"I've missed you, too," JT said, zipping his pants.

"You're everything to me, baby, and no man could ever take your place. You hear me?"

"I'm glad you feel that way."

"I love you more than I've ever loved anyone, and I can't wait until you leave Alicia. I can't wait until you and I are married."

"I know, baby, I'm looking forward to that day as well," he lied. "But you know you're going to have to have a little patience."

"I do, but I'm still so, so excited about the life we're going to have together. I'm going to make you so happy. I'll be the best wife in the world. I'll do any and every thing you want me to without any questions."

JT put on his shirt in silence. He wasn't even sure how to respond to such a dimwitted statement, so he let her continue talking.

"So, when are you coming back to see me?"

"Sometime next week?"

"I know, but when exactly?"

"Maybe Thursday evening or Saturday morning."

"That's too long, baby. So, what about Monday afternoon, the way you always used to?"

"This coming Monday is Memorial Day, and I won't be able to get away," he said, glancing at her in the mirror and seeing the angry look on her face. She'd turned on him faster than he could blink.

"I'm so tired of this. I'm so tired of spending every holiday all by myself."

"I'm sorry, but Alicia and I are going over to her mom's, and there's nothing I can do to change that," he said, and then saw what looked to be Alicia's manuscript sitting on Carmen's dresser. "What's this?"

She responded in a curt tone. "What's what?"

"This," he said, picking up the first few pages and turning toward her.

"What do you think it is?"

"It looks like Alicia's novel, so I guess I'm sort of wondering where you got it from."

"I got it from the little wifey herself when she took me out to lunch today. Happy?"

"But why would you go anywhere with her when I've asked you not to visit her anymore or spend time with her, period?"

"Alicia's my friend," she said. "She's my very dear friend. We're such good friends that I could make her believe just about anything at all if I wanted. I could tell her all sorts of stories. The kind that would leave her devastated."

"Why are you doing this?"

"No, the question is, why shouldn't I? I mean, why shouldn't I do whatever I want, because it's not like you're breaking your neck to see me on a regular basis, anyway."

JT saw how upset she was and knew it was time for damage control.

He sat down on the bed next to her and placed his arm around her. "Maybe I don't get to see you every day, but, baby, what matters is that I'm with you right now. And I promise you I'll try to be with you a lot more than I have been."

"But I need more than that. What I need is to know that you're serious about me and that you really do still love me."

"I do."

"But, JT, how do I know you're telling me the truth?"

"Because I am. And if you can't trust me, then things will never be right between us."

Carmen gazed at him with watery eyes but didn't speak.

"Look," he said, caressing her back. "The reason I can't be with you as much as you want is because I'm doing everything I can to move the ministry forward. I'm working on it day and night because the sooner I can get everything in place, the sooner I'll be able to leave Alicia like you want me to. The sooner I work everything out, the sooner you and I will be free to be together."

Tears fell down her face, and JT hugged her closely.

"I'm so scared, JT," she said, sniffling. "I'm so scared that all you're doing is leading me on again and that you're not going to follow through on your promise."

"Baby, believe me. I'm really telling you the truth this time. I'm being open and honest about everything. As a matter of fact," he said, preparing to lay his words on as thick as possible, "I was just thinking earlier how I never should've married Alicia over you in the first place because now I realize that money and success don't mean anything if I can't be with the woman I love."

"Do you really mean that?"

"I do. I mean it with all my heart."

"I love you, JT. And it's like I just told you, I would do anything for you."

"I'm glad, baby," he said, sounding as sincere as he could. "Because the feeling is definitely mutual."

Chapter 19

The banquet facility for the tenth annual Pastors' and Wives' Luncheon was as elegant as Alicia had expected. She and JT had arrived at the hotel about twenty minutes ago, had valet-parked, and had then taken the escalator straight up to the third floor. There must have been at least fifty linen-covered round tables situated throughout the room, all adorned with exquisitely arranged white lily floral pieces at the center and each surrounded by ten plush chairs. Alicia loved this kind of setting, and while she'd really wanted to attend Matthew's track meet, she was also glad to be in the midst of five hundred people.

"Here's our table right here," JT said, pointing his finger at the tall, skinny metal stand that held a place card displaying the number thirteen.

"Pastor Valentine?" an older, distinguished-looking gentleman said, and Alicia and JT smiled.

"Oh my goodness," he said. "Pastor Jacobs, it's really wonderful to see you. It's been a very long time, hasn't it?"

"A very long time indeed. So, how have you been, my boy? From the looks of this beautiful young lady you have with you, it seems you're doing just fine."

The two men chuckled and JT said, "Well, I guess you got

me there, and you're right. Pastor Jacobs, this is my wife, Alicia. Alicia, this is Pastor Jacobs, one of the best men I know and the person who gave me a lot of great advice when I first founded NLCC."

"It's very nice to meet you," she said, smiling and reaching out her hand to him.

"The pleasure is all mine, and I'm sorry we weren't able to make the wedding. We'd already scheduled and paid for our annual vacation to Hawaii, and it would have been a bit on the expensive side to change our plans."

"We completely understand."

"You did receive the gift, though, right?"

Alicia looked at JT because she honestly had no idea. As a matter of fact, they'd invited so many guests to witness their nuptials and had received so many gifts by mail, there was no way for her to remember the names Pastor and Mrs. Jacobs, let alone what they'd sent them. But JT said, "Yes, and it was very, very generous of you."

"We really appreciate your kindness," Alicia said, so she wouldn't sound so clueless. "And you should have received a thank-you card right after we returned from our honeymoon."

"Oh, I'm sure we did," he said. "But you know how we men are. We don't really pay much attention to all that women-related stuff."

They all chuckled and then Pastor Jacobs said, "Alicia, if you don't mind, I'd like to steal your husband away for a few minutes so I can introduce him to a couple of the newer pastors in the city."

"Oh, of course. Please go ahead."

"Are you sure, baby?" JT asked.

"Yes. Absolutely."

JT kissed her on the cheek. "Okay, then, I'll be back in a while."

Alicia walked back closer to their assigned table and saw three women sitting in place, two side by side and one straight across from them. They all looked to be in their late thirties or early forties and were each dressed very stylishly. They looked as though they were married to successful men, the same as she was, and she was looking forward to meeting them.

"How are you ladies this afternoon?" she said, speaking against all the chatter in the background and sitting down next to the woman who was alone.

The two women sitting together acted as though they didn't want to be bothered and barely uttered the word "Fine." Alicia wasn't sure why they were being so rude, but she wasn't going to get herself all worked up over it.

"I'm doing well," the woman next to her said, "and it's very nice to meet you. I'm Tamara Jackson, first lady of Lakeview Christian Center."

"It's very nice to meet you as well. I'm Alicia Black Valentine and my husband, JT, is the pastor of New Life Christian Center."

"Yes, I figured as much when I saw him kissing you," she said jokingly.

"Oh, so you know him?" Alicia asked, placing her dainty, off-white satin, rhinestone-trimmed shoulder purse across the back of her chair. She'd purchased it specially to go with the off-white Armani suit she was wearing.

"Yes. My husband and I have visited New Life a few times over the years, and for the most part, most of the pastors with churches on the South Side of Chicago tend to all know one another."

"Oh, okay," she said, and then looked over at the other women, who seemed as if they could take her or leave her. Still, she smiled and tried making small talk with them. "So, which churches are you the first ladies of?"

The women looked at each other, slightly laughed, and shook their heads. Alicia wasn't sure why they didn't like her because it wasn't like she'd ever done anything to them. It wasn't like she even knew them.

Tamara sipped some water from her glass and set it back down on the table, and Alicia could tell this whole scene was just as awkward for her. "So," Tamara said, "how are you settling in as a new first lady?"

"Very well. Everyone at NLCC is wonderful. They're all very kind, and they're constantly making me feel welcome. I'm really very blessed to have found someone like JT and also to be a part of such an awesome ministry."

"Ha!" one of the other women said, obviously the most aggressive of the two. "You know, ever since you sat down, I've tried my best not to say anything, but the more you sit here acting all blissful and like you're on top of the world, I can't help but feel sorry for you."

Alicia leaned farther back in her chair. She didn't like the indignant look the woman was wearing but said, "Oh, really? And why is that?"

Alicia waited for a response, but the woman just gawked at her.

Tamara repositioned her body in her seat and attempted changing the subject. "It's always great when the congregation loves you and they go out of their way to make you feel at home."

"It really is."

"They can love her all they want," the rude woman mumbled to her friend. "But that still won't stop JT from whoring around the same as always."

Alicia stared at the woman in silence, trying to hold her tongue, but enough was enough. "What in the world is your problem?"

"You wanna know? Well, I'll tell you. My problem is that even though JT runs around here acting all holy, he messes around with every tramp he can get his hands on. Then, to think he might have had something to do with his first wife's death, well, that makes me even sicker. So, sweetheart, make no mistake about it, JT is as pathetic as they come, and if you married him, you must be just as lame as he is."

Alicia swallowed hard and wondered why yet another person was accusing JT of murder and cheating. It just didn't make any sense, but Alicia would never let on that the woman's words were unnerving her. "You know what?" she said angrily but not loudly. "You need to mind your own business. What you need to do is spend less time worrying about my husband and more time worrying about your own."

The woman frowned. "Honey, you don't even *know* my husband. But on the other hand, I know plenty about JT. I know more than I care to know about that rotten creep. But if you want to be naïve enough to believe he's such a saint," she said, standing up, "then by all means, you go right ahead and do it. Although, it would seem to me that since your father slept around on all three of his wives, you would know better. I would think you'd know a true whoremonger from the moment you first saw one. But I guess not." The woman eyed Alicia in disgust, and then her sidekick stood up, too. Seconds later, they both strutted away.

Alicia was so embarrassed and could barely look at Tamara face-to-face.

"I am so sorry," Tamara finally said. "That woman needs to mind her own business just like you said."

"Do you know her?" Alicia asked, looking across the room and watching her mingling and talking with two other women as if nothing had happened.

"Just as an acquaintance. But I may as well tell you that the only reason she's so angry and envious of you is because years ago, she basically ran herself ragged chasing after JT. Sadly, though, all he did was use her and then move on to someone else."

Alicia sat still, contemplating what she should say next. She was hurt, to say the least, and certainly didn't want anyone thinking she had any doubts about JT, but right now she needed a friend. She needed to talk to someone, and she had a feeling Tamara could be trusted. "So, have you heard some of the same things about my husband? Because if you have, I really need to know."

Tamara sighed and then said, "Come on. Let's step outside the banquet room for a few minutes."

Alicia got up and grabbed her handbag, and the two of them made their way through various groups of people. More and more attendees were coming inside and taking their seats, but Alicia and Tamara continued on outside of the room, into the main corridor, and down to the very end of the building.

When they arrived, Tamara wasted no time telling what she knew. "First, I just want to say that I am definitely no trouble-maker, but because I am a pastor's wife myself and have witnessed so many other pastors' wives being treated so terribly, I feel I have an obligation to tell you everything I know."

"I really appreciate your honesty," Alicia said, knowing that whatever Tamara was about to say wasn't going to be good. She knew it without question.

"I'll just start by saying that while I don't know a thing in terms of whether JT had something to do with his first wife's accident, what I do know is that he's always been known to mess around with lots of women. I won't say that I have any specific proof, but if you ask any of the pastors' wives on the South Side and even some in other areas of Chicago, they'll tell you the same thing."

Alicia was heartbroken. Her father had basically tried telling her the same thing, but she hadn't wanted to believe him. Not because she thought her father would lie for no reason, but because she really believed JT was in love with her. She believed that his feelings for her were very real and that he would never be unfaithful to her.

Now, though, she couldn't help thinking a little differently. She couldn't simply dismiss what Tamara was saying to her, because Tamara didn't seem like the kind of woman who would intentionally try to deceive her. Tamara was warm and seemed like the kind of person who cared about everyone, and Alicia's gut told her that Tamara honestly did mean well. Alicia had only met her a short while ago, but there was something very sincere about her demeanor. Something very genuine.

"I just don't know what to say."

"I know. Hearing something like this about the man you love is very painful, and I'm sure even more so because you just got married to him."

"Maybe he's not like that anymore."

"Maybe. And I actually pray he's not. But at the same time, you need to keep on top of things. You need to know that your husband has a pretty tainted reputation and that this probably won't be the last time you hear someone talking about it. You won't hear it as much at your own church because most people who are loyal members of any church are not going to say bad things about their pastor. But when you attend events such as this, people can be very cruel."

"This is just horrible," Alicia said, refusing to shed any tears.

"I know. Believe me, I know," she said as if she literally did understand, maybe from personal experience. "But when you're talking about some of the pastors around here, it's more common than not."

Alicia didn't respond, so Tamara continued. "The luncheon should be starting in a few minutes, so let's head back down the hallway."

Alicia did what Tamara suggested, but they walked in silence. As they got closer to the entrance of the room, however, she saw JT chatting with a group of ministers and winking at her. She smiled dryly and kept going.

She proceeded inside and over to their table and pretended she couldn't have been happier.

She pretended as hard as she could, even though she was completely beside herself.

Chapter 20

They hadn't been home more than ten minutes, and already JT was removing his suit and preparing to head back out again. According to him, he needed to go visit some church member whom he had supposedly known for years, which was fine, but what Alicia couldn't understand was why she couldn't go with him.

"Baby, I already explained this to you before we left for the luncheon."

"I realize that, JT, but all you said was that you had to go visit one of your charter members in the hospital, and you never said anything about my not being able to go with you."

"I'm sorry I didn't clarify that, and normally it wouldn't be a problem for you to come, but this particular member asked if I'd come alone because he wants to confide a few things to me. He wants to confess some very serious sins he committed in the past and then go about asking God to forgive him."

"So, he can't do that on his own? He can't do that without you helping him in person?"

JT pulled on a dressy-casual, navy blue round-neck shirt. "I guess not, because when he called me, he sounded pretty bothered about whatever it is he's done. He also said he wanted me to advise him on how he should begin making amends to the people he's hurt in the process."

Alicia didn't like the sound of this and said, "So, what's his name?"

JT sighed. "Baby, I just can't tell you that. I wish I could, but I can't."

"Why? Because it's not like I would ever repeat his name or his situation to anyone. Plus, I thought we agreed that we wouldn't keep any secrets from each other."

"We did, and when it comes to our personal business or the church business, I don't have any, and I will always be up-front with you about everything. But as far as our members go, it just wouldn't be right to betray their trust. Not when they've specifically asked me not to disclose their names or what they're experiencing."

Alicia sat on the chaise, watching her husband step into a pair of pants, and thought about her father and all the times he'd told her mother he needed to visit the sick or bereaved. He'd told her these lies on a pretty regular basis, sometimes more than once a week, and Alicia couldn't help making the comparison between those lies and the one she had a feeling JT was telling. She didn't want to believe he was literally standing there lying straight to her face, but after hearing all those dreadful things earlier from those women at the luncheon, it was hard not to. It would be difficult believing anything JT said from this day on. Alicia did love him and until this morning couldn't have been happier with her marriage, but she wasn't stupid. She wasn't like some of the first ladies she'd known and heard about, the kind who were willing to take whatever their husbands dished out. No, she was just the opposite and had always sworn she would never tolerate infidelity from any man she was married to—especially if that man was a pastor—because with these particular men, it was never just one random mistake. It never happened with just one woman, and the philandering seemed to go on indefinitely. She'd thought the same thing about her father, and while he had changed for the better and had been faithful to Charlotte for two years now, who was to say he would actually remain that way? She prayed for his sake and for her stepmother's that he would, but she knew there were no guarantees—she also knew, too, that since JT had already admitted to messing around on Michelle, he might be just as questionable.

JT worked his left foot into an Italian leather slip-on, put on the other, and walked over to where Alicia was sitting. She gazed at him, and then he leaned down and kissed her on the lips. "I know you're not happy about not being able to go, but, baby, please try to understand."

She ignored his last statement and asked, "When will you be back?"

"As soon as I can, but it might take a few hours because I don't want this man to feel that I'm rushing him to get everything off his chest just so I can get back to my daily life. He wants me to be there for him, and as his pastor it's my responsibility to help him get things right with God. It's my job to help him work toward getting his soul saved."

Alicia didn't bother responding but had a mind to tell him everything that that awful woman had told her this afternoon. She wanted to tell him, too, how Tamara, the first lady she'd been sitting next to, had even confirmed his womanizing history. She especially wanted to tell him that, once again, someone had insinuated he was a murderer. However, she decided that maybe this wasn't a good idea. She wasn't sure why exactly, but something told her it was better to keep all the information she had to herself—better to wait and see how all this eventually played out.

It was better to keep a closer eye on JT, the way Tamara had suggested.

When Alicia finished speaking to Melanie and then to her mom, she went into her office and sat down at her computer. This morning, before she'd begun getting ready for the luncheon, she'd signed in to her e-mail account and had been shocked by one of the messages she'd opened and read multiple times. She'd even felt guilty about the content of it and also about the warm feeling it had given her, but at the moment, she didn't feel an ounce of remorse. She didn't feel bad about it at all, and she knew it was because she now had valid doubts and reservations about her husband.

Alicia read the e-mail again.

> Hi sweetheart. It's me. I debated whether I should contact you since Darrell said you didn't want to see me but I couldn't help it. Alicia regardless of who you're with now I still think about you daily. After all this time you're still the first person I think of when I wake up in the morning and you're the only person I fantasize about before going to sleep at night. You are absolutely my everything. Yes I know you're married and that the last thing you need is to have someone trying to cause problems for it but the love that I have for you hasn't changed. If anything it's grown stronger and so much deeper and I really need to talk to you. We don't have e-mail access through the correctional facility but one of the staff members who looks out for me was cool

enough to let me use his personal account. But I do have to say I definitely don't have any typing skills so it took me way too long to type this. I also didn't dare try guessing where I should add commas! I've always been a great speller but terrible with that other English stuff, so will you call me between four and five this afternoon at the number below? Please if you don't mind do me this one favor. Because I really need to talk to you. I really need to hear your beautiful voice and tell you how different things are going to be for me when I'm out of here. Okay? I love you sweetheart and can't wait to hear from you. Levi.

When Alicia finished the last word, she read the e-mail one more time but still hesitated responding. Not because she didn't want to, but because she knew that once she did, there would be no turning back. She also didn't trust the excitement and nervousness that was overtaking her body. She didn't like how thrilled she was to be connecting with Levi.

So, she waited. She stalled for a few seconds, trying to forget about her ex-lover, and then finally browsed some of her favorite department store websites. Strangely enough, however, she wasn't interested in anything she saw. She still loved shopping, but what she'd been noticing more and more, specifically ever since marrying JT, was that shopping was no longer the most important thing in her life—maybe because she could do it whenever she wanted to. She still loved nice things, expensive ones for that matter, but she was finally starting to realize that there was so much more to life. There were so many other things to worry about. There were so many people to worry about—namely, two-timing husbands and the women who slept with them.

Alicia browsed the Internet for another fifteen minutes, voluntarily yielding to temptation, and dialed the number Levi had given her. The phone rang three times before someone answered.

"Hello?" a deep voice said.

"Uh, hi. Is Levi available?" she said, thinking how weird it sounded asking for a prison inmate no differently than she would a free man.

"Sure, he's right here."

Alicia heard Levi thanking the owner of the phone and then heard a door shut. A second later, he was greeting her.

"Hi, beautiful. How are you?"

His voice gave her the same kind of comfort as it had in the past, and she felt like melting. For a moment, she wished Levi could be any normal everyday guy and not a convicted felon. She wished he'd never even thought to begin selling drugs.

"I'm good," she finally said. "And you?"

"Well, the facility isn't as bad as it could be, but being locked down means exactly that, and it's not the kind of thing I could ever be okay with."

Alicia wasn't sure what to say next and waited for him to continue.

"So, it's been a long time, huh?" he said.

"Yeah, I guess it has."

"Were you shocked to hear from me?"

"Actually, I was."

"I figured you would be, but I had to take a chance. You know?"

"It was good hearing from you."

"So, how's married life treating you?"

Alicia wanted to tell him how worried she was about JT and what he might be doing behind her back, but she didn't.

"Everything's good."

"Are you sure?"

"Yes. I am."

"Then why don't I believe you?"

"Probably because you don't want to. Maybe you'd rather believe what you want to believe."

Levi laughed. "Come on, sweetheart, this is me you're talking to. Remember, I don't play games or say things I don't mean. I deal only with reality, and I can tell from the sound of your voice that something's troubling you. I can tell you're not all that happy."

"You're wrong," she said, knowing he'd assessed her true feelings to a tee.

"Whatever you say, but I know better."

"So, tell me, really," she said, changing the subject. "How are you?"

"I'm hanging in there and pretty much just praying for this appeal process to progress. Darrell told you about that, though, right?"

"Yeah, he mentioned something like that."

"My attorney says I have a very strong case in terms of the way they violated my rights, so hopefully I'll be out of here in just a matter of months . . . hey, hold on for a second," he said, and Alicia heard someone talking in the background. "Cool. Thanks, man."

"Who was that?" she asked.

"That was my boy who's letting me use his phone. He was just saying the coast was clear and that I could talk for another thirty minutes if I want."

"Then he must be a really good friend."

"Sweetheart, in here, money can buy you a lot of privileges. The kind of privileges you would never be able to have otherwise."

"But I thought all of your money was confiscated."

"I guess you really don't know me as well as I thought you did."

"I guess I don't."

"Okay, enough about prison and me, though, because what I want is to talk about you."

"What is it you wanna know?"

"Whether it's going to be possible for me to see you or not. I mean, I know you're married, but, Alicia, I can't help the way I feel. I can't help the fact that I'm still in love with you, girl."

"I just can't, Levi. I can't come there."

"I don't mean here, because this is definitely not an environment for someone like you. Not even as a visitor. I never wanted you to do that, and the only reason I'd had Darrell ask you a few weeks ago was because I was having a really lonely moment. So, when I say I want to see you, I'm referring to when I get out."

Alicia held the phone in silence, and for a second or two Levi said nothing either. Then he spoke.

"I know you have a husband, but, sweetheart, even if you're happy with this JT guy, deep down I know you still care about me. I know you have to still love me in at least some sort of way because no man will ever treat you as well as I did."

"JT gives me everything I want."

"I'm sure he does. Materially. But are you the most important person in his life next to God? Is he being completely faithful to you? Does he love you so much that he would never even consider being with another woman, let alone actually doing it? I mean, can you honestly answer yes to every one of those questions?"

He'd said a mouthful, and sadly, he was right, because she couldn't answer yes to any of them and be confident about it. But she wouldn't admit that to him.

"Levi, I know this might be hard for you to believe, but JT and I really do love each other and we're very happy."

"If I recall, you said the same thing right after you married your first husband. Remember?"

"We did love each other."

"But you weren't very happy. Maybe in the beginning but not when it came to the kind of money you wanted to spend. It sounds to me like your first husband gave you love and dedication and now this one is giving you a lot of luxury."

"He gives me a lot more than that."

"Like what? Sex?"

"You're being unfair. You're judging JT, and you don't even know him, so can we talk about something else?" she asked in a defensive tone, but she knew Levi's mental assessment was probably right on the mark.

"Look, sweetheart, I'm not trying to upset you, okay? Because I would never do that intentionally. I guess I just got a little carried away because I'm still so in love with you and because when I'm out of here, things are going to be very different for me. I'm completely done with that old life I was living, and for the first time in years, I've been reading my Bible every day. I've been studying and meditating, and I decided late last year that if God could forgive me for all the horrible mistakes I've made and then give me another chance at doing the right thing, then I was going to make good on it."

"I'm glad you feel that way."

"I've always believed in God, but when you're locked away like this for months and months, you find yourself talking to Him continuously. You find comfort in knowing that you still have at least Him to depend on."

Alicia had never heard Levi speak this way before, and she was truly happy for him. Of course, it was common knowledge that many inmates found God while serving lengthy sentences and sort of lost Him along the way once they were released, but she had a feeling Levi was very serious about his new sense of spirituality. Partly because he was the kind of person who only said what he really meant, but mostly because she could hear the realness and the excitement in his voice. They talked about nothing else before hanging up, and now Alicia wished she really could see him.

But she wouldn't. Not when she was married to JT, and as his wife, she needed to give him the benefit of the doubt. Yes, those women at the luncheon had caused her to be suspicious, but she and JT were still newlyweds. They'd only been married for seven weeks, and it simply wasn't right for her to jump to so many conclusions. She did wonder if he'd been telling the truth about where he was going this afternoon, but if he'd planned on messing around, would he really do it in broad daylight? It was only five o'clock and the sun still beamed brightly, so she couldn't imagine him taking that kind of a risk. It was the reason she told herself JT might merely be a victim of lies and vicious rumors. She told herself she was probably worrying for nothing.

Chapter 21

JT lay in bed, his body turned slightly to the side, with Veda's head resting against his chest. They'd made the most gratifying love to each other, and now she was sleeping peacefully. She slept, and all he could think was how he wished he didn't have to leave this hotel near O'Hare Airport until sometime tomorrow morning. He knew this clearly wasn't possible, but after being with Veda on two separate occasions, he also knew there was no way this would be the last time he saw her. He wasn't sure if it really was because she looked so much like Michelle, but regardless, his attraction to her was fierce. He'd been attracted to Alicia right away, too, but for some reason his attraction to Veda seemed even more immediate. He'd known from the moment they'd finished making love two nights ago at The Ritz that he couldn't simply forget about her, and it was the reason he'd stopped her from flying home yesterday afternoon. They'd hung up just as she was preparing to walk onto her plane, but then he'd called her right back, asking her not to leave. At first, she'd paused and then told him she really needed to get home, but JT had convinced her to remain in Chicago for at least another couple of days. He'd known he had to go spend time with Carmen shortly after he'd ended his call with Veda and would have to attend the luncheon with Alicia this afternoon, but he'd promised Veda that if she could just be patient, he'd find a way to spend all evening with her now. Needless to say, she'd told him she was fine with it, and JT had been in bed with her for three hours.

Still, he couldn't understand why his desires for Veda were so deep and why they had so instantly come about—especially since he really did love Alicia. He didn't know why any of this kept happening to him, why he couldn't just be happy with one woman. He'd been thinking he could, or at the very least, that he could get rid of Carmen and keep only one mistress, namely Diana. But now he knew otherwise. Now he knew he simply couldn't help who he was, and if Veda agreed, he was planning to see a lot more of her. There was the problem of her living miles away in Minneapolis, but he strongly believed in the old cliché his aunt used to love saying, "Where there's a will, there's a way." Which was why all he had to do was map out a more extensive and more detailed plan for his life and ministry.

Next week, he would give Janet the final okay to send out the introduction packages to the churches she'd compiled a listing of, he would bypass setting up a marketing committee the way he'd originally discussed and settled on with Minister Payne and Minister Weaver, and he would hire an ad agency himself so the agency could schedule the media campaign as soon as possible. After that, he would have Diana transfer the hundred thousand dollars he needed into one of his personal bank accounts and convince her to transfer the same amount at least another two or three times. Then, on the personal side of things, he would see Carmen once per week and would do the same with Diana, but once the campaign began, maybe about a month from now, and the speaking offers started coming in, he would slowly but surely cut off all communication with Carmen and would limit his meetings with Diana to maybe once every two weeks. Diana would certainly be upset but wouldn't make much of a commotion because she would never want her rich husband to find out what she'd been doing. She wouldn't want him finding out that she'd been having an affair with a much younger man who just so happened to be their trusted pastor. She would never want him finding out that she'd given her young lover loads of their money.

Carmen would be a different story, however, and she had already made it clear she would never walk away so easily. But when the time was right, JT would see to it that she was no longer a threat to him or the life he wanted to have. After that, he would welcome all the new church members he was positive his citywide media campaign would bring in, he would travel to as many speaking engagements as possible, and he would make a motion to double the annual salary he was receiving from the church. He would exercise his right to do whatever he wanted, since he'd been the one to found NLCC in the first place. There would surely be a few officers and associate ministers who might have a problem with it, specifically Minister Weaver, but they would each soon get over it—either that or they'd be booted out of the ministry altogether and onto the street. Then, when he was making a million dollars a year from his church income alone, he would purchase a nice, comfortable home in a suburb far away from where he and Alicia lived. He'd purchase something only he knew about and would begin flying Veda in for weekly visits. At the same time, he'd be able to give Alicia the extravagant life he'd been promising her all along, and this meant he'd finally have the best of three worlds: a beautiful wife and first lady of his church, an out-of-town mistress who made him feel better sexually than any woman had ever made him feel, and a local mistress who gave him sex, too, plus all the financial support he could ever want. He'd have everything and that got him excited.

Veda gently turned her body, looked up at him, and they smiled at each other.

"So, I see you finally woke up, huh?"

"How long was I asleep?" she asked.

"I don't know, maybe about an hour."

"All this morning, I worked on some reports I had been putting off, and they were very intense. But I guess I was more tired than I realized."

"Well, you didn't seem all that tired earlier," he said, slightly laughing.

"Yeah, I guess not."

"You were full of energy, and I loved it," he said, stroking her hair.

"I loved it, too."

"And you know what else?"

"No. What?"

"My feelings for you are a lot stronger than I realized. I knew I liked you a lot, but I don't think I'm going to be able to stop thinking about you."

"I feel the same way, and the strange thing for me is that this has never happened before. I mean, not only was the other night the first time I'd ever slept with any man only an hour after meeting him, but it was also the first time I had ever messed around on my husband."

"Sometimes situations like this can't be helped."

"Yeah, but this is so out of character for me and dangerous, too, because for all I know you could be some serial killer."

"Okay, I admit that you definitely have a point," he said, laughing. "But I promise you, I'm far from being anything like that."

"Well, that's good to know."

"So, tell me," he said, caressing her back, "exactly how bad is your marriage? I mean, did the two of you basically just grow apart over the years or did something else happen?"

"I don't know that we were ever what you would call desperately in love with each other, and now I realize the only reason we got married was because I got pregnant during my sophomore year in college."

"So, you went to the same school?"

"Yes, and even though my parents took care of our son until we graduated, my husband still wanted us to do the right thing. Actually, I wanted us to do the right thing, too, so that our child would be able to grow up with both his parents. But now it's time we go our separate ways."

"That's understandable. So, you were about twenty when you had him?"

"Yes."

"Well, you certainly look a lot younger than thirty-eight."

"Thanks. And since we're on the subject, how old are you?"

"Thirty-three."

"Just a baby, huh?"

"Not in the least."

"Does age matter to you?"

"Nope. Does it matter to you?"

"No. Not at all."

"Then that's that," JT said, kissing her on her forehead. "Because all I want is to make you happy."

"You say that now, but once I'm gone you'll quickly forget about me."

"Not a chance. And if things go my way, we'll be seeing each other all the time."

"Hmmm."

"What? You don't believe me?"

"Well, it's not like you don't have a wife."

"True. But that won't change the way I feel about you."

"We'll see. I do have a question for you, though."

"Which is?"

"What is it that you do for a living?"

JT paused and then said, "I'm not sure I should tell you."

"Why?"

"I'm just not."

"Well, I really want to know."

"Why?"

"Because as shallow as this may sound, if I'm going to take a chance on messing around with a married man, knowing full well that he'll probably never leave his wife and marry me, I want to make sure I at least get to enjoy some of the finer things in life. I know it may sound bad, but I think it's only fair that I be honest with you."

"I'm a minister."

"Whoa. Do you have your own church?"

"As a matter of fact I do, and it's a pretty sizable one at that."

Veda didn't respond.

"Does that bother you?"

"Sort of. I mean, I know it's wrong to sleep with any married man, but somehow, having an affair with a pastor makes it seem even worse."

"Look, baby, we're both human and no one on this earth is without imperfections. Every person alive is flawed in some sort of way, and God understands that. He understands, and He still loves us anyway."

Veda breathed deeply, seemingly still uneasy about what they were doing, so JT moved her chin closer to his and kissed her. Then he said, "Plus, if you think about it, how could something that feels so right really be all that wrong?"

Chapter 22

Alicia listened as the choir sang, but mostly she sat thinking about JT, how late he'd gotten home last night and the shady excuse he'd given her. All this morning, she'd been trying to think on a rational level and not rely on unfounded assumptions, but JT was making it very hard for her. It was one thing for him to be gone for two to three hours, but leaving right after four P.M. and not returning until shortly after midnight, well, that was another. Sure, he'd claimed he'd gotten caught in traffic during his drive to the hospital because of some accident on I-294 West and hadn't arrived until almost two hours later, but she hadn't believed him. Then, when she'd asked him what time visiting hours were over, he'd told her that the staff had given him special permission to stay much longer because the man he'd gone to see was very ill. This, of course, was a story Alicia might have accepted had she not told a similar one to her first husband. She still remembered the day Phillip's father had passed and how she'd concocted this huge lie once she'd realized she hadn't been there for him. She'd told him how there had been bumper-to-bumper traffic on the freeway and that her car had broken down, when actually she'd really been shopping at the mall. She'd told Phillip everything she'd thought he might want to hear without the slightest flinch, and she had a feeling JT was doing the same thing.

When the choir members took their seats, JT stood and strutted up to the glass podium. Alicia smiled, but for the first time since marrying him, she wasn't all that happy to be there.

"This is the day the Lord hath made, so let us rejoice and be glad in it," he began for the second Sunday in a row, and Alicia wondered why he was all of a sudden beginning his pastoral observations with Psalms 118:24. Interestingly enough, it was one of her father's favorite scriptures and JT certainly looked up to him as a minister, so maybe he was simply trying to mimic him.

"Before I begin my sermon, I want to talk a little bit about temptation."

Alicia looked around as parishioners nodded and mumbled in agreement.

"I wasn't planning to talk about this particular subject, but when God lays something on my heart to share with His people, I'm obligated to do it."

"Speak, Pastor," Minister Payne said.

"See, most of the time," JT continued, "we can be going about, minding our own business, and then Satan will jump right out of nowhere, armed with all sorts of tricks. He'll taunt you and harass you until you fall into his trap, and then the next thing you know, you find yourself committing one sin after another."

Alicia wondered where all of this was coming from. She wondered if his words were the result of a guilty conscience, but since she had no proof, she tried staying positive.

JT gazed out into the audience, scanning the entire church. "Then, if he's not tempting you and causing you to go against God's will, he'll instead try to cause problems in your marriage, with family members, and even with friends. Husbands, he'll have your wives thinking you're up to no good when you haven't even thought about another woman. And wives, he'll have you accusing your husbands of all sorts of terrible things when, in reality, they haven't done a thing at all."

Members of the congregation whispered to their neighbors and seemed to love all that their pastor was saying. Alicia wished she could feel the same way, but she didn't. As a matter of fact, she was even more taken aback now that JT had spewed all this jargon about wives falsely accusing their husbands because it made her feel as though he was speaking directly to her. It was true she had grilled him in a pretty assertive manner last night and that their mild discussion had quickly become their first real argument, but the reason she'd become so irritated with him was because he'd given her more than ample reason to. He'd stayed out late, his story had sounded phony, and yes, all those rumors she'd heard at the luncheon were still floating in her head. There were so many marks against him, and all she could hope was that her intuition was way off base. She hoped she couldn't have been more wrong about anything.

It had been a long while since JT had stayed out after midnight, especially the night before having to deliver the Sunday-morning message, and he felt a little exhausted. He and Veda had practically worn each other out, but if he had to do it all over again, he would. If she wanted him to, he would drop whatever he was doing on a moment's notice just to go be with her, so it was definitely better for her to be gone. He'd been thinking that her living in Minneapolis was the downside to his budding relationship with her, but not after arguing with Alicia when he'd arrived home. She'd been so upset, and it was all he could do to try to convince her that he really had been visiting with and praying with some anonymous congregant. He didn't feel good about all the lies he kept telling her, but every one of these lies was very necessary if he wanted to keep her happy. He had to lie in order to keep himself satisfied. He lied because he needed so much more than his marital vows would afford him.

JT and Alicia stood next to each other out near the main exit, greeting hundreds of members as they left the church. JT always loved making personal contact with the people who supported him, and he could tell Alicia enjoyed it as well. Especially when they raved over how good she looked or what she was wearing.

"Just as cute as a button," Lacey Jordan, a sixtysomething spry and very outgoing woman, said, and Alicia blushed.

"Isn't she, though?" the woman behind her agreed.

"Well, thank you," Alicia told them. "You both are way too kind."

"Son, I know I've told you this several times now," Lacey said to JT, "but you really did pick a lovely bride. I mean, she's just beautiful."

"I agree, and I'm glad you think so, too, Sister Jordan."

"Is he taking good care of you, sweetheart?" she said, looking at Alicia.

"He really is. He's very good to me, and I'm very blessed to be married to him."

JT hadn't been sure how Alicia might respond to such a question, what with the little lovers' quarrel they'd had, so he was relieved by the way she'd answered it.

"Well, you both be good now," Lacey told them. "And I'll see you on Wednesday night."

"You take care," Alicia said.

JT shook a couple of other hands but did a double take when he spied Carmen. He was stunned but knew she was only trying to be funny and that this was all because he hadn't returned any of her phone calls yesterday. But how could he? He'd been with Alicia during the afternoon and with Veda all evening, so what was he supposed to do?

"Oh my God," Alicia said, clearly elated to see whom she thought was a trusted friend of hers. "Carmen, girl, why didn't you tell me you were coming to service this morning? You could have sat right next to me."

Carmen hugged Alicia. "I know, but to be honest, I didn't decide until the last minute. I was planning to go to my own church, but since my mom wasn't feeling well, I decided it would be nice to visit you guys for a change."

"Well, I'm so glad you did, and actually, I wish you would think about joining NLCC anyway."

"You know, I just might think about doing that," she agreed, and JT wanted to strangle her. She was jeering at him on the sly, and he couldn't stand it.

"You really should."

"Well, hey, I don't want to hold up the line too much longer, but the other thing I wanted to tell you was that I finished reading your novel."

Alicia beamed. "Really?"

"Yes, and I absolutely loved it! After we spoke on the phone last night, I knew I was going to at least get to start it, but I had no idea I would read the entire story. Anyway, it was a page-turner, and I can't wait to talk more about it. So, I'll just call you at home."

"Sounds good," Alicia said, and they hugged again.

But before leaving, Carmen stopped in front of JT. "Your sermon was truly wonderful. And I really look forward to hearing you speak again sometime. Maybe next week even."

"I'm glad you enjoyed it," he said, realizing she was going too far. She was crossing the line, and it was time he ended all dealings with her. If he didn't, he knew he would be sorry.

Chapter 23

*I*T bit into one of the ribs his other father-in-law had just given him and wasn't sure he'd ever tasted better barbecue. "Man, you're a master at this, and you can cook for me anytime. Not to mention, this is just a sample and the sauce hasn't even been added to it."

James laughed like most men do when they've been patted on the back by another one. "I'm glad you like it."

"Like it? I love it. Man, this meat couldn't be seasoned any more perfectly, and it's so tender it's practically falling off the bone."

James stepped a bit closer to the oversized charcoal grill, removed a few more ribs from the fire, and turned the last few pieces of chicken and Italian sausage on their opposite sides. "So, have you been keeping up with the conference finals much this week?"

"Actually, I haven't, but I have to say I was a little disappointed about the Bulls not making it past the first-round play-offs. Especially when they came so close."

"I was pretty bummed about it, too. Mainly because they haven't won an NBA championship since 1998, which, of course, was just before Michael Jordan retired and Phil Jackson left as well."

"Yeah, things have definitely been different since then, and it'll be interesting to see when they might win again."

James forked up a few more pieces of meat and set them in the foil-lined Teflon pan. "So, on a different note, how's married life treating you?"

"To be honest, it couldn't be better and we couldn't be happier."

"I'm glad to hear that, because I became Alicia's stepfather when she was just a small girl, and I love her just like she was my own child."

"She loves you the same way," JT said, gazing toward the patio and watching Alicia and her mom bringing food out and placing it on the table.

"She's a very special young lady, and I just hope the two of you can have the same kind of relationship Tanya and I have. My wife means everything to me, and after all these years, we still love each other like we did in the beginning."

"If I have it my way, I can assure you, Alicia and I will be together and very happy until the day one of us leaves this earth."

"I like your attitude and you'll certainly be able to do just that, as long as you keep each other first in your life—after God, that is—and you never allow anyone else inside your marital circle. I'm telling you this because there is a ton of temptation out there, but if you ignore it and stick together as a couple, you'll be okay."

"I agree, and I won't ever let any woman cause me to be unfaithful to my wife," he said, but when he looked back over toward the patio and saw Carmen and her mother walking onto it, a heat wave swept through his body. Alicia had told him early this morning that she'd invited Carmen and her mother but that since Carmen's mother still hadn't been feeling well, they probably wouldn't be able to make it. Then, when JT had phoned Carmen, insisting it wasn't a good idea for her to visit NLCC again, he'd been pretty sure he'd also convinced her not to drop by his in-laws' either. He'd thought he'd made himself very clear, but apparently he hadn't.

"Hi, Dad James. Hi, JT," Carmen yelled out to both of them.

"How's it going?" JT said dryly.

"How are you, Miss Carmen?" James said, smiling, obviously glad to see her. "It's been such a long time. And how are you, Rita?" he said to her mother.

"I'm fine, James, how are you?"

"Wonderful."

"Baby, come up here for a minute," Alicia said to JT, and he walked closer to where they were all standing. "Sweetheart, this is Carmen's mom, and Mom Rita, this is my husband, JT."

They shook hands and Rita said, "It's a pleasure to meet you, and congratulations on your recent marriage to Alicia."

"Thank you."

"Also, if I might add, you're even more handsome than Carmen told me you were."

"That's what I thought when I first met him, too," Alicia said.

Everyone laughed, but JT had never felt more uncomfortable. This whole scenario was teetering toward a possible disaster, and he didn't like it.

"Everything looks wonderful, Tanya," Rita said. "And thank you for having us over."

"Oh, please. We haven't seen each other in forever, so I'm excited to have you."

JT shot a glance at Carmen, who seemed very full of herself, but then he quickly looked away when his mother-in-law called his name.

"JT, if you don't mind, can you go out to the garage to get the card table we have stored toward the back of it? I was thinking we wouldn't need it, but I can see now that we do."

"Of course," he said, and started toward the glass patio doors. But once he'd walked inside the kitchen, he heard Carmen say, "Alicia, could I use the restroom?"

"Girl, you know you don't even have to ask something like that. Go ahead."

JT walked as fast as he could toward the door leading to the garage, opened it, and then closed it behind him once he was on the other side of it. He hoped Carmen wasn't planning to follow him, but to his regret, she didn't waste any time.

"So, are you glad to see me?" she asked.

"Carmen, why are you here? Why did you come when I specifically asked you not to?"

"I came because I wanted to see you and it's like I told you on Friday: I'm tired of spending all my holidays without you. And anyway, doesn't a girl have a right to change her mind?"

JT moved closer to where the table was stored and picked it up. "You've got to stop showing up like this."

"I'll stop coming around just as soon as you stop ignoring me the way you did yesterday. I tried calling you at least twenty times, and I never heard back from you."

"Didn't I already explain that to you earlier? I was with a very sick man, and there was no way I could get back to you."

"But you could have called me when you were on your way home."

JT lifted the table, making sure it didn't touch his starched khaki shorts. It wasn't excessively dirty, but it would definitely have to be wiped down before they used it. "I'm sorry I didn't call you back."

"Can I see you tomorrow evening?"

"Fine," he said, but only so Carmen would leave him alone and let him get back to the patio. He told her what she wanted to hear; however, he knew he couldn't make good on his words because he'd already promised Diana he would be with her. There was no doubt Carmen would probably go ballistic once she realized he wasn't coming to her apartment, which was the reason he'd have to have some sort of an excuse ready before then.

When JT finished setting up the card table and cleaning it with soap and water, he scanned the main table and couldn't wait to dig in. Tanya had prepared everything from potato salad, baked beans, and spaghetti to coleslaw, tossed salad, and some sort of fruit concoction that was drenched in whipped cream. Then there was all the meat James had finished up as well, and JT couldn't have been more content than he was right now. He hadn't been blessed to have parents like Tanya and James, and he was thankful just to have them as in-laws.

After listening to another twenty minutes of small talk, mostly between Alicia and Carmen and then Rita and Tanya, they all held hands and JT said grace. Seconds later, they began reaching for various dishes and started filling up their plates.

"Everything looks great, baby," James said to Tanya.

"I wish I could have done more. Especially with the decorations."

"The whole setting is wonderful," Rita added.

"And these baked beans are to die for," JT said.

"Why, thank you, son-in-law," Tanya said, smiling.

Alicia and Carmen offered their compliments as well to both Tanya and James, and then Tanya said, "Carmen, I really am glad you decided to contact Alicia after all these years. She told us how you looked her up on the church's website and e-mailed her."

"I'm glad, too, because now I realize just how much I missed her."

"I missed you, too. That's for sure."

JT forked up a helping of potato salad and wanted to kill Carmen. She was acting as if she were Alicia's best friend, and he hated the way she was deceiving her. He hated that he'd allowed this whole mess to spin way out of control.

"I'm thrilled about it, too," Rita said. "Because you girls were so close when you were children."

Tanya drank a couple of sips of tea. "You really were, and you used to spend the night with each other all the time."

"You were just like sisters," Rita said, and then grabbed both sides of her head and leaned back in her chair.

Carmen slid her chair back and turned toward her. "Mom, what's wrong?"

"My head is killing me."

"Is it worse than it was yesterday?"

"Yes," she said, now moaning with her eyes shut tightly. Then, in a matter of seconds, she passed out and slumped down into the chair.

"Oh no!" Carmen screamed. "Mom? Mom? Wake up!" she said, shaking her arm. "Mom, can you hear me? Oh my God, somebody call nine-one-one!"

Chapter 24

The five of them had been waiting for at least an hour but still hadn't heard anything from the doctors. James had called for an ambulance, which had arrived in a matter of minutes, and the paramedics had rushed Rita straight to Covington Park Memorial. Thankfully, Carmen had been allowed to ride with her mother, because the last thing JT had wanted was to be in the same vehicle with both his wife and the desperate woman he was messing around with.

"This is just horrible," Carmen said, sobbing. "And what in the world am I supposed to do without my mother? How am I supposed to go on if she doesn't make it?"

Tanya pulled Carmen closer, and Carmen laid her head on Tanya's shoulder. Alicia looked on with tears filling her eyes, and JT wished he could go home. He did feel bad for Carmen's mother, but it wasn't like there was a whole lot he could do. There wasn't a lot *any* of them could do except be there for Carmen, but at the moment, he wanted to be as far away from her as possible.

They sat, waited a while longer, and watched a number of gurneys wheel by them, some at normal speed and some in a hurry. They watched frustrated patients who obviously didn't have life-threatening ailments because they still hadn't been called into an examination room yet. They looked on in total silence, and then finally they were all directed into a conference room and two East Indian doctors in their midfifties dressed in scrubs walked in afterward.

"Miss Wilson?" the first one said, trying to identify who Rita's daughter was.

"Yes," Carmen said.

"Miss Wilson, I'm Dr. Mehta and this is Dr. Nigam."

"It's nice to meet you both."

"It's nice to meet you as well," Dr. Mehta said, and both doctors shook everyone's hand and took a seat. "Although I'm sorry it's not under better circumstances."

"So, is my mother going to be okay?" Carmen asked right away.

"Well, the thing is, she's had a massive brain aneurysm, and we're prepping her now for emergency surgery. We need to get in there as soon as possible to prevent any further damage."

Carmen burst into tears again. "So . . . what . . . are . . . her . . . chances?"

Dr. Mehta took a deep breath. "Unfortunately, it's pretty serious, but we're going to do all we can for her, and we'll keep you posted all the way."

Carmen was too upset to respond, so Tanya said, "Thank you very much, and we appreciate your coming out to update us."

"You're quite welcome," he said, and then he and Dr. Nigam stood up.

"How long do you think the surgery will take?" James asked.

"It's hard to say but probably a few hours. It just depends on what we find once we get in there."

"Well," James said. "We'll be here."

Be Careful What You Pray For

Both doctors exited the room, and tears drenched Carmen's face. She was distraught, and JT could tell Alicia was glad her mother was there helping to console Carmen because Alicia hadn't said more than a few words since they'd arrived.

"Now, come on, sweetie," Tanya said. "You have to try and settle down because your mom is really going to need you when this is over. She's going to need you to be the very strong daughter she raised you to be, and instead of crying, you have to focus on prayer. As a matter of fact," she said, looking at her son-in-law, "JT, can you please say a few words for Rita right now?"

JT wanted to say no but knew that wasn't an option. "Sure."

Carmen looked at him for the first time since they'd come into the conference room, and JT hurried to bow his head. "Dear Heavenly Father, we come right now, recognizing that You are in control of everything. We come asking for Your awesome grace and wonderful mercy. Lord, we ask that You please guide the doctors through this entire process and that You give them all the skill and knowledge they need. We ask that You heal Rita's body completely. Then, Lord, we ask that You watch over all of us who are here and that You give strength and understanding wherever it is needed. Father, we thank You for all that You've done and for all that we know You'll do in the future. We ask for all these and many other blessings, in Your son Jesus's name. Amen."

JT glanced at his Rolex, the one his church had given him for his birthday about a year ago, and breathed deeply. They were now back out in the family waiting area, but after sitting for yet another couple of hours, he was starting to feel exhausted and wished this would be over very soon. About twenty minutes ago, one of the surgical nurses had come out with an update, but all she'd said was basically that there had been a lot of bleeding and that the doctors were still working. JT hadn't known what that meant, but for Rita's sake, he did hope she was going to be fine.

He leaned his head against the wall and thought about Veda. He wondered what she was doing for the holiday, and he wished he could see her. Maybe he would ask her to fly back down in another week or so, even if only for a day trip.

"I wonder what's taking them so long," Carmen said suddenly, and then got up. She stood for a couple of seconds and then paced back and forth.

"We just have to be patient," Alicia said. "I know it's hard, but I felt the exact same way when my dad was shot, and you see how things turned out for him. Everything worked out fine."

Carmen walked over near the television that was hanging from the wall, looking distraught, and for a second JT felt sorry for her. But it was only for a second, because while he was sad for Rita and for what she was going through, he could also see the positive side of things: If Carmen's mother survived the surgery, Carmen would be so consumed with taking care of her, she wouldn't have time to harass him. JT would be the least of her worries, and what an astounding reprieve that would be.

Four more hours passed and then finally both neurosurgeons came out and spoke to them again.

"Well," Dr. Mehta began, "as it turns out, it was a little worse than what Dr. Nigam and I had originally thought, and I want to be honest with you. Your mother only has a fifty-fifty chance of surviving this."

Carmen sniffled and tears fell instantly.

Dr. Nigam looked at her sympathetically. "Had your mom been complaining of any headaches?"

"Yes. She's been having them on and off for a week or so, but she wouldn't go get them checked out. But then, this morning, she felt a lot better. Better than she had over the last couple of days."

"Had she spoken about any chest pains or anything? Because there was a period where we had a little difficulty keeping her heart stabilized."

"No. She's never mentioned anything like that."

Dr. Mehta placed his hand over Carmen's and said, "Well, we'll be keeping a very watchful eye over her, and we'll be hoping for some major progress as your mom recovers."

"Can I see her?"

"She's still in recovery and probably won't be conscious for a while, but I'll have one of the nurses come out to get you as soon as she's situated."

"Thank you, Doctor. Both of you," she said, looking at Dr. Nigam, too.

"You're very welcome, and please take care."

When both men were out of sight, Carmen's face turned serious. "She's going to die."

Alicia frowned. "Carmen, don't say that. The doctor said she had a fifty-fifty chance and we have to believe that she's going to be fine. We can't just give up on her."

"That's right," Tanya said. "What we're going to do is keep praying for a miracle. We're going to keep our faith in God, no matter what."

JT felt a little awkward because, as a pastor, he knew those were the kinds of words he should have been saying. He knew he should be the first person to comfort anyone who had a seriously ill mother, but he couldn't bring himself to do it. He couldn't force himself to comfort the woman he'd been cheating with, not in front of his wife and her parents.

"Maybe you should get something to eat," Alicia suggested to her.

"No."

Alicia turned to JT. "Honey, I'm going to stay here with Carmen for the night, but if you want, you can go on home."

JT had thought he would never hear those words and wanted to jump for joy. "Are you sure? Because I can hang around for as long as you need me to."

"No, go on. We'll be fine."

"Well, I guess we'll get ready to leave, too," Tanya said. "But we'll be back tomorrow."

Carmen forced a smile and then stood up and hugged her. "Thank you so much for being here with me all this time. And I'm so sorry your cookout was ruined."

Tanya wrinkled her forehead. "Don't you even think twice about that. Your mom is the priority right now."

James hugged Carmen next. "We're here for you, and you just let us know whatever you need, okay?"

"I will, and thank you for everything."

"JT, if you want to leave your car here for Alicia, we can drop you off at home."

"That would be great, if you don't mind."

"Of course we don't."

JT pulled his wife into his arms. "Now, baby, you call me if you need me."

"I will," she said, kissing him.

Then JT looked at Carmen, figuring he'd better say at least something to her prior to leaving, before the rest of them got suspicious. "I'll be praying for your mom."

"Thanks," she said, grabbing hold of him, and he was sorry he'd said anything to her. "That really means a lot, JT. More than you could possibly ever know."

JT pushed her away in a subtle manner, and he and Tanya and James proceeded down the corridor leading to the parking lot. He looked back at Alicia and Carmen and prayed that Carmen wouldn't do or say anything stupid. In times of heartache or loss, most people tended to become extremely sentimental and were much more apt to come clean about their wrongdoings. If they had betrayed a close friend or family member, they were more prone to confessing everything. He had to believe, however, that Carmen was different . . . and that she had sense enough to keep her mouth shut.

Chapter 25

JT read off the number of the account he wanted Diana to transfer his marketing funds into, and she repeated it back, making sure she had it right.

"That's correct," he said.

"Then I'll get this taken care of this afternoon."

"I really appreciate what you're doing, because I know six figures is a lot of money."

"As a matter of fact it is, and I just hope you're worth it."

"Hey, come on, now. Why do you say that?"

"Because once again, I only saw you one time last week and that's just not enough for me."

"I know, and I'm sorry. But I promise you, things will be very different this week," he said, knowing he really would be able to make good on his word since he was pretty sure Alicia would be spending most of her time at the hospital with Carmen. Now that he thought about it, it was kind of strange how some things tended to work out, because who would have guessed that the reason he now had more free time to be with one mistress was because his wife was busy trying to comfort another one?

"I hope you mean that."

"I really do."

"Okay, I'm holding you to it, and of course I can't wait to see you in a couple of hours."

"I can't wait to see you either, which is why I've been thinking about you all morning."

"Well, I guess I'll see you when you get here then."

"See you soon."

JT ended the call and set his cell phone down on his desk. He thought about calling Alicia to see how things were going at the hospital, but his phone rang before he could pick it back up. The word "private" was displayed on the screen, which made him a little uneasy because there was a chance Alicia had left the waiting room or the hospital for a while, leaving ample opportunity for Carmen to call him.

"Hello?"

"Well, well, well," the woman said. "It certainly has been a very long time, hasn't it?"

"Excuse me, do I know you?"

The woman laughed. "I can't believe you don't recognize my voice, especially with all the history you and I have."

"Look, I'm very busy, and I think maybe you have the wrong number."

"No, I don't think so. And by the way, did your wife tell you I saw her at the mall? Did she tell you *Donna* stopped and had a nice little chat with her?"

JT's heart pounded heavily. This just couldn't be. Not now. Not when he finally had the perfect long-range plan in place and was experiencing no obstacles.

"Are you still there?"

"Why are you calling me?" he finally asked.

"JT, JT, JT," she sang. "Now, why does anyone contact a person they haven't spoken to in over two years? They do it because either a family member has died or because they need money, and I'm here to tell you that every one of my family members is alive and well."

"But once I paid you that fifty thousand you asked for, you agreed to never contact me again. You said we had a deal, and I trusted you."

"Well, unfortunately, I need more. Unfortunately, I need *another* fifty thousand, and I need it by the end of this week."

"You must be crazy. And it's not like I have that kind of money, anyway."

"Then I'm really sorry to hear that, because if you can't meet my demands, I'll have no choice but to go public with some of your past transgressions. And that's putting it nicely. I'll have to tell everything I know and, sadly, that would mean you'd be finished as a pastor. You'll lose everything you've worked so hard for, and what a shame that would be."

A thousand thoughts flashed through JT's mind, and he couldn't believe this was happening, not after all this time. He was also stunned by the way she'd run into Alicia and had given her a phony name. He was even thrown by the description Alicia had given him because the woman he remembered had very short hair, but maybe she'd had on a wig or weave that day Alicia had seen her. There was just no telling when it came to Barbara—or Barb, as she preferred to be called—but it really didn't matter either way because the bottom line was that she was trying to blackmail him all over again. He'd paid her off per their agreement; however, now she was back and was demanding another stack of money, and he wasn't sure how he should go about handling her.

Barb continued. "So, when can I expect my money? Tomorrow, Thursday, or Friday?"

JT frowned. "Didn't I just tell you I don't have it?"

"Well, you'd better find it, or else. You'd better find it, or I'll be telling your wife a lot more than what I already have. When I'm finished, the police will be reopening that investigation relating to your first wife's accident."

"But you know I never had anything to do with Michelle's death, and the police already confirmed that."

"Hmmph. It's amazing, though, what they'll believe if they're given the right kind of evidence and are told the right kind of information."

"Maybe, but I'm not worried about that. I'm not worried about anything, and if that's all you have, I'm hanging up now."

"You know, actually, you should be very worried. But even if you're not, I wonder what your congregation will think once they find out about those two little businesses you had going on the side—those businesses you ran for the first three full years after you founded New Life Christian Center. I also wonder what they'll think when they learn about the baby you conceived with another woman barely a year after you and Michelle were married."

JT cringed. "Barb, why are you doing this?"

"Because men like you make me sick. Men like you who chase innocent women, fool them into bed, and then simply toss them aside when you're finished with them."

"Look, as much as I'd like to help you, there's no way I can get my hands on such a large sum of money in just a few short days."

Barb chuckled but then turned serious. "You can and you will. I want my money by Friday, and I'll call you back on Thursday to set up a time and place for us to meet."

JT shook his head. "Look, I'm going to need at least—" he said, but Barb hung up before he could finish his sentence.

This was totally and completely insane, and JT hated that he'd placed himself in a position where he could be blackmailed by two different women. First Carmen had made her threats and now Barb was making hers, and he couldn't deny that Barb could do a lot more damage than Carmen because she knew the kinds of secrets he would never want anyone, not another living soul, to find out about. Which was why he had to pay her what she was asking and hope she would go away for good this time. He hoped she would go about her business and pretend she'd never even known him.

As soon as JT strolled into Diana's condo, he sat down on the mauve leather sofa and started lying. "I really hate having to ask you, but just before I left the church, I received a tentative budget amount from the ad agency, and it looks as though the campaign is going to cost quite a bit more than what I'd been counting on. So, instead of the original hundred thousand dollars we talked about, I'm now going to need a hundred and fifty."

"Whoa," she said, sitting next to him. "So, is this because radio and TV rates have gone up, or is it because you want to do more stations and for a longer period of time?"

"I do want to do a few more spots, but, yes, this is mostly because the rates are much more expensive than I had imagined."

"Well, advertising is never cheap."

"So, you don't have a problem with it?"

"Not with the money, but before I commit to increasing the amount, I need to talk to you."

"Okay. What about?"

"Us. Because even though you told me earlier that you're going to spend a lot more time with me from now on, I sort of feel as though you've been purposely avoiding me. I've also been wondering if maybe it's because you have another mistress who's keeping you occupied."

JT wasn't sure where this was coming from but knew he'd better say whatever necessary to reassure her. "Another mistress? Are you kidding me? Because why would I need anyone else when I'm completely satisfied with you?"

"I don't know."

"Well, I *do* know. And the only reason I haven't been able to see you as often is because of all the responsibilities I have at the church. I'm being pulled in every direction, and there are some days when I'm completely wiped out. Plus, while I would love nothing more than to be with you every day if I could, I can't ignore the fact that I have a wife at home."

"I understand that, but as of late your time with me has been a lot less, and if I'm going to continue supporting you in such a major financial way, I have to know for sure that you're going to be a lot more committed to our relationship."

"I am committed, and you're going to see a huge difference from this point on. Once I have this whole marketing blitz in place, I'll be able to see you at least twice every single week the way you want."

"I'm going to hold you to that, and I hope you don't disappoint me, because my feelings for you have become a lot stronger than I'd planned on. So much so that I look forward to our time together more than I do anything else."

She moved closer to him, loosened his tie, and kissed him up and down his neck, but he didn't like how serious she was sounding. Diana was a wonderfully nice woman; JT enjoyed her company and loved sleeping with her, and interestingly enough, this was all he'd thought she'd wanted out of the deal as well.

Still, though, he needed that hundred and fifty thousand dollars she was giving him, so he would do and say whatever that hundred and fifty thousand dollars required.

"I feel the exact same way," he said as she kissed the other side of his neck. "I think about you practically every hour of the day, and I always hate leaving you when I have to go home."

"I'm glad to hear it," she said between kisses, and then stood up, grabbed his hand, and led him toward the bedroom.

JT went along willingly and could tell she was content with all that he'd just confessed to her. It was clear that the only thing she was expecting from him now was hot, passionate love. And needless to say, hot, passionate love was exactly what he was going to give her.

Chapter 26

*J*T had left Diana's about an hour ago and was heading back to the church, but when Alicia had called to say she'd come home from the hospital to shower and change, he'd stopped by to see her for a few minutes.

"Hey, beautiful," he said, hugging and kissing his wife and then leaning against the armoire, watching her finish getting dressed. "It's a shame when a person can look as good as you do even in jogging pants and a T-shirt."

"Why, thank you, sir," she said, smiling. "Actually, it's a little too warm outside to be wearing this, but it won't be once I get back to the hospital because they have it freezing in there. It's the reason I'm taking my jacket with me, too."

"Yeah, they do keep it pretty cold. They do it because of all the germs sick people tend to have."

"Yeah, that's for sure."

"So, there's still no change in Rita's condition?"

"No. None at all."

"I'm really sorry to hear that."

"So am I, and I really feel bad for Carmen. Which is why I was thinking that if her mom doesn't get better very soon,

I would really like to invite her to come stay with us for a while."

JT swallowed the massive lump lodged in his throat and tried keeping his composure. "I don't think that's a very good idea."

Alicia squinted her eyes, clearly upset about his response. "And why is that?"

"Because, baby, we're still newlyweds, and I don't think we should be sharing our household with any outsiders. I mean, I know Carmen is a childhood friend of yours, but it's not like you've been around her on a regular basis for years."

"But she doesn't have anyone else. She's an only child and the few relatives she has all live out of town. And I just don't think it's good for her to be alone."

"I'm sorry, baby, but moving her in here won't work for me. I just can't agree to something like that."

Alicia walked over to him and locked her hands inside of his. "Honey, I realize you don't really know Carmen, but she's a good person and she really needs me right now. So, can you at least just think about it?"

"We can discuss this later, but I may as well tell you now that there's no chance of me changing my mind."

Alicia sighed. "Baby, why are you being so selfish? Especially at a time like this?"

"I'm not. But I've also never been in the habit of opening up my home to just anyone."

"Carmen isn't just anyone, and I thought this was my home, too."

"Of course it is, but I'm not going to allow someone to stay here when I don't even know if they can be trusted."

Alicia released his hands and walked away from him.

"Baby, come on. Please don't be upset with me about this."

"You're wrong," she said, sitting down on the side of the

bed, slipping into her gym shoes, and tying them up. "I mean, where's your compassion?"

"My decision has nothing to do with that. I empathize with both Carmen and her mother, but letting Carmen move in here like she's some loyal family member, well, that's just not something I can do."

Alicia didn't say another word, so JT followed her downstairs. When she walked out to the garage, he set the alarm system and closed the door behind him.

"So, I guess you're not speaking to me, huh?" he asked, realizing this was officially their first major disagreement. They'd had a few discussions that weren't the most cordial, specifically the day she'd wanted to know about those accusations Barb had made, even though she thought Barb was someone named Donna, and also last Saturday when he'd lied and told her he had to go see a sick church member—that day when he'd actually spent the entire evening with Veda, but this argument was much more severe.

She opened her car door. "There's not a lot else for me to say."

"Can we talk about this some more when we get home tonight?"

"If you want," she said, putting on her sunglasses.

"I do. And I love you."

Alicia got in her vehicle, started the ignition, backed out of the garage, and drove off. JT did the same, but as he left their subdivision, he knew it was time to get rid of Carmen. It was time to cut her off and also find a way to end her relationship with his wife.

When JT steered his car into the church parking lot, closed the convertible top, and stepped out onto the asphalt, he saw Minister Payne and Minister Weaver heading inside. He had asked both of them to come in for a short meeting so he could update them on the marketing agenda, and he was glad they were right on schedule.

"Have a seat," JT said when the three of them walked into his office, and JT went around and sat behind his desk. "This won't take very long but since I've decided to go a slightly different route with the marketing plan in comparison to what we discussed three weeks ago, I wanted to fill you in. That way you can share it with the other ministers and officers when you have your weekly meeting with them this evening. Actually, I may stop in for a few minutes just in case they have questions."

"Sounds good," Minister Payne said.

However, Minister Weaver was a lot more forthcoming. "So, what's the change?"

"Well, for one thing, I've hired a firm to coordinate and schedule a full broadcasting blitz. We'll have spots promoting the church and myself, as well as what we can offer the overall community."

"That sounds like a great idea," Minister Payne said. "Are we doing both radio and TV?"

"Yes, we're doing both, although I've asked the ad rep to gear more of the money toward radio, specifically during the morning and evening drive times."

"Good."

"How long will these ads run for?" Minister Weaver asked.

"For at least a month."

"On how many stations?"

"All the top stations in Chicago. Gospel, R&B, pop, and talk radio."

Minister Weaver raised his eyebrows. "That sounds awfully costly, so how are we going to pay for all of this?"

"Well, that's the good news," JT said, smiling. "I've located several private donors who really believe in what we do here."

"Who?" Minister Weaver asked. He was starting to annoy JT.

"I wish I could say, but these contributors have asked that I keep their identities confidential. Every one of them has made it clear that, while they are very happy to help get out God's Word, they don't feel the need to make their names known."

Minister Weaver glared at JT, his eyes practically screaming the word "liar," but JT ignored him.

"So, are both of you okay with this?"

"I'm more than fine with it," Minister Payne said. "We need some daily publicity, and I think it's a blessing that you've found a few good people who are happy to pay for it."

"So, what about the committee we talked about creating?" Minister Weaver asked.

"We're going to do that, too. Just not right away. Maybe in about a month or so. When this media blitz has completed, we'll focus a lot more on the other things we discussed."

Minister Weaver seemed skeptical, but this wasn't the first time he had silently disagreed with something JT had come up with. In the end, though, Minister Weaver would basically back down because one fact always remained: JT was the founder of NLCC, and he really didn't owe anyone any explanations about anything. Keeping the two of them, along with the others, abreast of any new business was mainly just a courtesy, but it definitely wasn't something JT was required to do.

They reviewed the rest of this week's schedule as well as this coming Sunday's, and then JT said, "Well, unless you have something else, Glenn, Steve needs to speak with me on a private matter."

"Of course," Minister Weaver said, and stood up. "Also, have you had time to take a look at the information we spoke about at our last meeting?"

JT knew he was referring to his and the other ministers' possible salary increase but said, "No, not yet. And with everything I have going on, I probably won't get to that for a long while."

"If I recall," he stated matter-of-factly, "you said you would review it by the end of the month, and today is already the twenty-sixth."

"Well, unfortunately, this isn't a good time," JT replied, his voice curt.

Minister Weaver made no attempt toward hiding the disgruntled look on his face and soon turned and left the office.

JT pursed his lips tightly. "Sometimes that man really gets under my skin."

Minister Payne cracked up. "He's a trip all right. And what is he worried about now?"

"Money. He wants more of it, and he wants me to take a look at all of your salaries. He says you're not getting paid nearly what you deserve."

"I disagree. We get paid fine."

"Well, clearly Weaver begs to differ. But on the other hand, I think *you* actually do deserve a bonus, and especially if you agree to do a small favor for me."

"Sure. Whatever you need."

"Well, I've sort of gotten myself into a jam, and you're the only person I can trust to help me out of it."

Minister Payne sat up straighter in his chair. "Go ahead. I'm listening."

"It's really bad, Steve. To be honest, it's the worst."

"This sounds serious."

"It is, and there's no sense beating around the bush. I've been sleeping with this woman named Carmen for the last four years, and now she's saying that if I don't leave Alicia and marry her, she's going to go public about the affair we've been having. She's threatening me more and more, and she has to be stopped. This woman is crazy, and I have to get her out of my life."

"Man, Pastor, that's pretty deep."

"I know. And if I could do things over, I definitely would, but it's too late for that."

"I guess you're right. So, what do you want me to do?"

JT gave him more details, mainly about how she'd slithered her way back into Alicia's life and how she'd never bothered telling him that she and Alicia were childhood friends. Then he said, "I've thought about this long and hard and since I can't kill her, although it would be nice"—he chuckled—"the only way I can see getting rid of her is by sending her to prison. So, what I was thinking was that maybe you could contact one of your boys from your old neighborhood, purchase a batch of weed, cocaine, and crack, and then plant it inside her apartment. That is, if you're willing."

Minister Payne nodded in agreement. "Of course I am. Whatever it takes."

"I'm glad to hear it," JT said, happy he'd chosen to mentor and groom such a loyal and dedicated subject.

"All I need is about five grand, an address, and a key if you can get me one."

"Done," JT said, remembering how quickly Carmen had given him a key the same day she'd moved in and how he would gladly take the money from one of his personal accounts. He would withdraw it from the one Alicia didn't know about.

"So, when do you want this taken care of?"

"Soon. And, Steve, if you do this, I'll owe you for life."

"I appreciate that, but you know I'm glad to serve in any way I can. I'm glad to do it free of charge."

Chapter 27

Rita's bed was surrounded by monitors and all sorts of other equipment, and a breathing tube was secured down her throat. From her left arm ran an IV tube, and from the looks of the minimal amount of fluid left in the hanging bag, it was time for it to be replaced.

Alicia stood next to Carmen and wished there was something she could do to make things better. Rita looked as pale as ever, and still, there were no signs of improvement. Her heart still beat, but with the exception of that, her body wasn't doing much else on its own.

"So, how are you young ladies today?" Dr. Mehta asked, walking in.

"Okay," Carmen said, forcing a smile.

"How are you, Doctor?" Alicia added.

"I'm fine. A little tired, but I'm good."

Carmen rubbed her mom's forehead and then looked at Dr. Mehta. "So, how long do you think she's going to be like this? How long will it be before she wakes up?"

"I wish I could say, but unfortunately, I just don't know. Sometimes it can take a lot longer than we would like."

Carmen's eyes turned teary, and Alicia placed her arm around her.

Dr. Mehta flipped through Rita's chart and glanced at her vitals on the digital screen. "For the most part, all we can do is give her more time."

Carmen sniffled. "I just don't understand why this is happening. My mom is only forty-five years old. I mean, who would ever expect something like this to happen to their parents when they're my age?"

"I know," he said. "And I'm very sorry."

Alicia wanted to ask him if Rita really did have a chance of recovering, but she didn't have the nerve to question him in front of Carmen.

"Well, I'm going to head out to see a couple of my other patients, but I'll be in bright and early in the morning before I begin my surgery schedule for the day."

"Thank you so much for everything," Carmen told him.

"You're quite welcome."

After Dr. Mehta left, Alicia and Carmen stayed for a few more minutes and then went back out to the long-term family waiting area, which, interestingly enough, was empty right now. This particular room was a lot more relaxed; it offered more of an at-home kind of atmosphere and was utilized by families who had very sick loved ones. It was even furnished with a microwave, a refrigerator, and a huge flat-screen television, and there were board games and puzzles stacked inside a large wooden entertainment center.

Alicia sat down in one of the plush recliners, and Carmen settled into the other one.

"You know," Carmen began, "I can't help but wonder if this is all my fault."

Alicia looked at her. "How do you mean?"

"Well, I certainly haven't been perfect, and I've done a lot of things I'm sure God isn't happy about. So, I have to wonder if my horrible sins are the reason my mom is ill."

"I really doubt that, and you shouldn't blame yourself for any of what's going on. I can't explain why your mom had that aneurysm, but what I do know is that God doesn't purposely cause any of us a lot of pain and suffering. He does allow some bad things to happen, but He would never intentionally try to hurt anyone."

"But not only have I committed sins, I'm still committing a lot of the same ones right now."

"I've committed sins as well, but last year, I completely turned my life around, and I truly believe God has forgiven me. Which means he'll do the same thing for you, too."

"You really think so?"

"I honestly do. It's never too late to confess our sins, ask for forgiveness, and then live our lives the way God wants us to."

Carmen reached for Alicia's hand. "You are such a good friend to me, and I'll never be able to repay you enough for being here with me."

"I'm here because I love you, and I'll stay by your side for as long as you need me."

Carmen breathed deeply and then paused for a few seconds. "Alicia, there's something I really need to tell you," she said, but they both looked behind them when they heard someone calling Alicia's name.

"Oh my God," Alicia said, smiling at her ex-husband and then standing and hugging him. "Phillip, what are you doing here?"

"I was going to ask you the same thing. You're not here for your mom or stepfather, are you?"

"No," she said, touching Carmen's shoulder. "This is a very

good friend of mine, and her mother had an aneurysm yesterday."

"Oh my. I'm really sorry to hear that."

"Thank you," Carmen said, and Alicia could tell she was wondering who he was.

"Carmen, this is my ex-husband, Phillip."

"Oh, it's very nice to meet you."

"It's nice meeting you as well."

"So, who are you here for?" Alicia asked him.

"One of our church members. When I moved back to the area, I resumed my old position as assistant pastor, so I try to go see as many members as I can on Tuesdays and Wednesdays."

"Oh," she said. That was just like Phillip. Always trying to do right by others and always going out of his way to show how much he cared about people.

"So, how are your mom and your dad James doing?"

"They're doing well, and actually we were visiting them yesterday when Carmen's mom fell ill. How's your mom?"

"She's doing great. As busy as ever."

"Good, and you'll have to tell her I said hello."

"I will."

Alicia and Phillip smiled like two teenagers who'd just met for the first time, and it was obvious that neither of them knew what to say next. Thankfully, Carmen broke the silence.

"I'm going to go back in to check on my mom for a few minutes. I know we just left her, but I really want to see her again. Then I'm going to run down to the cafeteria to get something to eat."

"Do you want me to go with you?"

"No, you stay here and visit. I'll be fine."

"Are you sure? Oh, and wait. There was something you said you wanted to tell me."

"I know, but there's no rush. We can just talk about it later."

"Okay, well, I'll be right here when you get back."

"So," Phillip said without hesitation. "How have you been?"

"Good. And you?"

"I'm doing well. Although, maybe not as well as you, because I hear you just got married."

"Yeah, I did."

"Are you happy?"

Alicia didn't mean to pause before answering but finally said, "Yes. I am."

"I'm glad, because happiness is all I ever wanted for you."

"That's very kind of you to say. But what about you? Are you seeing anyone?"

"Sort of."

"Is it Shandra?"

Now Phillip hesitated. Then he said, "Yes."

Alicia knew it was wrong for her to care one way or the other, but she wasn't thrilled to hear about his dating another woman. She definitely didn't like hearing that he was seeing his high school sweetheart, and she couldn't help feeling a little envious. She had no right, of course, but Phillip still held a special place in her heart. She'd tried telling herself that she no longer loved him, but now that she was seeing him face-to-face, she wasn't so sure.

"So, did you already see the person you came to visit?" she asked, changing the subject.

"No. I was on my way to his room and as I was passing, I just so happened to look in here. I wasn't positive it was you until I opened the door and came in, but I'm so glad I did."

"I'm glad you did, too."

"So, have you spoken to your dad lately?"

"Yeah, I called him earlier to ask him to pray for Carmen's mom. What about you?"

"I haven't talked with him since this past weekend, but we try to stay in touch as much as possible."

"I guess I shouldn't be surprised, because everyone knows that Daddy thinks the world of you."

"And the feeling's mutual. I may be here in Chicago, but Curtis is still my mentor and I'm still learning a lot from him."

"I can imagine," she said, but was at a loss for words again. Phillip seemed to be searching for something else to say as well and Alicia knew why. He still had feelings for her, and God forgive her, she still had very strong feelings for him, too.

"So, your dad tells me you finished your novel and that you've signed with his agent."

"I did, and now she's in the submission process with editors."

"Wow, baby . . . I mean . . . well, you know what I mean. Anyway, I'm really happy for you."

"Thanks, and actually, you should take some of the credit because you always encouraged me to keep writing until I finished. Even when we weren't getting along."

"I did it because I knew you were good and that you deserved to be published."

Just then two sixtysomething women who looked like sisters walked in, said hello, dropped a couple of overnight bags on the floor, and went back out.

"They must be planning to be here for a while," Phillip said.

"Probably so. I'm sure a lot of people stay for days just like Carmen is planning to do. I guess it just feels better to stay close when someone you love is fighting for their life."

"There's no doubt about it," he said, and the moment between them became awkward again. Not in a bad way but in a bashful, nervous, and uncharted-territory sort of manner—uncharted because while they'd once been completely in love with each other and had taken marital vows before God, this whole seeing-each-other-for-the-first-time-after-the-divorce-and-still-experiencing-intense-chemistry thing was a bit overwhelming. Not to mention Alicia had a new husband. She was married to a man she loved and one who cherished her very being, so none of what she was feeling made any sense.

Alicia and Phillip sat watching CNN and made small talk, and Carmen soon returned.

"So, what did you get to eat?"

"I had a tuna croissant and some fries."

"Good. Because it really was time you ate something."

"Well," Phillip said, standing up, "I guess I'd better get going. But before I do, would you like me to go say a prayer for your mom, Carmen? Because I would be more than happy to."

"Yes. My mom needs all the prayer she can get, so if you don't mind, I would really appreciate that."

"I don't mind at all," he said, and the three of them headed toward the intensive care unit. They strode down the corridor, Carmen walking slightly in front and Alicia and Phillip walking side by side. They continued on their way, and it wasn't long before Alicia felt a wonderful sense of comfort. But then she thought about JT and felt a tremendous sense of guilt.

Chapter 28

JT typed in his user ID and password and waited for his account details to pop onto the screen. He'd already browsed it late last evening, but he couldn't help looking yet again. First he saw a transfer amount of one hundred thousand dollars and then a second for fifty thousand. It was all there, every single dollar, and now he really would be able to pay for the hundred-thousand-dollar media campaign and also give Barb the fifty thousand she was demanding. Everything was working out exactly the way he wanted it to, and he couldn't have been happier.

Although he did wonder if this really would be the end of Blackmailing Barb, and sadly, he knew there was no way to guarantee it. He knew her word basically meant nothing and that all he could do was hope the money he was preparing to give her would more than suffice and that she would disappear. He couldn't be sure one way or the other, but he would pray for that kind of outcome just the same.

JT scrolled through his account information, clicked on a few other general banking items, and then signed out. He was all set on the financial front, and that made him think about Veda and how it wouldn't be long before he'd be able to search for

and purchase that nice little getaway property he'd been thinking about. It would be his home away from home and the place
where he could spend all his private time with Veda whenever
she was able to fly in from Minneapolis, and also with any other
women he might connect with from time to time. He wouldn't
go looking for another mistress, but he was slowly beginning
to accept the fact that he needed to be with *different* women.
He needed a variety of them to choose from, and there was no
use trying to fight the inevitable. He wasn't sure why, but this
morning, he'd done a lot of soul searching and had come to the
same conclusion over and over again: He loved or cared about all
the women in his life, but none of them was enough. Not Alicia,
not Diana, not Veda, and certainly not Carmen. So, in the end,
he was who he was and there was simply no changing that.

JT pulled out his BlackBerry and dialed Veda's cell number.
It rang three times before she answered.

"How are you?" he said.

"I'm well. How are you?"

"Fine, now that I'm talking with you."

"I saw that you called me, but on Monday, I was with my son
and some of my relatives, and then yesterday I had meetings
back-to-back."

"I figured as much, but you know I missed hearing your
voice, though, right?"

"I missed you as well."

"Did you have a good holiday?"

"I did. It was actually better than I expected it to be. And
yours?"

"It was okay. One of the people in attendance had a medi-
cal emergency, but before that, the day had turned out pretty
nicely."

"Oh, I'm sorry to hear that. I hope it wasn't too serious."

"Unfortunately, it is, but we're praying for her to get better. So, tell me," he said, no longer wanting to focus on Carmen or her mother. "When will I get to see you again?"

"I don't know. Hopefully soon, though."

"What about this coming weekend?" he asked, seeing no reason to wait any longer than that.

"I wish I could, but remember, my son's graduation is on Friday, and I'm throwing him a party on Saturday."

"Oh, that's right. You did mention that, but I totally forgot. Well, then, how about next weekend?" he asked, removing the phone from his ear. He'd heard the Call Waiting signal but now that he saw it was Carmen, he frowned and ignored it.

"I'll check my schedule and will let you know as soon as I can. I think I'm pretty open, though."

"Good. Because I really need to see you. I've been thinking about you a lot, and if we don't get together soon, I'm afraid I'll die from withdrawal symptoms."

Veda laughed and so did JT, but then he said, "You think it's funny, girl, but I'm serious."

"Whatever you say," she said, still chuckling.

"I really do miss you, Veda. I miss seeing you, holding you— I miss everything about you."

"Well, the truth is, I miss you, too. I'm not sure why, but I do."

"Meaning?"

"That I don't even know you. And you don't know me, so it's not normal for two people to feel this way about each other so quickly."

"Yeah, but stranger things than that happen all the time, and for the most part none of us has any control over who we fall for. It's pretty much just the nature of the beast, so to speak."

"I guess."

The two of them paused for a few seconds and then JT said, "Well, I suppose I'll let you get going, but definitely call me once you know if you're able to come down."

"I will."

"Take care, love."

"You, too."

JT hung up and wished Veda was right there in his office. If she had been, church building or not, he probably would have torn her clothes right off of her. He wanted her badly, and the sooner she was able to fly back to the Windy City, the better off he would be. At least for that moment, anyway.

After sorting through a few files on his desk, JT summoned Janet into his office so she could give him an update.

"So, how's the mailing process moving along?"

"Wonderfully," she said, standing just a couple of feet away from him. "All the packages are stuffed, sealed, labeled, and ready to be shipped."

"Great."

"I'm planning to send everything out by UPS this afternoon, and they should arrive at each respective church either by Friday or no later than Monday. Then, if I don't hear anything within the first couple of weeks, I'll begin following up with each church secretary, making sure they received the information."

"I hadn't even thought that far ahead, but that's an excellent idea. Also, just so you know, I've been speaking with an ad executive at a well-known agency downtown, and he's compiling a listing of top radio and TV stations here in the Chicago area. He's also creating a proposal for me, but for the most part, I'll want you to be the primary contact. I'll want to see everything before any final decisions are made, but I'll want you to communicate with him by phone and e-mail. I'll also have you sit in on any physical meetings I might schedule with him as well."

"No problem. I'll be glad to."

"There is one other thing that you should know, though. I've given him a budget of one hundred thousand dollars to work with."

Janet looked at him quietly, but he could tell she was taken aback. She was clearly shocked, and before she could ask any questions or think suspiciously, he said, "I know that sounds like a lot, but I've been saving money for something like this all along. I mean, I always knew we could raise the money from our parishioners, but since that could take months, I decided to just go for it. I want to move now, and to be honest, I really do believe that this is what God wants. He wants me to use my own money for this entire project."

She nodded in agreement, and JT was sorry for lying to her. Although, maybe he wasn't lying at all, because in reality, Diana had given him that money free and clear and wasn't expecting to be paid back, so technically this was his *own* money. It was all his, and this meant every word he'd just told Janet was true.

"I know this is sort of out of the blue," he said, "but I'm really excited about it."

"It really is a huge sacrifice, but if this is what God wants you to do, then you know it's the right thing."

"I know. And that's all that really matters, anyway. Being obedient and doing His will."

"Well, just let me know whatever you need."

"I will, and thanks for everything, Janet. You do so much, and I just want you to know how much I appreciate it."

"Don't even give it another thought. I love God, and I love my job, and that means I'll do anything I can to preserve and help this ministry."

JT smiled and then Janet said, "Well, if that's all, then I'm going to get back to the mailing. The other girls have pretty much got it handled, but I still want to look in on them to make sure all the packages will be ready before pickup time."

"Thanks again," JT said, watching her leave his office.

Then he thought about how rich and famous he was going to be and got tickled. It was only a matter of time because, once those commercials began running, people from all over would be flocking in to hear him speak on Sunday mornings. They would come, hear how good he was, and quickly invite their family members and friends. Before long, he would be the most popular minister in the Midwest, and after that there would be no turning back. And he couldn't forget all the megachurches nationwide that would soon be calling him to come speak, and this would all be thanks to his infamous father-in-law. Every bit of his blessings would all be a result of his forging Curtis's name on that recommendation letter and his masterful ability to sweet-talk Diana out of six figures. Doing both would soon prove to be well worth his while, and JT couldn't wait to reap all the benefits. He could barely wait to begin living the fabulous life he was fast on his way to securing.

Chapter 29

Alicia read the latest e-mail from Levi and debated how she should respond. There was no doubt that the proper and honest thing to do would be to end all contact with him. But deep down she really didn't want that—she didn't want it, and she was ashamed to say there was a certain level of excitement Levi Cunningham filled her insides with. Yes, he was locked away in prison and certainly wasn't the kind of man any decent person would recommend she consort with, but Alicia had seen the real good in him. She had experienced firsthand how gentle and considerate he was when it came to women, namely her, and she couldn't simply forget about that. She couldn't write him off like he didn't matter to her, because he did.

Still, after contemplating for nearly twenty minutes, she replied with the following:

Hi Levi,

It's really good hearing from you again, but I don't think our communicating with each other, even by e-mail, is a good idea. You are a truly wonderful person, and of course, I'll be praying for your release, but that's pretty much where our relationship will have to stand. I'm sorry, I hope you understand, and I pray that you will take good care of yourself.

Wishing you all the love and blessings possible,
Alicia

Alicia reread her note, hit the send button, and then scanned the rest of her inbox. She read a few new ones from more members at the church, but then smiled when her cell rang and she saw that it was Melanie.

"Hey, girl," Alicia said.

"Hey yourself. And can I please ask why you didn't bother calling to tell me you saw Phillip yesterday?"

"Oh my goodness, I guess news travels pretty fast, doesn't it? And who told you that, anyway?"

"Phillip. He called and left me a voice message this morning, and I just now got a chance to call him back."

"What did he want?"

"To talk about you, of course."

"I don't get it," Alicia said, trying to play innocent.

"Well, he gets it, and based on how shady you're sounding, you know exactly what I'm talking about."

"Whatever."

"Oh, so are you saying you don't want to know what we talked about?"

"Not really. Unless you're just dying to tell me, that is," she said, and they both laughed.

"Well, first of all, he admitted that he was way out of line for asking, but he wanted to know if you really were happily married. He wanted to know if things were really that great with you and your new husband."

"And what did you tell him?"

"That as far as I knew, you and JT were very happy."

"Good. And then what?"

"He went on about how good you looked, something about you looking even more beautiful than when he first met you and that as soon as he saw you, he knew he loved you more than before. He said he knew he shouldn't, not after the way you slept with Levi behind his back and especially not now that you're married to someone else, but he can't help how he feels. He said he knew he'd never stopped loving you, but when he saw you in person, he could barely handle being around you."

Alicia's heart thumped more noticeably, and she wondered why this was happening—why her ex-husband had shared all of this with her best friend. Mainly, though, she wondered why she was feeling the same way about him. She'd also felt similar feelings when she'd spoken on the phone with Levi as well as when she'd read his e-mails, so this was all terribly confusing. None of it made any sense because she really did love JT. Her current husband. The man who loved her back. The man who gave her everything she wanted and who was working tirelessly to give her even more than that.

"Helloooo?" Melanie sang.

"I'm here," Alicia finally said.

"I guess this was a lot of information to take in for one conversation, huh?"

"You're telling me."

"Well, all I know is that Phillip is still head-over-heels in love with you, and he pretty much talked about nothing else."

"But the only thing is, Mel, I'm married. I'm married, and I'm completely committed to JT."

"Which is why I debated telling you any of this. But after

I thought about it, I knew you would be upset with me if you found out about it later."

"You're right. Still, though, I wish Phillip hadn't told you any of that, and now I wish I hadn't seen him."

"Why? Do you still care about him?"

"I won't even lie to you, Mel. I do. I wish I didn't, but it is what it is. Phillip and I have a lot of history, both good and bad, but if he'd never left me and filed for a divorce, I know I would still be with him."

"That's really gotta be tough."

"Yeah, but it's much too late for all that now. We both have very separate lives, and that's how we're going to have to continue them."

"I hear you."

"Anyway, how's everything else going?"

"Fine. I've been working a lot of hours this week, but Brad and I just decided last night to head down to South Beach for a four-day weekend. We're leaving tomorrow and coming back late on Sunday."

"Good for you, girl. You deserve a vacation, and there's nothing more fun than being in Miami."

"I know, and I can hardly wait."

"Well, if I don't talk to you before you leave, you guys have a wonderful time."

"We will, and if I get some time, I'll call you."

"Sounds good, and travel safe."

"Talk to you soon. Oh, and wait, girl, I'm so sorry. How is your friend's mom? I told Phillip that you'd called me yesterday morning to tell me what happened, but he said when he was there yesterday, not much had changed."

"No, there's been no improvement at all, and actually, I just came home this morning so I could get a little rest and take care of a few to-do items. I'm going back in a couple of hours or so, though."

"I know this must be tragic for Carmen because it certainly would be for me. Here at the hospital, I see illnesses like this all the time, but I know it would be a lot different if it happened to one of my own loved ones."

"Definitely."

"Well, even though I've never met her, please tell Carmen I'm praying for her mom."

"I will, Mel, and thanks so much for that."

"Okay, talk to you later."

Alicia set her phone down and started out of her office, but now the home phone rang. It was her agent, and Alicia hurried to answer it.

"Hello?"

"Hi, it's Joan."

"How are you?"

"Great. And the reason I'm calling is to let you know that I've already heard back from all the editors I submitted your manuscript to, and they each want to make offers."

"Oh my God. This is wonderful."

"It certainly is, and we're already in the process of setting up all the meetings, which will probably span a two-day period. Most likely, next Wednesday and Thursday, so I can hold the auction on Friday."

"Gosh, Joan, I've wished for this for a long time, but now that it's happening, it just doesn't seem real."

"I can imagine. I'm very excited for you and all that I know this will lead to."

"Also, thank you again for agreeing to represent me."

"No, thank you, and I'll be in touch again very soon."

"Take care."

Alicia quickly pressed the off button, turned the phone back on again, and dialed JT. She was thrilled beyond her wildest dreams and couldn't wait to tell him the news.

"Hey, you," he said when he answered.

"Hi, sweetheart, guess what?"

"Talk to me."

"Joan just called and all six of the editors she submitted to want to make an offer."

"That's wonderful, baby."

"And I'll be meeting with each of them next week. I mean, can you believe that?"

"Of course I do. I knew all along that things would turn out great."

"It really is happening, JT. And now I'm wondering what kinds of offers will actually come in."

"Well, with them obviously reading your novel this quickly and already saying they want it, I really can't see them offering anything small."

"I hope you're right."

"Aren't I always?"

"Yeah, as a matter of fact you are."

"I'm really proud of you."

"Thanks, baby. But hey, I just wanted you to be the first to know, but now I need to call my dad."

"I know he'll be just as excited as I am. Oh, and before you go, are you going to make it to Bible study tonight?"

"I wanted to, but because I've been home most of the day, I really want to get back to the hospital to sit some more with Carmen."

"That's what I figured, and I definitely understand."

"Sorry."

"No, don't be sorry about it at all, and I'll just see you when I get home."

"I love you," she said.

"I love you, too, baby, and congratulations."

Alicia hung up the phone and called her dad, who was ecstatic, and then got ready to head back out to the hospital. But as she gathered up her Gucci shoulder purse and the black and white tote bag she'd filled with a few magazines she'd been wanting to read, the doorbell rang. So she walked through the foyer and opened the door, and a FedEx driver smiled at her. Interestingly enough, she hadn't ordered any clothing, shoes, or jewelry by mail in the last couple of weeks, so as far as she knew they weren't expecting any deliveries.

"Hello," she said, greeting him.

"Hi. I have a letter for you, so can you please sign here?" he asked, passing her a white envelope with orange and purple lettering.

"Sure." Alicia took the package and signed where he told her.

"Thanks so much, and have a good day."

"You, too," she said, closing the door. First, she looked to see who the sender was and got a little nervous when she saw the name "Donna" and no last name. Still, she pulled the strip back, opened the envelope, and started to read the handwritten note inside.

Hi there. I hope this letter finds you doing well but I must say, I've really been thinking about you a lot. Truthfully, I've been very worried for your safety. I'm afraid because if JT did in fact stage his first wife's accident, you could be the next person on his murder list. I'm terrified of what he might do, so I suggest you watch your back at all times.

Be Careful What You Pray For

I'm sure you're probably thinking how none of this is really any of my business and that's why I've tried keeping my mouth shut. But where I come from, women always stick together and look out for one another no matter what. They feel a strong obligation to try to protect anyone who might be at risk. So, what you need to do is watch JT every waking moment and make him accountable for everything he says or does. You need to watch that whoremonger like the dog that he is and call him on anything that even seems remotely suspicious.

Take care, my friend,
Donna

Alicia wondered who this woman really was and why she felt such ill will toward JT. She also wondered if maybe this had less to do with his alleged part in Michelle's accident and more to do with something else. For all she knew, maybe this Donna person had previously been in some sort of relationship with JT and hadn't gotten over him. Maybe JT had dumped her for someone else or possibly even for Michelle. Alicia had no way of knowing for sure what her reasons for revenge might be, but what she did know was this: No matter what Donna kept insisting and no matter what JT might be capable of, Alicia knew JT could never kill anyone. She wasn't claiming he was a saint, but in her heart, she didn't believe he would even consider taking someone else's life. He just wouldn't do anything like that. Never. Not for any reason.

She told herself she didn't have a single thing to be concerned about when it came to her own well-being.

Chapter 30

Alicia went inside the hospital, walked through the lobby, and continued down the glass-encased corridor. Until now, she hadn't paid much attention to how beautiful the garden outside these windows was, and if she ever got a chance, she would spend a little more time admiring it.

She strolled past nurses, doctors, nursing assistants, and many other hospital personnel and finally arrived at the west elevators, which would take her to the intensive care unit. An older gentleman stood in front of them, and the up button was already lit. Alicia stood patiently, but then she thought about her conversation with JT. She'd called him as soon as she'd gotten in the car to tell him about that FedEx package, but all he'd basically said was that this Donna woman was scary and needed to be admitted to a nuthouse. In a sense, Alicia tended to agree, but she also knew that no one would spend this much time writing a letter, finding out her and JT's home address, and then paying to send it by an actual shipping carrier for no reason. The woman wouldn't have come up to Alicia when she'd run into her at Nordstrom that day either.

The elevator system chimed, the up arrow illuminated, and the door slid open. Alicia and the guy she'd been waiting with stepped on, he got off on the third floor, and she continued on to the fifth. When she arrived, she stepped out, walked a few feet, turned the corner, and went inside the family waiting room. Carmen sat there alone but looked up as soon as she heard Alicia entering.

"I really wish you would have let me bring you something to eat."

Carmen smiled at her but wore an odd look on her face.

"What's wrong?" Alicia said, sitting down adjacent to her.

Carmen smiled again. "She's gone."

"What?"

"She's gone. She went into cardiac arrest, and they couldn't revive her."

Alicia placed both her hands in a praying position and brought them toward her chin. "Oh no, Carmen, I'm so sorry," she said, tears streaming down her face. "I'm so sorry I wasn't here."

Carmen looked at her, still smiling. "Everything is going to be just fine."

Alicia thought it strange that Carmen was acting so nonchalantly and seemed so at peace. She acted as if she hadn't just been told very devastating news.

Alicia wiped her tears away and said, "When did it happen?"

"About two hours ago."

Alicia frowned. Two hours ago? Well, if that was the case, then why hadn't Carmen told her that her mother had passed when Alicia had called to see if she needed anything? She hadn't said a word, and now this made things even more eerie.

"My mom is now in a much better place, and I'm happy for her. She no longer has to suffer or worry about anything, and that's why I have to be strong. I have to be the kind of woman she raised me up to be, just like your mom told me the other day."

Alicia understood that wholeheartedly, but she was still confused about Carmen's overall reaction to her mother's death.

"Everything happens for a reason," Carmen went on. "And instead of mourning the loss of my mom, I'm going to celebrate the wonderful life she lived and then go on with my own life just like she would expect me to. I'm going to do whatever I have to to get everything I've ever wanted, and I'm going to be happier than I've ever been."

Alicia sniffled and smiled and was glad Carmen had taken on such a positive attitude, but she *still* didn't think any of this was normal. Finally, though, she asked her, "Is there anything I can do right now?"

"No. Girl, you've done more than enough just by being here the last two days. Plus, there's not much else to do because I already told the nurse which funeral home to call, and once they arrive, I'm going to go back in to see my mom one last time. After that, you can drive me home."

Alicia took both of Carmen's hands into hers. "I'm here for you, okay? I'm here, and I'll do whatever you need me to do for you."

Carmen smiled again and said, "Thank you, but really, girl, I'm fine."

Alicia stared at her and then wondered if Carmen was having a nervous breakdown.

Right after they left the hospital, Alicia drove Carmen to her apartment and they both went inside. On the way there, Carmen had talked about seemingly everything she could think of, but all Alicia had done was mainly listen.

"Have a seat," Carmen said, and then dropped a duffel bag onto the sofa, the one Alicia had placed a change of clothing inside and brought to her yesterday afternoon. Thankfully, Carmen wore a size six, the same as Alicia did, so Alicia hadn't had any problem finding something to loan her.

Alicia took a seat and then Carmen went into the bathroom, returning minutes later.

"There's something I really need to talk to you about."

"Of course. What is it?"

Carmen took a deep breath. "Okay. First of all, there's a reason I'm not as sad as most people will probably expect me to be."

"Which is?"

"I'm not very sad because even though I've lost the one person who loved me unconditionally and I'll miss her terribly, I'll soon have another person in my life who will love me just the same."

"And who is that?"

"Well, in about seven or seven and a half months—that is, if my calculation is right—I'll be giving birth to a precious little baby," she said, smiling. She was beyond excited, so Alicia smiled with her.

"Really? When did you find out?"

"I knew my period was pretty late, so right after you left for a while yesterday, I went down the street to the pharmacy. I went there so I could get a pregnancy test, and when I came back and took it, the results showed positive."

"So, is that what you wanted to tell me yesterday just before Phillip walked in?"

"Yes. And, Alicia, I'm so excited. I mean, I do wish my mom was still here so she could get a chance to see her first grandchild, but I'm still very happy about all of this."

"So, who's the father?" Alicia asked without thinking.

Carmen paused and then said, "Actually, that was the other thing I was going to tell you about yesterday, but now I think it might be better if I waited on that. I mean, don't get me wrong, you know I trust you completely, but, again, for right now, I really think it's best I don't say. At least not until my relationship with him becomes a lot less complicated than it has been."

Alicia wondered if he was married and couldn't imagine any woman being careless enough to get pregnant by someone else's husband. She kept her thoughts to herself, however.

Carmen nestled farther into the sofa. "I know I probably should have waited until I was married before trying to get pregnant, but I really wanted this baby."

Alicia tried masking how astonished she was. "So, it wasn't an accident?"

"No. I planned the whole thing from beginning to end because I knew how much my man wanted to have a child. Which is also why I know we'll be married long before our baby gets here."

Alicia hoped for her sake she was right, but she didn't comment one way or the other. Instead, she sat quietly and pretended she was just as elated as Carmen.

Chapter 31

JT turned onto his street, pulled in front of his house, and frowned when he saw Carmen's vehicle. It was ten P.M., so he had no idea what she was doing there so late. It didn't add up because when he'd spoken to Alicia again in the late afternoon, she'd told him Carmen's mother had passed and that she was going to stay with Carmen at her apartment for a few hours, helping her make calls to relatives and do whatever else was necessary. She'd told him all the general details, but she hadn't said anything about Carmen coming home with her.

After JT drove inside the garage, he stepped out of his vehicle and Alicia opened the door leading to the kitchen. Then she closed it behind her.

"Hi, sweetheart," she said. "Before you go in, I need to talk to you about something."

He leaned against his car door. "I'm listening."

"When I called you earlier, Carmen was actually taking her mother's death pretty well, but as time went on this evening, she became a lot more emotional. As a matter of fact, she pretty much cried her eyes out just before my mom and Dad James came by, but then while they were there, she laughed and joked about just about everything. So, needless to say, I'm very worried about all these mood changes she keeps having, and I didn't think it was a good idea for her to spend the night all by herself."

"That's all fine and well, baby, but I've already expressed to you how I feel about this."

"I know, but, honey, she really needs me right now. She needs us."

"No, she needs *you*," he said, trying not to sound as pissed off as he felt. "Because I don't know a thing about her."

"But you know she's my friend and that I care about her, right?"

"Nonetheless, I still don't want her here."

Alicia tossed him a dirty a look, something JT hadn't seen her do before. "What's wrong with you?" she asked loudly. "I mean, how can you be so cruel?"

"I'm not. But it's like I told you before, I don't want someone staying here when I don't know if they can be trusted."

Alicia folded her arms. "You know, JT, I'm really shocked to see you taking such a strong stance about this because this is so totally unlike you. You're acting as though Carmen has done something to you personally or like she's one of your worst enemies, and I don't get that."

JT wondered if Alicia was simply trying to make a point or if maybe his negative attitude toward Carmen was beginning to make her suspicious. Either way, he couldn't take any chances.

"Okay, fine, baby," he said. "She can stay."

Alicia hugged him and then pecked him on the lips. "Thank you for understanding, and I'm sure she'll feel well enough to go home by tomorrow or the next day."

When they went inside and into the family room, Carmen stood up. "JT, I hope you're not upset about my staying over here."

JT gritted his teeth. "Of course not. You just lost your mother, and we're glad to have you."

"Oh, bless you," she said, smiling, and JT wanted to smack that grin from her conniving little face.

"You're welcome," he said reluctantly.

But he had barely gotten the words out before Carmen rushed over and hugged him. "You and Alicia really are lifesavers, and I don't know what I would do without the two of you."

JT pulled away from her and glanced over at his wife, checking to see her reaction. Interestingly enough, she was smiling with the utmost approval. She was actually thrilled beyond measure and clearly had no idea her "good friend" was scheming and doing everything she could, trying to take her place.

This whole scenario, though, was too much even for him and the reason he finally said, "Hey, baby, I'm beat. So, I'm gonna head upstairs to take a shower and get ready for bed."

"That's fine. I'm going to sit and chat with Carmen for a while, but after that I'll be right up."

"Take your time," he said, and went on his way.

JT slipped off his suit jacket, plopped down onto the chaise, removed his tie, and flipped on the television. A few minutes ago, he'd told Alicia how tired he was just as a way to escape Carmen and whatever she was plotting, but now he realized he hadn't been lying. He truly was exhausted, and if he hadn't been a stickler about always showering before turning in, he would have skipped freshening up altogether and would have fallen straight to sleep.

So he sat only for a short while, then finished undressing and went into the bathroom. He opened the glass door, threw his plush bath towel over the side of it, turned on the steamy-hot water, and stepped in. This felt good already, and this was one of the days when he was glad he'd insisted the builders install a very high-pressure showerhead. It could easily be adjusted so that the water flowed less powerfully, but he always kept it at this position. He loved the way it massaged his muscles and how rejuvenated he usually felt once he finished lathering down and rinsing off. It was one of the small luxuries he'd requested but one that had been well worth asking for.

JT stood still for longer than normal but then finally turned off the water and stepped out. He dried himself off, secured the towel around his waist, and strutted back into the bedroom. It was then that his heart skipped a beat and began pounding rapidly.

He couldn't believe his eyes but knew he wasn't hallucinating. Carmen stood in front of him, dropping to the floor what appeared to be one of Alicia's bathrobes, and then moved closer. She had not a stitch of underwear on.

She placed both arms around his neck, but JT pushed her away. "What are you doing? And where is Alicia?"

"She's out. Yeah, I sent the little wifey off to fetch me something to eat. I told her I was finally hungry and that I had a huge taste for some Giordano's deep-dish pizza, and she was in her car and on her way in no time. She'll be gone for at least an hour."

"You're sick, Carmen. You know that? You're sick and you need help."

"Why? Because I know what I want, and I'm not afraid to go after it?"

"No, because you've got my wife thinking you're her friend, yet here you are standing in her bedroom, butt-naked, trying to seduce her husband."

Carmen smirked at him. "I guess I don't see what the problem is."

"You know exactly what I mean, and I want you out of here."

"But your wife wants me to stay, remember? She told me I can stay for as long as I want, and before she left to go get me something to eat, she told me to come right on up to that gorgeous guest bedroom I'll be sleeping in . . . but I decided to come satisfy my man instead."

"Carmen, I'm only going to say this one more time. Get your crazy behind out of here."

"Geez. You're so testy these days," she said, stroking the side of his face.

JT slapped her hand away as hard as he could.

"And violent, too," she said, laughing at him. "But I forgive you."

Now JT wanted to laugh himself, because this whole travesty seemed more like a bad joke. It certainly didn't seem real, but what he worried about most was how he was going to bully Carmen back to that room Alicia had set up for her.

"You know, baby," she said, laying across JT and Alicia's bed and resting her head against two pillows, "you really should answer my calls or at least have the decency to call me back. We've had this very conversation before, but you still don't seem to understand."

"I understand perfectly. But in case you forgot, Carmen, I'm a very busy man with a lot of important responsibilities, and it's not like I can drop everything I'm doing just because you want me to."

"You drop what you're doing whenever that little tramp calls you."

"What tramp?"

"Your wife, of course."

"Oh, so now you're back to calling her names again."

"I've never stopped. I mean, maybe for a little while, but she'll always be a tramp-trick in my book."

"Look, Carmen," he said, "Alicia could walk in at any time, so do you really want her to catch you lying in our bed like this?"

"Do *you* want her to catch me?"

"Of course I don't."

"Well, then I suggest you drop that towel and make love to your *real* woman."

"Yeah, right. You must be crazy."

"Make love to me or else I'm telling her the truth about this baby I'm carrying."

JT took two steps backward. "What baby?"

"The baby I told her about this afternoon. The baby that belongs to her loving, faithful husband, Pastor JT Valentine. Right now, she has no idea who the father is, but if you don't give me what I want, I'm telling her everything."

JT glared at Carmen and wanted to choke the life out of her. He wanted to end her existence, dump her body, and read that she'd been classified as a missing person.

But he knew his thoughts were nothing more than wishful thinking and that he had to do what Carmen wanted. He wouldn't have sex with her in his and his wife's bed, and he would instead insist they go back to her guest room, but he would do whatever else she wanted just to keep her quiet. He would play all her ruthless games until Minister Payne took care of things. JT would sit back, waiting patiently, until his gracious protégé brought this nutcase to her knees.

Chapter 32

It was just after seven, but Alicia lay quietly with her back toward JT and couldn't stop thinking about that FedEx delivery. She'd thought about it on and off quite a bit yesterday, but with Carmen's mom passing, she hadn't focused on it nearly in the manner she was now. Then, last night when she'd returned with Carmen's pizza, sat, eaten a couple of slices with her, and had finally gone upstairs to bed, she'd come into the room and found JT sound asleep. For a moment, she'd considered waking him up but had decided she just didn't have the energy or desire to talk about Donna and the terrible things she'd said about him.

Alicia sighed and turned onto her back. She looked over at JT and surprisingly, he smiled at her. Still, all she did was look up at the ceiling, refusing to say anything.

"What's that about?" he asked.

"Nothing."

"C'mon," he said, reaching over and caressing her stomach. "Tell me."

"I don't wanna talk about it."

"Don't wanna talk about what?"

Alicia pretended she didn't hear him.

"Wait. I know you're not still upset about this whole Carmen thing and the fact that I don't want her staying here."

"No. Well, yes, I'm still not happy about that, but right now that's the least of my worries."

"Baby, please don't do this."

"Okay, fine. I'm upset because, for the life of me, I don't get why this Donna woman sent me that package."

JT moved his arm away from her. "But, baby, we already went over all that when you called me yesterday."

"Maybe so, but I'm still bothered by the whole thing. I mean, who does this kind of crap for no reason?"

"Someone who is simply trying to cause problems for us, and as far as I'm concerned, this Donna person is nothing more than some raving lunatic."

"But, JT, why is she continuing to make all these accusations if there's no truth to what she's saying?"

"Honey, pastors and their wives have to deal with this kind of madness all the time. I've told you that before, and at some point, you're just going to have to get used to it."

"Maybe, but just to be safe, I want to file a report with the police."

"No," JT said abruptly, and Alicia looked at him. He seemed dead set against the whole idea of pressing any charges, and that made no sense to her.

"Why not?"

"Because this really isn't all that serious. I know it has you upset, but I don't think it's necessary to involve the authorities."

"I disagree, JT, because this woman told me flat-out that when it comes to you, I should definitely watch my back. So, to me, this is beyond serious."

"I understand how you feel, and if for some reason this

woman contacts you again, I promise we'll call the police. We'll report everything."

"Good," Alicia said but had a feeling JT was hiding something. She wasn't sure what exactly, but she knew that whenever her father would lie to her mother, he would either become defensive or would become angry and would blame everything on someone else—people who were crazy or who were simply just trying to make trouble for them. He would respond almost precisely the way JT was.

JT pulled his wife closer to him and hugged her. "I know this whole pastor, first lady, church situation can be a little trying at times, but please know that I am completely in love with you and only you, and that I would never do anything to hurt you. Sweetheart, you are my world, and I'll do whatever necessary to protect you at all costs. You hear me?"

Alicia gazed into his eyes, wishing she could believe him. But her intuition insisted there was more to the story and that it was only a matter of time before Donna exposed it. Then, without warning, Alicia thought about Phillip and how he never would have caused her this kind of worry. He never would have caused her any kind of pain or suffering, and she was sorry she hadn't appreciated how wonderful he was when she'd been married to him. She was sorry she'd acted like a spoiled brat, the kind who had to have everything she wanted or else, and that she hadn't realized what it truly meant to have a caring, compassionate, and honest husband. She hadn't taken the time to notice just how perfect Phillip had really been for her. She hadn't valued his strong character or his obvious desire to do the right thing— she hadn't cherished the man any woman in her right mind would long to be with. She'd made a huge mistake in terms of the way she'd betrayed him, and now this, these accusations and suspicions about JT, was the result of it. She finally had all the material possessions she could want and the ability to buy even more if she so chose, but sadly, she no longer had the most important thing of all: true happiness.

JT picked up his cell phone and answered it.

"Good afternoon," Barb said in a chipper tone. "So, how's my favorite pastor today?"

JT gritted his teeth. "What is it that you want, and why did you send my wife that pathetic letter?"

"First of all, you know full well why I'm calling. But to answer your other question, I sent it so you would know I'm not joking around with you. I told you I'm not playing, and I needed to make sure you understood that."

JT wanted to curse her into oblivion but said, "Well, let that be your last time contacting her."

"Well, actually, that'll depend on you and whether you have my money. So, do you?"

"Yeah, I have it," he said reluctantly.

"Good boy. So, now all I need you to do is go get a cashier's check the same as you did last time, but instead of making it out to me, just make it out to Jessica Valentine."

"Excuse me?" JT said, frowning.

"You heard me. Jessica Valentine."

"And who on earth is that, Barb?"

"Well, according to the photo on my State of Illinois driver's license, it's me."

JT laughed but wasn't amused in the least. "So, first you tell my wife your name is Donna, and now you're supposed to be someone named Jessica? And on top of that, you now have *my* last name?"

"Is that a problem for you?"

"Actually, it is."

"Well, it's too bad, because my change of identity is a done deal."

"So, I guess Valentine was the only name you could come up with?"

"No, but if for some reason the bank decides to question me about my deposit, it'll certainly make things a whole lot easier. I'll simply explain that every penny came from a very generous family member, and then I'll give them *your* number, so you can verify it."

"Whatever," JT said, losing all patience with her. "So, where is it you want to meet?"

"The same place as last time."

JT hadn't gone to that particular park in years, partly because it was pretty far out and was very secluded, but mostly because he hadn't wanted to be reminded of Barb and the way she had blackmailed him. He hadn't wanted to think about the history he had with her or anything relating to it. "What time?"

"Ten A.M. See you then," she said, and hung up.

JT slammed his fist against his desktop and couldn't wait for tomorrow to be over. Although, the more he sat thinking, the more he realized he had much bigger problems than ruthless, no-good Barb. He allegedly had a baby on the way and no idea what to do about it.

Chapter 33

As traffic slowed and merged into one lane, JT decelerated his vehicle. For over an hour now, he'd driven in a constant stop-and-go manner and was glad he'd left the house early enough, so he wouldn't be late. Construction on I-294 South seemed to stretch for a couple of miles, but thankfully, he was only a few feet from his exit. Of course, it wasn't like he was in a hurry to see dirty Barb, but at the same time, he knew it wasn't smart to keep her waiting—not when she had all the goods on him and could ruin everything in a matter of minutes.

JT drove down the ramp, took a left at the first light he came to, and headed down a two-way road. Not ever did he think he'd be in such a defenseless state, but if he could help it, from now on he would be a lot more careful in terms of whom he dealt with. He would certainly never deal with lowlifes such as Barb or with any other common criminals, because he was finally above all of that. JT was a successful and very reputable pastor with a massive amount of potential, and he could no longer consort with anyone who wasn't on the same level.

JT drove another five miles or so and then turned into the park entrance. For the most part, it still looked the same, and just being there brought back a lot of memories. When he was a teenager, he'd sneak off in his aunt's car, pick up one of his many girlfriends, and bring her out there to have sex. Sometimes they would climb into the backseat and sometimes he would bring a couple of blankets, so they could spread them out in this little hidden section he'd discovered after going there a few times. He would take a different girl with him every single week and most of them practically begged for the opportunity. Interestingly enough, not much had changed today and the only difference was that instead of having his pick of girls, he had a wide range of women to choose from.

After cruising around a number of curves, JT saw a lone black Cadillac parked in an isolated area and pulled over next to it. Barb immediately rolled down her window, but JT was more interested in the man in sunglasses who was sitting next to her. At first, he had no idea who it could be . . . until this mystery person opened the passenger door and got out . . . and he saw that it was Minister Weaver.

"Wow," he said, walking directly over to JT's vehicle. "You look like you just saw a ghost."

JT didn't say a word. He was too shaken to even try.

Minister Weaver walked closer. "It just goes to show, though, doesn't it? You simply can't trust anybody."

JT finally snapped out of his trance. "What is this all about, Weaver?"

"The pay raise I told you I deserved. You know, the one you basically blew me off about."

This was all too much for JT. He couldn't fathom any of what was happening, but mostly he couldn't believe someone like Weaver would even associate with the likes of Barb. He wondered how Weaver even knew her, but before he could ask, Weaver said, "I'm sure you're wondering, too, how I know your good ole buddy Barb. Am I right? Well, imagine my surprise when my long-lost sister—yes, believe it or not, Barb is my biological sister. But imagine my surprise when she contacted me last month, told me how she'd been one of six high-priced call girls you had pimped all while being pastor of NLCC, that you did it until you married Michelle, and also how right after your wedding, you manipulated our baby sister, got her pregnant, and then forced her to have an abortion. You forced our nineteen-year-old sister to kill her baby, and then you just dumped her."

JT was still at a loss for words. He knew he couldn't deny any of what Weaver was saying, so he just listened.

"You see, I always knew you were capable of criminal activity, but not once did I ever think my own sister would be the one to expose you."

JT finally spoke. "Weaver, man, that's all in the past, and I'm a totally different man now."

Weaver laughed out loud. "No, you're exactly the same, JT, only sneakier. You're the same low-down minister you've always been, but most people just can't see it. Although, I will admit, I was pretty low-down myself for cutting off my sisters the way I did. I separated myself from them years ago because they didn't lead the most respectable lives, but now I'm going to do whatever I can to make up for the way I've treated them. And you're going to help me."

"And how am I supposed to do that?"

Weaver looked over inside JT's vehicle. "First, you're going to hand over that fifty thousand dollars you brought today, so I can give it to my baby sister. You know . . . for all the pain she had to endure. But next week, I'll be expecting another fifty for Barb and also fifty for myself, and then maybe I'll consider us even."

JT stared at him, trying to see if he was joking, but Weaver never cracked a smile.

So JT finally said, "And where is it exactly you expect me to get a hundred thousand dollars?"

Weaver's face turned cheerful. "From the same place you got the fifty, I guess. Now, pass it over," he said, reaching his hand out.

At first, JT hesitated, but he knew there was no way out of this and did what he was told.

Weaver took the envelope and took a quick look at the bank draft. "And just to make things easy, you can have the other check made out to Jessica Valentine the same as you did for this one."

JT looked at him. "Weaver, I know we didn't always see eye to eye on everything, but I trusted you. I believed in you, and I honestly thought you were a true man of God."

"I am. Just as true as you are."

"You're wrong."

"Call it what you want, but you just make sure you get the rest of our money. All of it. And we'll be in touch next week regarding a day and time to meet."

Weaver turned and went back around to the passenger side of the Cadillac and got in. He looked at JT through the driver's-side window. "Oh, and by the way, Pastor, I'll see you on Sunday," he said, readjusting his sunglasses and then looking straight ahead. Barb grinned and winked at JT. Then she sped off.

She and her brother left with not a care in the world about what they'd just done, and JT knew he had no choice but to give them every dime they were asking for. Initially, he'd wondered how he would get another large sum of money, but then it came to him. The ad agency would get everything scheduled, he would go ahead and pay them up front, he would charm Diana and convince her that the campaign was much more than a hundred and fifty thousand dollars and then tell her he needed more money. She might question him, but what he would do is have the agency draw up a proposal that totaled two hundred fifty thousand dollars, the one he would show Diana, but then once she gave him the additional funding, he'd tell the ad agency he'd changed his mind and now only wanted to spend a hundred as planned. That way, he could pay for the media spots, cover the fifty thousand he'd just given Weaver for his youngest sister, and then pay the remaining one hundred thousand to Weaver for himself and Barb. He hated deceiving Diana this way, but with the kind of money she and her husband had, two hundred fifty thousand dollars was mere chump change to both of them. They probably wouldn't miss it one bit, and just knowing that made him feel a lot better about what he was doing.

So, really, this wasn't as bad as he'd been thinking, and now all he had to do was fix this whole baby issue Carmen was burdening him with. He wasn't sure how he would get her to see that she just couldn't keep it, but he would. Somehow, some way, he would get her to do the right thing. He would pressure her to do what was best for him, the same as always.

Chapter 34

Rita had been gone for two days now, and yesterday, Alicia had gone with Carmen to meet with the funeral home representative. Thankfully, Rita had owned more than enough life insurance and had already purchased her burial site, so the only thing left for them to do was order flowers and buy her a new suit. Carmen had mentioned how her mom had a number of very stylish outfits but that she still wanted to buy her this one last thing. She wanted to do something very special for the woman who had loved and supported her to the fullest from day one.

Now, though, they were having lunch at a charming little eatery not far from downtown, which was only partially full.

Carmen ate one of her waffle fries. "You know, I just can't believe my mom is really gone and that her service is only three days away."

"Neither can I."

"She was such a wonderful person. Always had a kind word to say to everyone and always treated people with the utmost respect."

Alicia nodded in agreement. "She really was a very caring lady, and I don't ever remember her being any different. Not even when we were children."

"She's always been the same. Even when my idiot father left her for some woman he worked with, she never acted as though she hated him. She would speak to him, and it was as if she had nothing against him."

Alicia sipped some raspberry lemonade. "Some people try to see the good in everyone, no matter how much they may have hurt them, and I admire that."

"She was definitely one of the most forgiving women I ever met," Carmen said, leaning back in her chair. "Because I could never forgive my husband for messing around on me. That is, if I had one."

Alicia thought about JT but didn't comment.

"Although, I guess it's easy to say what you would or wouldn't do if you've never been in a certain situation."

"This is true."

Carmen scanned the restaurant, saw what appeared to be a mother and her adult daughter laughing about something, and then looked back at Alicia. Seconds later, tears streamed down her face.

Alicia reached across the table and grabbed her hand. "I'm so sorry, Carmen. I'm so sorry that this has happened to you."

Carmen sniffled and then pulled a tissue from her purse. "It's just that it hurts so badly."

Alicia remembered how devastated Phillip had been when he'd lost his father, and it made her think about her own parents. She tried imagining how she would feel if she ever lost either of them, but the pain became so real in her mind, she was glad Carmen changed the conversation.

"But regardless of what's going on, I have to be strong for me and my baby."

"That's right," Alicia said.

"Mom would have been so excited for me."

Alicia wondered how, when Carmen didn't even have a husband, but pretended to agree. "I'm sure she would have."

"She would have been just as thrilled as I am, and, girl, just as soon as the baby's father and I are married, I'll be as happy as you are right now."

"So, have you told him yet?"

"Yes, but now he has to get a divorce."

Alicia had already suspected this the day Carmen had first told her but tried sounding surprised. "He's married?"

"Yes, but not for long."

"So, has he already filed?"

"No, but it's only a matter of time before he gets rid of that uppity little whore once and for all."

"Have you met her?"

"Yeah, I've been around her on a number of occasions, and it's pretty obvious why he prefers being with me over her."

Alicia listened but wasn't sure what to say.

"Anyway, she's practically history," Carmen continued. "And there isn't a thing she can do about it."

Alicia looked away but suddenly thought about that Donna woman again and how she had to have some sort of connection to JT. He'd denied it to no end, but Alicia wasn't as naïve as he may have thought and knew what men were capable of.

"Alicia?" she heard Carmen say, and then returned to reality.

"Yes?"

"What's wrong?"

"Nothing. Why do you ask?"

"Because I called your name three different times."

"Oh, girl, I'm sorry. I guess I was in another world."

"Why? Is everything okay?"

Alicia hesitated, but for some reason, she needed to confide her problems to someone. Melanie was her best friend, but she just couldn't tell her about all these accusations against JT. She couldn't tell her or any of her family members, but again, she felt compelled to tell someone. Not just anyone, of course, but someone like Carmen, whom she could trust. So she divulged everything that had been going on. She told her about the women at the luncheon and all the horrible things one of them had said about JT and also what the nice one had confirmed about his past reputation with women. Then she told her about that Donna person and how she'd even claimed that JT planned his wife's death.

Carmen widened her eyes. "Do you think any of that is true?"

"At first, I didn't, but now I've heard so much, I don't know what to think."

"Well, what does he say?"

"That it's not true, and that he would never do anything like that."

"Then why would anyone make such terrible claims?"

"I don't know. I don't understand any of this, and on top of that, my dad never wanted me to marry him in the first place."

"What? Your dad doesn't like him?"

"No."

"Girl, that's pretty deep."

"Yeah, tell me about it."

"So, what are you going to do?"

"I don't know that either, but I do know that I'm not going to just ignore all of this or act as though it couldn't be possible."

"I don't blame you. I mean, I really like JT and all, but unfortunately, men are going to be men. They are who they are, and you never know what they might be up to."

Alicia thought about the man Carmen was messing around with, whomever he was, and how he was proof of that very thing. She also thought about how wrong Carmen was for being involved with him.

"You're right," Alicia finally said.

"Sadly, I am, and that's why I can't sit back and sugarcoat my opinion. I don't want to be negative or say anything bad about JT, but I also don't want to see you getting cheated on or staying with a man who might be dangerous."

Alicia heard what she was saying and was glad she had someone to talk to about this. "I appreciate your honesty, girl, and thank you so much for listening. Especially since you have your own worries right now."

"I do, but you can talk to me about anything, anytime."

"I know, but still."

"But still nothing. You and I are friends for life, and you can count on me no matter what. You can depend on me the same as if I were your blood sister."

Alicia smiled at Carmen and knew she meant every single word.

Chapter 35

The funeral had taken place yesterday, and Alicia, JT, and both sets of her parents had attended. They'd met over at Carmen's apartment, along with some of her family members and fellow parishioners, and had driven to the church in the processional. Strangely enough, Carmen hadn't shed many tears and had stood at the podium and spoken at great length about her mom. The entire service had been beautiful and hadn't lasted more than an hour and fifteen minutes, but Alicia was glad this phase of the mourning process was behind Carmen. She knew Carmen would never get over losing her mother, but Alicia prayed that God would give her all the strength and understanding she needed to go on with her life and live it to the absolute fullest.

Of course, though, this would take time, and it was the reason Alicia had asked Carmen to come stay with her and JT again, at least for a couple of days. But Carmen had insisted she wanted and needed to be alone. Alicia had practically pleaded with her to reconsider, but Carmen had said she just wanted to spend some time quietly reflecting on all the wonderful memories she and her mother had shared.

Alicia sat down at her desk, opened her word processing software, and opened the outline she'd begun working on for her next novel. She'd debated whether she would write a sequel to her first but had ultimately decided she wanted to write about all new characters. She wanted to write about two women who'd been best friends as small children, lost touch with each other, and then became close once again as adults. Of course, she would incorporate lots of Melanie's personality into one of the characters, since Melanie was her best friend of best friends, but she would also base a lot of the story line on her and Carmen's relationship. She wanted to tell this story because she really did feel blessed to be so closely connected with Carmen after not seeing or talking to her for so many years.

After mapping out a couple of additional chapters, Alicia stopped and checked to see if her agent had sent her any last-minute messages. The auction for her book was scheduled for Friday, and all six meeting times with the editors and their respective publishing groups had now been confirmed. When Alicia had read Joan's note from yesterday, outlining all the details, she'd barely been able to contain herself and she couldn't wait to leave this evening for New York. She'd known how exciting this whole process was probably going to be, but she hadn't thought she'd feel so nervous and overjoyed.

Alicia scanned her inbox, deleted a few junk messages, and saw a new e-mail from Levi. She opened it right away.

> Hey you. I hope all is well but I really need to speak
> to you this afternoon when my friend is back on duty.
> Please call around 2 P.M. Love you. Levi

Alicia wondered if Levi just wanted to talk to her or if he needed her to phone him for a reason. Either way, she knew it still wasn't right for her to be contacting him. On the other hand, however, it wasn't like things were wonderful between her and JT, not the way they'd been over the last few months. Their honeymoon stage was basically over, and even yesterday, she'd noticed how uneasy and impatient he'd seemed at the funeral and also while they were at Carmen's, acting as if there was some other place he needed to be. Then, this morning, he'd left earlier than normal, claiming he had all this church business to attend to. Alicia didn't know if he was up to no good or not, but with everything that was going on, maybe there actually wasn't anything wrong with communicating with Levi. So she e-mailed him back to say she would call the cell number he'd listed at the time he requested.

Over the next few hours, Alicia jogged on the treadmill, took a shower, got dressed, worked more on her outline, and called her mom and then her stepmother for a chat. She did everything she could to pass the time, but now she was finally dialing Levi. Today, he answered the phone himself.

"Hi, sweetheart," he said.

"Hey. How are you?"

"Well, not as good as I'd like to be, because yesterday, I received a little bit of bad news from my attorney. He told me that there's been a slight setback toward getting me released."

"Oh no. I'm really sorry to hear that because I know you were so looking forward to getting out."

"Yeah, I was. But it'll happen in due time. It'll take longer than I thought, but my attorney thinks we'll be all set with what we need to present to the judge in about six months. At the latest, I should be free in maybe nine months to a year."

"Good. I'm glad."

"But that's not the only reason I wanted you to call," he said without hesitation.

"Oh, okay. So, what else is going on?"

"I've got a couple of very close Chicago buddies on the outside, and I'm sad to say they told me a ton of information about your husband."

Alicia held her breath, fearing whatever Levi was about to disclose.

"And, sweetheart, please know that I thought long and hard in terms of whether I should tell you, but once I was able to confirm that everything I'd heard was true, I decided that even though I can't get out of here right away to be with you myself, I still want you to be happy. I also want you to be fully aware about the man you're married to."

Alicia closed her eyes, wondering just how bad this news was going to be.

"Are you there?"

"Yes."

"I really hate doing this, but, sweetheart, JT used to pimp top-shelf call girls—you know, the kind who only sleep with wealthy businessmen or filthy-rich criminals. From what I hear, that's how he got the money to start his first church, but then he continued doing it for about three years after that . . . but that's not the worst part."

Alicia wasn't sure how much more she could take and tried bracing herself for the rest of the story.

"Word on the street is that JT is still sleeping with one of them now. Someone by the name of Carmen Wilson, and I hear her mother just died last week."

Alicia covered her mouth with her hand, felt lightheaded and almost like she was dreaming. She knew she really was on the phone with Levi, but she felt as though she was living someone else's life. Certainly not her own, that she was sure of.

She sat, not saying anything, but then it dawned on her. Carmen was pregnant.

"Oh my God," she said. "Oh my God."

"Baby, I'm really sorry. I'm sorry I had to do this, but you really needed to know."

"No. I'm glad you told me."

"Are you going to be okay?"

"Eventually."

"Is there anything I can do? I know I can't come to you in person, but if there's anything you need, all you have to do is say the word, and I'll have someone take care of it."

"No. I'll be fine."

"Okay, but if anything changes, you e-mail me."

"I will. And actually, I'm going to hang up now, okay?"

"I understand. But you take care of yourself, all right? Remember that you deserve so much better than someone like JT and that I'll always love you."

"You take care, too, and I'll talk to you later," she said, and hung up.

Alicia set the phone down and tried digesting all that Levi had told her.

How could JT do this? And Carmen ... how could she smile in my face and pretend like she was such a loyal friend? How could she sit listening to me a few days ago, pouring my heart out about JT and all these allegations I've heard, when all along, she knew she was sleeping with him and carrying his baby?

Alicia replayed all of Levi's words, and tears finally flooded her face. She cried loudly, her body shook, and she felt like she was dying. She sobbed, wiped volumes of tears, and then sobbed again. She did this on and off for nearly thirty minutes but then got angry. She was outraged and wanted JT dead. She wanted the same for Carmen. What a rotten, manipulative, self-serving whore she was.

Alicia tossed a plethora of violent thoughts through her mind but then calmed herself down so she could think a lot more clearly. The pain she felt was atrocious at best, but she took a few deep breaths—and signed on to verizon.com. When the home page displayed, she entered all of JT's personal information that was requested, registering him as an online user, and then she pulled up his account.

She clicked on a few different pages but then found the one that listed details for the current statement's incoming and outgoing calls and saw both Carmen's home and cell numbers. Next, she pulled up the archived information for previous months and saw that there was a time when JT spoke to Carmen multiple times per day, especially during the months when Alicia was dating JT—months when she'd thought JT was so completely in love with her, he would never be with any other woman again.

Alicia scanned more listings, printed out pages of details, and immediately slipped into revenge mode. Her father had preached loads of sermons on forgiveness and had quoted Romans 12:19 more times than she could remember. "Dearly beloved, avenge not yourselves, but rather give place unto wrath: for it is written, Vengeance is mine; I will repay, saith the Lord."

She knew that scripture well and had always worked hard to uphold it. She had lived by it pretty religiously and had never seen a need to pay people back when they'd wronged her.

Until now.

Chapter 36

"Either you deliver our money by tomorrow afternoon, promptly at three P.M., or it's whistle-blowing time," Minister Weaver threatened.

"I said you'd have it, and you will," JT declared.

"That's what you claimed last week, too, but we never got it."

"But you'll have it tomorrow for sure. You have my word."

"I hope you're right, because if I find out you're trying to stall on us again, the situation won't be pretty. It's going to turn into something very ugly and unbearably humiliating. A lot of people are going to be hurt, particularly those five thousand members of yours who so blindly believe in you, and you'll be kissing that lavish life of yours completely good-bye." Then he paused and said, "You have a nice day."

He never even gave JT a chance to respond, but it was fine, because in twenty-four hours, this would all be over with. It would all be a done deal, and JT wouldn't have to worry about Weaver, Barb, or any other person from the past he no longer wanted anything to do with. Carmen was still a major issue that needed handling, but over the last eight days, she'd remained pretty calm—partly because he'd gone along with whatever she said and mostly because he'd given her sex whenever she'd asked for it. He'd slept with her at least five times, starting with the day after her mother's funeral, but the good news was that it hadn't posed much of a problem for his marriage. It hadn't caused any strain because Alicia was now working day and night on her next novel and was always too tired by the time she got in bed. Nonetheless, this baby dilemma had to be dealt with once and for all. But first, he had to get the rest of that money from Diana.

"Another hundred thousand dollars is a lot more than I anticipated," Diana said, clearly not happy about JT's latest request.

"Baby, I know," he said, sliding closer to her on the sofa and showing her the media proposal—the one he'd had the agency working on for a whole week now and the one he'd had e-mailed over to him first thing this morning when he'd gotten to the church. It had been the reason he'd left the house so early this morning, so he could download it, print it out, and then go over every figure and small detail. He'd needed some extra time to review it, so he could explain things as articulately and convincingly as possible to Diana.

"Does the campaign really require all this? I mean, are all these spots really necessary? Because based on what I'm seeing here," she said, flipping to the next page, "they've got you airing spots during every single commercial break, all day long. So, what it sounds like to me is that this agency you're working with is blatantly overselling the amount of spots you actually need."

JT had to think fast. Why? Because this meeting with Diana was turning out to be a little harder than he'd expected. He'd known she would need proof of what she was paying for, but he hadn't counted on her asking so many legitimate questions. He hadn't even considered the possibility that she might read and debate every single page he'd brought to her.

"I know it's a lot of money," he said. "But, baby, you have to trust me. You have to believe that I know what I'm doing. I mean, sure, we could definitely do a lot less publicity on each station or eliminate some of the stations altogether, but I really want to do the kind of media blitz that everyone will have an opportunity to hear. I want them to hear these spots on the radio, see them on TV, and take notice. I want the words 'New Life Christian Center' and 'JT Valentine' to become household names. I want people to wonder what they're missing by not attending our services, so they'll be dying to come visit."

"I understand that, but again, a hundred thousand dollars more is a lot. I already gave you one-fifty two weeks ago, so a quarter of a million dollars is a little over the top."

JT took the proposal from her and slid into victim mode. "Fine. Look, I only came to you because you said you would help out and that you were behind me all the way. But let's just forget it. Let's just forget everything," he said, standing up. "As a matter of fact, let's cancel this whole campaign and pretend like it never happened . . . and actually, if you want to know the truth, I'm really not surprised by this at all."

"What do you mean?"

"Remember how I told you about my mom dying when I was a child and then my aunt dying when I was a teenager? Well, all my life, people have been forcing me to fend for myself, so I really didn't expect you to be any different."

Diana got up and wrapped her arms around his neck. "Now, honey, you know that's not true. You're the most special man I've ever met, and I think I made it pretty clear a while ago that I would do just about anything for you."

JT kept his hands at either side of his body, refusing to embrace her.

"Baby, please don't act this way," she said.

JT unlocked her arms and backed away from her. "I don't think I can do this anymore."

"Do what?"

"This. Us."

"Why not?" she asked, and JT heard the worry in her voice.

"Because I see now that I can't trust you. I can't depend on you, so it's time for me to move on."

"You don't mean that."

"I do," he said, grabbing his suit jacket and heading toward the door. "You take care, okay?"

"JT, wait," she hurried to say. "Okay. I'll do it. It's a lot more than I'm comfortable with, but if you really think this is going to help bring in hundreds and hundreds of new members, then I'm behind you."

JT grinned before turning around and facing her. "You really mean that?"

"Yes. You've been keeping up your end of the deal by spending more time with me, at least for the last couple of weeks, anyway, so I'm going to do the same."

JT squeezed her body close to his and said, "I promise you, you won't regret it. And once things really take off, I'll even begin paying you back."

"Really?"

"Yes."

"Well, actually, you can do that right now."

"And how's that?"

Diana's laugh was beguiling. "Take a wild guess, cowboy."

JT smiled and couldn't have been prouder. Of himself, that is.

It was already after six P.M., and as far as JT was concerned, the day simply couldn't get any better. Tomorrow morning, Diana was going to transfer the remaining money he needed, he would then be able to make good on the funds Weaver and Barb were demanding from him, and he was all set with doing a six-figure marketing campaign. But if that wasn't enough, he'd already gotten two calls from pastors in Atlanta and Cleveland who wanted to bring him in as soon as possible. JT had been sure he'd get a number of responses, but not ever had he expected to receive two on the same day and so soon after the packages had gone out. It hadn't even been two full weeks yet, and here he was being invited to speak at churches that had a minimum of fifteen thousand members! Initially, when he'd gotten back from Diana's about an hour ago and Janet had told him the great news, he'd sort of thought this was all too good to be true. But then he quickly thought otherwise when he realized these engagements were just an inkling of all the blessings he had coming to him. It was all so amazing and proof that God truly did work in mysterious ways.

JT leaned back in his chair, feeling more pleased than he had in a long time, but then Janet rang his desk phone.

"Pastor, you're not going to believe this," she said with sheer excitement.

"What's that?"

"Pastor Braeden is on the line for you."

JT sat up straight. "Pastor Donald Braeden? From Vineyard Christian Center?"

"Yes, and he's calling you from home."

"Unbelievable. Okay, give me a few seconds, and then put him through."

"I will."

JT hung up and tried gathering his composure. This was crazy. *The* Pastor Braeden of Dallas. *The* Pastor Braeden whom he watched on television every Sunday morning before he left to preach at his own church. *The* Pastor Braeden who had a congregation that was twenty-five-thousand strong.

JT breathed in and out and then in and out again, and waited for Janet to ring him. Finally, she did.

"Pastor Braeden, sir, what an honor and a privilege to be speaking with you," JT said.

"No, son, the pleasure really is all mine because your father-in-law and I go way back, and I have the utmost respect for him. I'm a little bit older than him," he said, laughing, "but he's a friend for life."

"Yes, my father-in-law is definitely a very special man, and I love him to death."

"I haven't spoken to him in a while, but I'll have to make sure to give him a call."

"Well, right now, he's on a fourteen-day cruise with his wife, but I know he'll be very glad to hear from you when he's back home," JT said, telling the best lie he could think of at the moment. He knew there was no way he'd be able to keep Pastor Braeden or any of the other ministers he sent information to from contacting Curtis, but the longer it took for that to happen the better off JT would be.

"Good for him. Two weeks is a long time and the kind of break everyone needs to take every now and again."

"That's for sure."

"But back to you and the reason I'm calling. It just so happens that our scheduled afternoon speaker for our church anniversary has had to cancel. We just heard from his assistant a couple of days ago, letting us know he's taken ill. So, while I know this is very short notice, I was wondering if maybe you'd like to take his place."

JT wanted to yell, "Thank you, Jesus," but instead he said, "I'd love to, and I'm truly grateful just to have the opportunity."

"Wonderful. I know today is already Wednesday, but if you could fly out on Saturday evening I would certainly appreciate it. The service isn't until four P.M. on Sunday, but I'm sure you'll want to rest in a hotel overnight and not have to worry about flying in on the day of."

"Yes, definitely."

"Great. Our members are going to be pleasantly surprised when they learn that Pastor Black's son-in-law will be delivering the message. They love him here in Dallas the same as everyone else does throughout the country, so your visiting here will be a real treat."

JT was so ecstatic, he could barely sit still. "I can't wait. Also, if you don't mind, can I ask you something?"

"Of course. Go ahead."

"I can only imagine how busy your schedule is, but at some point maybe this year or next year, do you think you might have time to come speak at my church? I mean, it's nothing like yours, and we only have about five thousand members, but I know having you here would help our ministry tremendously."

"I would be happy to. You're doing me a huge favor, and I've always been a big believer in the idea that one good turn really does deserve another."

"Thank you so much for agreeing. When my father-in-law came to speak, it drew in more people than I'd ever seen here, and I know your presence will do the same."

"Also, young man, I must say how proud I am of you in terms of all the obstacles you've had to overcome. Losing your mother, not knowing your father, being tossed from one foster home to the next. Your letter was both saddening and powerful, and it was very brave of you to share it."

"Thank you, Pastor," he said, smiling, and was glad he'd exaggerated just about everything he'd written.

"No. Thank you. Because your story will be a blessing and an inspiration to everyone."

"I sure hope so."

"Okay, well, I'd better get going so my wife and I can get some dinner, but I'll have my executive assistant call yours first thing in the morning. That way, she can find out your airline and hotel preferences and get your reservations made. Oh, and by the way, I guess I forgot to mention your honorarium," he said, but JT certainly hadn't.

"Oh, that's no problem at all."

"Will twenty-five thousand, first-class airfare for you and your wife, and accommodations at a five-star hotel be sufficient?"

JT wanted to burst out laughing. God was so good. "It's more than sufficient, and thank you for being so generous."

"You're quite welcome."

"Also, just so you know, my wife has a women's event here at our church on Saturday evening that she has to attend, so unfortunately, she won't be able to travel out with me."

"Oh, I'm really sorry to hear that. But I certainly understand."

"Well, again, Pastor, thank you so much for everything."

"Of course, and please call if you have any questions."

"I will, and you have a good evening."

"You, too."

JT wanted to jump for joy, sing a song, and cut a jig. He was actually going to be ministering to the people of Vineyard Christian Center. It was a dream come true, and now he was even happier than he had been about including those recommendation letters from Curtis. They were doing wonders for him, and he was delighted to no end.

He picked up the phone and called Janet into his office.

"So, what's the deal?" she asked, smiling.

"Pastor Braeden has asked me to come speak this weekend."

"So soon?"

"Yes, the minister they'd invited has become ill and had to cancel."

"How wonderful . . . not that he's sick, but I mean, how wonderful this is for you."

"I know. Vineyard is one of the largest churches in the country, so I'm really going to have to be on top of my game. Which is why, instead of flying in on Saturday evening, the way Pastor Braeden suggested, I'd rather go early on Friday morning. That way, I'll be able to rest up some and then spend all day Saturday writing my sermon and doing a few dry runs with it."

"I don't blame you. This is going to be huge for you."

"No doubt, so I certainly want to make a good impression."

"So, are they going to contact me about your arrangements?"

"Yes, he said his assistant will call you in the morning. Also, unfortunately, Alicia won't be able to go with me."

"Oh no. Why not?"

"She has some sort of family get-together she and her stepmother have been planning for the last couple of months," he said, telling Janet a different lie than what he'd told Pastor Braeden, since Janet knew the entire church calendar without looking at it, meaning she'd clearly know there was no women's event taking place on Saturday evening or any other day this month.

"Wow, that's too bad."

"I know, but hopefully this won't be the last time I'll get to go there."

"No, I'm sure it won't be."

"And hey, I know I say this a lot, Janet, but thanks again for all your hard work."

"You're welcome. See you tomorrow."

JT watched her leave and then thought about the real reason he wanted to arrive on Friday and also why he didn't want Alicia traveling with him: He'd finally be able to see Veda again. He would fly her out from Minneapolis, and they'd be able to spend most of Friday and all of Saturday holed up in his hotel room. It would be a weekend to remember, and he couldn't wait to see her again.

Chapter 37

"Hey, baby, what's up?" JT said, sounding the same as always and like the loving, loyal, and faithful husband he'd always pretended to be.

"Hi, honey. Just sitting at my computer. What's up with you?"

"Well, actually a whole lot. You know Pastor Braeden in Dallas?"

"Yes."

"Well, I just hung up with him, and he wants me to come speak at his church this Sunday."

Alicia feigned how elated she was. "Oh my goodness. Really? That's wonderful."

"I know. It's the best news ever, and it's still very hard for me to believe."

"What made him call you?"

"Not long ago, I asked Janet to compile a listing of churches and then send out a letter of introduction, along with some other information about my experience. I also included a line saying if they ever needed a speaker, I would love to be considered."

"What a great idea."

"I guess it was."

"So, when do we leave?"

"Well, baby, you see, that's the thing. I would love, love, love for you to go, but since this is the largest church I've ever spoken at outside of the Chicago area, I'm really going to have to do more studying, praying, and writing than ever before. I'm going to have to come up with an unforgettable message and practice my delivery over and over again."

Alicia shook her head, wondering if he honestly thought she was that stupid. "You're right. You really do need to spend all day Saturday without any interruption, so you can meditate and concentrate in peace."

"So, you're not upset?"

"Of course not. It's no different than when I'm writing, and I sometimes slip away to one of the university libraries with my netbook. Sometimes you just need that kind of quietness."

"I'm really glad you understand because I was really worried about that."

"Please. I grew up with a pastor, remember? So, I know how important it is to have many hours of alone time."

"What would I do without you?" he said.

"I don't know, but the good news is that you won't ever have to find out because we're always going to be together. You are the love of my life, JT, and I'm so proud of you."

"I love you, too. And I'm so glad to have you as my wife. Anyway, I really need to get going, but I wanted to call you as soon as possible to tell you about Dallas."

"Oh, that's right, you have that publicity meeting you were telling me about this morning."

"Yep. I'm meeting my rep at his office in about forty-five minutes. But what about you? Are you coming to Bible study?"

"Yeah, I am."

"Okay, well, I guess I'll just see you later this evening."

"All right. Talk to you then."

"Bye, baby."

Alicia felt like patting herself on the back, what with how talented an actress she'd become. Here it had been a full week since Levi had told her about JT and Carmen, but she'd continued holding her own. She hadn't acted even the slightest bit upset and had gone out of her way to be the same trusting and caring wife he thought she was. JT didn't have a clue, and Alicia was planning to keep it that way.

Then there was Carmen, who thought she was as slick as could be, but in reality, she was just as oblivious. She had no idea Alicia was on to her, but it was probably because Alicia called her every single morning to see how she was doing and ask her if she needed anything, and over the last seven days, she'd even gone by to see her on three different occasions. Obviously not when JT was there, but earlier in the day so there was no way she would run into him—because make no mistake about it, Alicia was now fully aware of every time he visited that tramp.

This whole monitoring, acting, and planning thing, though, couldn't have come at a worse time because just one week ago she'd flown to the Big Apple, her auction had taken place, and all six editors had made very sizable offers. It had been an exciting time, but Alicia hadn't been nearly as enthused as she would have been, not after having found out about JT and Carmen the day before. But this week, she was feeling a lot better and was very thankful to have chosen an editor who seemed extremely passionate about her work and one who sounded as though she had exceptional character and notable integrity. If that wasn't enough, when Alicia had met her, the chemistry between them had been immediate and Joan had told Alicia that there were very few editors she knew who were more talented, personable, and completely on top of things. It also hadn't hurt that Joan was able to negotiate a two-book deal totaling a million dollars, something that was almost unheard of anymore for debut novelists—something Alicia knew probably wouldn't have happened had it not been for the kind of promotion and publicity interviews they were sure they'd be able to secure for her because of her father. Joan had already talked about this very thing, well before even submitting Alicia's manuscript to anyone, so it just went to show how right she'd been. It showed how blessed Alicia was to have Joan as well as her newfound editor.

As soon as JT walked inside Carmen's apartment, she met him at the door, kissed him, and sashayed back into the kitchen. "So, how was your day, baby? Are you ready to eat? I made your favorite. Chicken Parmesan."

Carmen acted as though the two of them were legally married, like JT had just gotten home from a long day at work and like she was some pampered, well-to-do housewife. This, needless to say, couldn't have been further from the truth, so JT wished she would cut it out. He wished she would accept reality and realize he didn't love her and that he was never going to leave his wife for any woman—not even for Veda, the woman he cared about a lot more than he did Carmen.

"I know I haven't cooked for you in a long time," she went on to say. "But I promise from now on, things are going to be different. I'm going to treat you better than both your other wives ever did, and you'll never, ever want to mess around the way you had to on them. I've been sitting here thinking all day how if Michelle and Alicia had treated you the way any good man deserves to be treated, you never would have had a reason to sneak and be with me."

JT had had enough of all this foolishness. "Carmen, we need to talk."

She walked back out to the living room. "Sure, baby. What about?"

"Come and sit down for a few minutes," he said, and she sat next to him on the camel-colored love seat.

"You seem upset," she said, caressing his face. "What's wrong?"

"Everything. I mean, I know you're really happy about being pregnant, and that's why I've tried my best to avoid having this discussion, but, Carmen, this isn't going to work."

She turned her body more in his direction. "I don't understand."

"I know you want this baby, but if you have it, it'll ruin my position in the ministry for good. I'll never be able to bounce back from this kind of a scandal, and I'll lose everything. All of my members at NLCC will leave, and I'll have no way of taking care of you or the baby."

"I can't believe I'm hearing this," she said, raising her voice.

"I know this doesn't make you happy, but I'm begging you to at least try and work with me on this."

"Work with you how?"

"By terminating the pregnancy."

Carmen got up. "Wait a minute. I *know* you're not asking me to kill my baby."

"No, I'm asking you to have an abortion."

Carmen laughed out loud in a deranged sort of way. "Like I said, I *know* you're not asking me to kill my baby."

"Sweetheart, look," he said, standing up. "Please try to understand what I'm saying. This is going to wreck my whole reputation as a minister. And if that happens, I'll never go national the way you and I talked about. I'll never make another dime."

"Of course you will. Ministers have babies all the time, and no one says a word about it."

"That's because most ministers have them with their wives and not with their mistresses."

"But that's just it; by the time I begin showing, you and I will already be married. I know I'd said I would give you a lot more time to divorce Alicia, but now that I'm carrying your child . . . well, that changes everything."

"Carmen, baby, please," he said, holding her hands. "I'll do anything you ask, if you'll just agree to have an abortion."

Carmen stared at him. "Oh my God. You're serious, aren't you? You really want me to kill our baby."

"Why do you keep saying that?"

"Because you do. You want me to commit cold-blooded murder."

JT decided to try a different approach. "All I'm saying is that we can't do this right now and that once we're married, we can have as many children as you want."

Carmen jerked away from him. "I'm having my baby, JT. I'm having it no matter what, and you'll either do right by me, or else."

"Baby, please, please try to see my side of this."

"I do see it. I see it very clearly. Years ago, you pimped me to other men, then started sleeping with me yourself, married two other women, got me pregnant, and now you're trying to dodge your responsibilities. But, JT, I want you to hear me and hear me good. You *are* going to divorce Alicia, marry me, and be the best father in the world to our son or daughter."

After seeing the I-will-not-be-moved-on-this look in her eyes, JT knew there was no reasoning with her. At least not tonight anyway, so he was through talking about it. He was done trying to win a losing battle, and for the rest of the evening, he would play the loving husband role just like she wanted him to. He would plaster a phony smile across his face, fabricate words he didn't mean, and force himself to have sex with her. He would do whatever it took to keep her quiet and somewhat happy—for now. He would continue biding his time until Minister Payne handled his business.

Chapter 38

*J*T hung up the phone and smiled. He'd just finished talk-ing with Veda for the second time this morning and also for the third time since yesterday, and her airline reservations were finally set. He could tell in her voice how excited she was to be making the trip with him, and he certainly couldn't wait to see her. At first, he'd thought it might be best if she flew on a sepa-rate plane, nonstop between Minneapolis and Dallas, but then once Janet had given him his travel itinerary, he'd decided he wanted to see Veda before then. He wouldn't sit with her at the gate or next to her on the plane, but now that she was connect-ing through Chicago, they would at least be able to share the same cabin—courtesy of JT's offering to reimburse her in cash for the first-class ticket he'd insisted she treat herself with.

JT glanced at his watch, saw that it was five minutes before noon, and went online to make sure Diana had made the wire transfer. He was still scheduled to meet Weaver and Barb at three but also needed time to stop at the bank to get a cashier's check.

He entered his user ID and password information and waited for his account summary to pop up. He scrolled through the page, but he could already see right at the top that the balance was still showing the same one hundred thousand dollars he was planning to use for the media buy. Maybe Diana had thought he didn't need it right away this morning and was planning to make the transaction this afternoon, so he picked up his phone and called her.

"Hello?" she said after three rings.

"Hey, dear. How are you?"

"I could definitely be better."

JT had no idea what she meant by that, but right now he didn't have time to inquire about it. "I only have a few minutes, but I just wanted to check in to see how soon you'll be able to make the transfer."

"That's just it. I won't be."

"Excuse me?"

"You're a real piece of work, you know that?"

JT repositioned his phone. "I don't understand what you mean."

"Well, then, just let me ask you one question. Did you really think I was that stupid?"

"That stupid about what?!"

"You."

"Diana, look. If you've changed your mind about helping me, then I wish you'd just say it and stop playing all these games."

"I don't play games. But you, on the other hand, are a master at it. Or so you thought you were, because, sweetheart, as of today, I'm completely on to you."

"What are you talking about?" he yelled, forgetting he was at the church and that Janet sat just outside his office.

"I'm talking about the private investigator I hired and the lengthy report he just gave me from the last two weeks. I mean, did you actually think I would give you a hundred and fifty thousand dollars and then not check up on you? And my only regret is that I didn't do it beforehand."

JT closed his eyes and leaned back in his chair but didn't speak.

"Yeah, that's right. He's been following you all over town, even to your other woman's house. Some chick named Carmen Wilson. He saw you going in and out of her building all this week and part of last week, so finally he followed you up to the floor she lives on to see what apartment you were going into. After that, he found a couple of her neighbors who were happy to confirm that you'd been visiting her for years. Interestingly enough, though, they didn't seem to know your name or that you were a pastor."

JT had no idea how he was going to recover from this one but said what any man would say in this kind of situation: "Baby, I can explain."

"No. But I'll tell you what you can do. You can give me back my money. Every single dime of it."

"Baby, please let me come by and explain this to you."

Diana ignored his pleas. "I want my money just as soon as you can get it back to me. Preferably today."

"I don't have it," he said, lying, because now that she wasn't going to give him the extra hundred for his media campaign, he'd have to use the hundred he had to pay off his blackmailers.

"What do you mean you don't have it?"

"I just don't."

"JT, I'm warning you. I want my hundred and fifty thousand dollars, and I want it now."

"And I keep trying to tell you, I don't have it."

Diana paused for a couple of seconds and then called him

everything but a child of God. She cursed him in ways he'd never heard before and sounded more like a woman of the streets than she did a millionaire's wife.

Still, JT tried saving face. "Look. I'm really sorry about this, and I promise I'll pay you back. I can't say when——" he said, but Diana interrupted him with another string of obscenities.

Then she hung up.

He finally laid his phone down, too. What a mess this had turned out to be, because without that other hundred thousand, he had to make a huge decision. Either pay for his radio and TV ads and push his ministry to brand-new heights or pay Weaver and Barb what they were commanding. If he did the former, Barb and Weaver would try to ruin him publicly, and if he did the latter he could forget about ever getting his name out to the masses the way he'd been dreaming about.

JT weighed all the advantages and disadvantages for both scenarios, and then it came to him. Pastors dealt with scandals all the time, and as long as they didn't each occur all at once, most ministers were able to work through them, regain the trust of their supporters, and move on. His father-in-law certainly had. Not to mention, JT's pimping days were long over, and actually, his congregation would probably have even more respect for him once they heard how terrible a sinner he'd been but had now turned his life completely around for the Lord. People loved hearing how sinners had bottomed out and had finally turned to God, and his members would feel the same way about him. Then, as far as Barb's baby sister and how he'd convinced her to have an abortion, well, he would deny that part of the story until death. There was no proof that he'd been the father anyway, so most everyone would chalk that one up to mere hearsay.

There was this issue with Carmen, though, but he had that

figured out, too. He would go to her, apologize profusely, and tell her he couldn't wait for their baby to be born. She would, of course, go on and on about his leaving Alicia and marrying her, but he would find some new way to put off their wedding. He'd been doing it for four years, anyhow, so what was another one or two of them? Then, if at some point Carmen finally decided to reveal their secret, enough time would have lapsed between that particular scandal and the one Weaver and Barb were surely going to initiate any day now.

So, his decision was made.

"Hello?" JT's media rep said, answering his phone.

"Jonathan, it's Pastor Valentine."

"Yes, Pastor."

"I know we're all set for the spots to begin airing on Monday, but I just wanted to let you know that I'll be sending over the check by courier in a couple of hours."

"Our agency has ongoing credit accounts with all the stations you're buying from, so we're good to go, anyway."

"That's all I wanted to hear. And, Jonathan, thanks for all the time you've put in on this."

"It was my pleasure, and I think you're going to be very surprised when you see how successful this campaign is going to be for you."

"I hope so, because at this point, failing isn't an option."

Chapter 39

One could never really go wrong when choosing a Four Seasons hotel, and it was the reason JT rarely stayed anywhere else. He loved The Ritz-Carlton, too, and a few other posh establishments he could think of, but when in Dallas, it was this particular brand he tended to enjoy the most. Not to mention, he certainly enjoyed the more extravagant suites, like the one he and Veda were relaxing in now, and he was thankful for Vineyard Christian Center's generous hospitality. There had been a slight change on his agenda, however, because while JT's original plan had been for him and Veda to come straight to the hotel right after their plane landed around ten thirty A.M. and not leave again, Pastor Braeden had scheduled lunch for the two of them, VCC's two head elders, and one of the assistant pastors. JT was excited to spend time with every one of these men, but by the time they'd eaten, laughed, and talked, he hadn't gotten back to the hotel until around four. Veda had been patiently waiting in bed for him, though, with nothing on, and now they'd just finished taking a shower together and were sitting in two complimentary bathrobes in the living room area, dining. JT had ordered steak and lobster, garlic mashed potatoes, and asparagus with hollandaise sauce, and Veda had gone with the same vegetable selections but had chosen crab-stuffed salmon for her entrée.

"I'm so glad you could make the trip," he said, drinking some ice water.

"I am, too, and actually it's a wonderful relief just to be here with you."

"So, it's that bad at home, huh?"

"The worst."

"I know you'd talked about wanting to wait until your son graduated, but have you now thought more about filing for a divorce?"

"I have, but I also want to make sure he's situated in college this fall because I don't want to cause him any unnecessary stress before then. It's bad enough that I'm stressed out all the time myself because of how miserable I am."

"I really hate hearing that."

"It's tough. I mean, as of late, I've been experiencing everything you can think of. From tension headaches to insomnia to heart palpitations. You name it, I'm having it."

JT shook his head. "All because you're in a miserable marriage."

"Yeah, that's pretty much what it is."

"I couldn't do it."

"What?"

"Be miserable all the time. I could never be in an unhappy household situation."

"Then why are you still with your wife?"

"Because for the most part, I'm very happy with her."

Veda looked at him, obviously questioning what he'd just said, but kept eating.

"Believe it or not, my wife is a very good wife. She also understands what it's like to have a husband in the ministry, and my congregation loves her."

"Do you love her?" Veda asked, breaking a dinner roll in two.

"Yes . . . I do."

"Then why are you here with me?"

"Because I can't help the way I feel and because I've never been one to believe that anyone should deny themselves when it comes to having something they really want."

"I'm not sure your wife would agree with that, though, right?"

"I'm sure she wouldn't, but you know that old adage—what you don't know won't hurt you," he said, thinking how careful he always was when he was with any of his women and even how today when they'd arrived at the airport, they'd taken separate car services to the hotel and Veda had shopped around in the hotel's gift shop until JT had checked in and called her on her cell phone. He'd had her wait in the lobby for a short and inconspicuous period of time, just to be on the safe side, and then a while ago, he'd also had her close the bedroom door when their room service order was being delivered.

They ate in silence for about a minute and then Veda asked, "So, tell me, what made you decide to become a minister?"

"Well, to be honest, I really didn't have a choice."

"I don't understand."

"I didn't have a choice because I didn't want to go against God's wishes. I didn't want to ignore the job He had for me to do."

"Oh, okay," she said, but JT couldn't tell whether she was impressed with what he'd said or not.

"So, does my being a pastor still bother you?"

"Sort of."

"Well, hopefully that'll change at some point, because overall, I'm no different than any other man."

"This is true, but I guess I would feel a lot better if you weren't married or if I could see you a lot more often."

JT wiped his mouth with his napkin and then set it down. "I know this isn't the most ideal situation for you, but I also think I need to be very clear on something. I really do care about you, and of course, I'm going to see you as often as I can, but I also need to make sure you understand that I'm not planning to leave my wife. Not now or in the future. I know this probably isn't what you're wanting to hear, but I also don't want to give you any false hopes about the two of us ever getting married."

"I totally understand that, and unlike most other women who see married men, I accept our relationship for what it is. All I want is to be treated well and with the utmost respect, and I'll be fine."

"I'm glad to hear that, because not every woman who sleeps with a married man can deal with the reality. They always end up wanting more, and when they don't get it, they practically lose their minds."

"You sound like you've already experienced something like that."

"I have," he said, thinking about Carmen.

"Well, you certainly won't have those kinds of issues with me, but I also hope you're not expecting to be the only man in my life either. Specifically, once I'm divorced."

Interestingly enough, JT didn't like the idea of her sleeping with any man besides him, but he knew he wasn't in any position to complain or object. So he jokingly said, "That's fine. But I still wanna go on record saying I'm totally against it."

They both laughed and ate more of their dinner. When they finished, they chatted awhile longer but then JT gestured with his forefinger for her to come around the table. But when she got up, the hotel phone rang.

"Come and sit down," he said, patting his lap and ignoring whomever was calling—although he knew it was Pastor Braeden, because he'd told JT he would call around seven, making sure he had everything he needed.

Finally, the ringing stopped, and JT untied Veda's robe and slipped it down her shoulders. He admired her nakedness and was planning to enjoy every inch of her for the rest of the evening and all day tomorrow. Then, on Sunday morning, he would get up early, work on his sermon for a few hours, and go deliver his message.

He would do an outstanding job, return to the hotel, and make love to Veda again.

He would spend the entire weekend doing exactly what he loved: having incredible sex and speaking to thousands of people.

Chapter 40

So, how are you?" Alicia asked Carmen as she drove onto the freeway, heading downtown to do a little shopping.

"I'm fine. What about you?"

"Hmmph. Worse than ever."

"Why? What's wrong?"

"I think JT is in Dallas with another woman."

"When did he go out there?" Carmen asked in a slightly edgy tone, and Alicia thought it was interesting how Carmen was more concerned about JT's whereabouts than she was about his having an affair—which meant JT definitely hadn't told her where he was going.

"Yesterday morning. He went early so he could prepare for a sermon he's doing there on Sunday."

"But why do you think he's there messing around?"

"Because he wanted to take the trip by himself, and that's how I know he's up to something. He gave what I'm sure he thought was a legitimate reason, but what he doesn't realize is that I heard my father tell lies like this all the time. When he was married to my mom, I was too young to know he was lying, but by the time he married his second wife and then

Charlotte, I was completely onto him. Even when his wives weren't."

"So, what are you going to do about it?" Carmen asked, acting as though she couldn't care less about what Alicia had just told her. This was also the reason Alicia gave her the answer she wanted to hear.

"I'm going to leave him."

"I don't blame you, girl," she declared. "Because if I thought my husband was sleeping around, I would do the same exact thing."

"So, you don't think I'm acting too hastily?"

"Not at all, and especially if you really feel in your heart that he's cheating on you."

"I do."

"Then there's nothing else to consider."

"Still, though. I can't believe JT would do this to me, and so soon after we were married. My father never trusted him, and with each day that passes, I'm more and more sorry that I didn't listen. Then, of course, there's the congregation. They've been so wonderful to me. So, I feel bad about having to divorce JT because it feels like I'm actually abandoning them. My mom talked about that all the time when she and my dad separated, and now I know how she felt. But what I think I'm going to do is ask JT for what will hopefully be an amicable and quiet divorce and then go to church with him next Sunday to say my good-byes."

"Gosh, girl, that's really nice of you and very diplomatic, because if it were me, I'd never tell them anything. I would leave both JT and his congregation and never look back."

Obviously. "I just think it's the right thing to do, and if you don't mind, I'd really like for you to be there. It's going to be a very tough time for me, and I'm really going to need the support of a good friend."

"Of course. I'm glad to do anything for you, and you already know that."

"I really appreciate it, Carmen," Alicia said, pulling her black Versace shades from the top of her head and down over her eyes. "More than you could possibly know."

Chapter 41

As soon as the choir finished singing, JT got up and went into the pulpit. He'd been sitting on the end of one of the front pews next to Alicia, and Carmen was sitting on the other side of her.

"This is the day the Lord hath made, so let us rejoice and be glad in it," he said, and most of the members nodded or spoke in agreement. "I first want to say how thrilled and overjoyed I am to see so many new faces here at New Life Christian Center, because it has been a long time since every single seat was filled. This has happened in the past whenever we have special services, such as the time when my father-in-law came to speak, but never on a normal Sunday morning. So, I just want to thank everyone for being here."

Alicia looked at Carmen and smiled and then looked back at JT.

"The other thing I wanted to share with you is how wonderful a time I had out in Dallas last weekend. Pastor Braeden is truly an awesome man of God, and his ministry is on a level like most of us have never seen before. So, I am very grateful to have had the opportunity to spend time with him at his church. My only regret, however, is that my beautiful wife wasn't able to make the trip with me, but you can be sure I'll be taking her with me next time around."

Carmen leaned over and whispered in Alicia's ear. "So, you didn't tell him yet?"

Alicia knew she was referring to their conversation last Saturday and wondering if Alicia had asked JT for a divorce the way she'd said she was going to, and so Alicia was pleased to say, "No. But I will."

"Are you still planning to address the church?"

Alicia nodded her head yes but kept her eyes and attention on JT, purposely not looking back in Carmen's direction.

JT made a few other observations and then said, "Before we continue on with the service, my wife would like to come and say a few words. I'm not sure what about exactly, but what I do know is that all this week, she's been going on and on about some women-only retreat down in Florida for the ladies of NLCC. So, if I had to guess," he said, chuckling, "I'm sure that's what she's going to be discussing . . . so, men, please, please bear with her."

Everyone laughed, and Alicia pulled out a set of documents and went to the podium. JT kissed her on the cheek and took his seat back on the pew next to Carmen.

Alicia scanned the huge audience and smiled. Over the last seven days, JT had run countless radio and TV commercials, and his timing couldn't have been more perfect. She hadn't even planned on him doing such a massive media blitz, but the more people who were there the better.

"Good morning," she said.

"Good morning," everyone responded.

"I want to begin by saying how honored I am to have served as your first lady and that I don't believe I've ever felt more welcomed by so many people in such a genuine way . . . which is why I am very sad to say this will be my last time seeing you."

Soft chatter flooded the room, and Alicia looked at JT, who was undeniably mortified. Carmen, however, seemed delighted beyond explanation.

"It is with great hesitation but also with a strong sense of duty that I also be completely honest with you about your pastor and my husband—my husband who has been sleeping with at least three different women since I married him."

Everyone spoke quickly and loudly.

"I know this is a lot to take in and that it's all very shocking, but if you'll please just give me a few more minutes, I promise I won't take much of your time," she said, waiting for them to settle down. "What I have here is a very thorough daily report that covers the last two and a half weeks, and I can confirm, without question, that one of the women JT has been seeing is Diana Redding," Alicia said, locking eyes with the woman, something that was very easy to do since the wealthiest and largest financial contributors of NLCC sat in designated seats up front. Alicia could tell this woman had never been more humiliated, but when Mr. Redding looked at his wife and exclaimed, "Diana, is this true?" all the mumbling in the sanctuary started up again. As expected, though, Carmen no longer seemed so elated.

"My husband has also been consorting with another married woman named Veda Scott who resides in Minneapolis . . . and interestingly enough, she accompanied him on his trip to Dallas—you know, the one he just told you about. The one he *regretted* I wasn't able to go on."

JT's face stiffened, but he never moved an inch. Carmen looked outraged.

"But what truly hurt me the most was when I learned that my husband was sleeping with one of my closest friends, whom

I've known since childhood," she said, staring at Carmen. "My wonderful friend, whom I trusted and who is sitting next to my husband at this very moment. My wonderful friend, who is newly pregnant with his child."

"Oh my goodness," a woman yelled out, and then laughed like this was some sort of a comedy show.

"What kind of man *is* Pastor Valentine?" another wanted to know.

"You just can't trust any of these preachers nowadays, can you?" someone else commented.

"How pathetic!" a man shouted from the back.

"Everyone, please. Can I have your attention for just another couple of minutes? Please," Alicia said, trying to speak over them. Finally they quieted down.

"As I said, I'm very hurt, but I'm also happy to know that something good has come out of all of this. I'm glad that justice will now be served."

JT left his seat. "This is ridiculous. Baby, why are you doing this?"

But Minister Weaver quickly stepped in front of him. "Sit down, Pastor. Or else."

JT continued standing but didn't move any closer.

Alicia looked at him and then at Carmen again. "My dear, dear friend here paid someone to rig Michelle Valentine's brakes, and that's why she was killed in that car accident."

"What?" JT said, frowning at his longtime mistress.

Carmen stood and rushed toward him. "She's lying, JT. You have to believe me."

"Get off me," he shrieked, pushing her away.

"JT, you know I would never do anything like that," she said, nearly having a fit.

"You did do it," Alicia reiterated matter-of-factly. "And I've already turned over to the police a taped conversation with you confessing everything."

"You killed my wife and my child?" JT asked.

Tears streamed down Carmen's face. "I did it for us, JT. I did it because I knew you wanted me to. Otherwise how were we ever going to be together?"

"Is this a church we're at or some evil den of sin?" an elderly woman asked, getting up and walking out of the sanctuary, and so did Diana Redding and her husband. A few others followed suit, but mostly people sat, waiting to see what would happen next.

"You're sick," JT said to Carmen, and then looked at his wife with pleading eyes. "Baby, I was going to tell you everything." He faced the congregation and spoke loudly, since his wireless mic was no longer turned on. "I was going to tell all of you the truth. About my past, about all the women, about every terrible thing I've done over the years. I know you might not believe it, but I was planning to do it today."

Alicia gaped at him, along with everyone else in the church, gathered her PI report, went and picked up her purse, and left JT standing where he was. As she made her way down the aisle, though, a group of plainclothes detectives and at least ten officers walked through the entrance. They proceeded into the church and Alicia wondered whom they were there for: Carmen, because of the part she'd played in Michelle's untimely death . . . or JT, because of the forgery charges Curtis had recently filed against him.

Epilogue

Six Months Later

*A*licia peered through the window of her condo, which was situated in a very nice community in Covington Park, the suburb she'd grown up in and the one where she'd hoped to have a nice life with JT. But so much for hoping and wishing, because her marriage to JT had turned out to be a total fiasco. First, she'd learned about Carmen from Levi, and then about Diana and Veda from JT's phone records, and then the private investigator she'd hired had confirmed all her suspicions.

It had been one thing to discover all the infidelity JT was involved in but quite another to find out that he'd once pimped a willing group of women and had gotten some other young woman pregnant when he was married to Michelle. It had also been terrible learning that he'd been sleeping with Carmen since her college years and that Carmen had been responsible for Michelle's death. Although these latter pieces of information hadn't actually come from the investigator but instead had come from Donna, or Barb, as she now admitted her name was.

About a week ago, Alicia had received another package from

her, but this time, she'd included a two-page letter that summarized exact details about Carmen and JT and also a CD that contained a fifteen-minute conversation. Unsurprisingly, Alicia had recognized the voice of her childhood friend immediately, and it hadn't been more than a few seconds before she realized the other person was Barb. Alicia had listened to their entire discussion, and when she'd finished, she'd decided she would never tell another living soul that Barb had also included a separate note explaining that the only reason she'd initially followed Alicia to the mall that day and tried making her believe JT had murdered his wife was because of the way he'd treated her baby sister. Barb had wanted to pay him back for forcing her sister to get rid of her baby and then completely dismissing her, but then, once her conscience had set in, she'd decided it was time she stopped protecting Carmen, her closest colleague from her call-girl days, and told the truth about Michelle's tragedy. Barb had decided to come clean, and now Carmen was facing a sentence of twenty years to life for first-degree murder—and some additional time because of the sizable amount of drugs the police had found stashed away in her apartment, something Alicia was still pretty amazed and confused about. Worse, she would have no choice but to give her baby up as soon as she had it. Be it to foster parents, adoptive parents, or even distant relatives, in the end, Carmen clearly wouldn't be the person raising her child.

Then there was JT, who'd done more dirt in the last five years than most criminals would do in a lifetime. Although Alicia was sure that of all the crimes he'd committed, not once had he expected forgery to be his ultimate ruin. But that's what he got for messing with the wrong man, namely her father, because it had only been when three ministers had called Curtis, saying they'd received a mailing from JT that included a recommendation letter from him, that Curtis had decided to bring him down. He'd debated how he was going to go about doing it but had finally decided not to confront him just then. In the meantime, however, he'd recontacted two of the ministers and asked them each to personally call and invite JT to come speak at their churches a few months down the road. After that, he'd phoned back Pastor Braeden, the minister he could trust the most, told him what JT was up to, and then asked if he would bring JT in to speak at his church as soon as possible. Pastor Braeden had readily agreed, and Curtis had covered the cancellation fee for the original minister Vineyard Christian Center had already contracted. Then, once JT had accepted payment for his services and deposited his five-figure check, and Curtis had received a complete listing of all the churches that that bogus letter had gone out to—thanks to Curtis making it clear to JT's executive assistant that if she cooperated, he would tell the authorities he believed her when she said she had no idea of what her boss had been up to—Curtis had gone straight to the police. Shortly after, Pastor Braeden had flown to Chicago and had given an in-depth statement, confirming that JT had purposely tried to deceive him and had gained financially by forging Curtis's name. Of course, this had only made the prosecution's case even stronger, not to mention some previous money scheme JT was also now being charged with, and he had a chance of spending up to seven years in prison.

Alicia had heard he was out on bond and still preaching every Sunday morning, business as usual, but that less than two hundred people actually showed up. So she couldn't help wondering how long he'd be able to continue. Although, to tell the truth, she honestly didn't care one way or another and was just happy to be finished with him. Their divorce was already final, she'd moved out of his house, and she had no intention of ever seeing or speaking to him again.

And why would she when she'd finally learned a truly valuable lesson—she'd learned it the hard way, no doubt, but still she'd learned it and learned it well. She'd also come to realize that *Phillip* and not JT was the best thing that had ever happened to her, and from this day on, she would do whatever it took to get him back. She would do all she could to regain his trust and show him that she would never again allow material possessions or money to come between them. And to begin proving it, she'd reimbursed her father for every dime of the money he'd spent paying off each of Phillip's credit cards last year, the ones she'd maxed out behind his back, and she'd opened a money market savings account and checking account and purchased a few investment products. This had all been made possible because of the two-hundred-fifty-thousand-dollar signing bonus she'd received from her publisher and also an additional one hundred thousand dollars they'd paid her now that her book had been revised and accepted for production. There was her agent's commission and federal and state taxes that had to be deducted, but there had still been more than enough money left over, and she was very proud of herself for managing it so well. She was happy because, for the first time in her life, she didn't have this great desire to shop or spend beyond her means. For the first time ever, she had her priorities in order and was working extra hard at doing the right thing. It was the reason Phillip, at this very moment, was hugging her from behind, and she couldn't have been happier. It was the reason she finally knew her fairy tale had nothing to do with men like JT, but had everything to do with her first husband, the man she loved and hoped to marry again. Yes, it was true that Phillip still wanted them to take things slow and wanted her to be completely sure about her new sense of satisfaction and total commitment, but

Alicia had the utmost faith in their relationship. She was even willing to spend the rest of her life making things up to him if she had to.

She would do this from now on.

And would forever be careful what she prayed for.